THE GUESTHOUSE

Abbie Frost has worked as a teacher, an actor and scriptwriter, and now reviews fiction for various publications and blogs. She is a published thriller writer whose work has been short-listed for various awards.

THE GUEST HOUSE

ABBIE FROST

HarperCollins*Publishers*

HarperCollins*Publishers* Ltd
1 London Bridge Street,
London SE1 9GF

www.harpercollins.co.uk

First published by HarperCollins*Publishers* 2020
2

A catalogue record for this book is
available from the British Library

ISBN: 978-0-00-832988-4 (PB)

This novel is entirely a work of fiction.
The names, characters and incidents portrayed in it are
the work of the author's imagination. Any resemblance to
actual persons, living or dead, events or localities is
entirely coincidental.

Set in Sabon by Palimpsest Book Production Ltd,
Falkirk, Stirlingshire

Printed and bound in the UK by CPI Group (UK) Ltd,
Croydon CR0 4YY

MIX
Paper from
responsible sources
FSC™ C007454

This book is produced from independently certified FSC™ paper
to ensure responsible forest management.

For more information visit: www.harpercollins.co.uk/green

To my wonderful family: those few I began with and the many more I acquired along the way

Prologue

Hannah's trainers skidded on the marble floor of the hall. She grabbed the wooden rail that ran along the wall to steady herself. Had to keep on her feet, had to get out.

Running on again, she strained to see through drifts of smoke. Sweat trickled down her neck in the heat. Smashed paintings and blackened chandelier fragments littered the floor. And the huge front door loomed at the end of the hall, smoke coiling around it in the gloom. She fumbled back the bolts, wrenched it open and sucked in a lungful of fresh air. Paused to listen for any sounds in the hallway behind her; any signs of life inside the house. Flames crackled and the building groaned as it began to crumble and fall apart in the heat.

Stepping outside, she pulled the door shut behind her, leaned against it and took in more clear air. The storm had calmed, but rain was still beating down onto the empty hillside that sloped away before her into the night.

She went to the heavy garden bench beside the door, gripped the cold metal of an armrest and dragged it forward. Her muscles burned, the iron legs of the bench screeched against paving stones. Hands shaking, she turned to the electronic security pad beside the door and tried to key in the code to lock it. *Hurry up. Hurry up.*

Then she heard something else, a noise that cut through the howling wind. Footsteps inside the house. Hard shoes beating against marble floor, coming towards the door.

She turned and started to run.

Down the long path, through the wide iron gates, groaning in the wind, and out into the green emptiness beyond. The grassy slope rose above, miles and miles of wilderness in all directions. She could still make it to safety if she moved quickly. Every step took her further from the house, its door still shut, and with every step she felt her mind becoming clearer than it had been in months. Thoughts of her mother, Ruby, came back to her then. Those shadows around her worried eyes. That look of disappointment that she couldn't hide whenever Hannah failed, broke down or threw away a chance to make something of her life. Not even Ruby could save her now.

A gnarled root jutting from the ground caught her foot. She stumbled, regained her balance, just stopped herself from falling. She began to cry and the wind whipped her sobs away into the empty bog. 'Help! Someone help.'

But there was no one left to help her.

She scrambled onwards, her drenched trousers clinging to her legs, her shoes still soaked through with water. Flashes of memory from the last few hours began to flicker through her mind: dripping cold walls in the pitch-black guesthouse; her helpless body sinking through murky water, struggling for air, drowning. Water filling her nose and mouth. Limbs moving in the dark. Water churning. Screams.

She glanced back over her shoulder, then ran faster, along a rutted track that cut through the bog and led down the hill towards safety. In front of her, a stretch of water blocked the path and she picked up speed. Leapt over the dark puddle but landed awkwardly. One foot slipped out from under her and she flew backwards. Slammed into the ground, her momentum carrying her onwards, slithering down through thick weeds and mud into a ditch full of icy water. She gasped, scrabbled at the earth around her. Let out another cry for help that nobody heard. Even she could barely hear it above the howling wind.

Her leg was trapped. With each jerk she could feel her trainer being sucked from her foot, the foul-smelling mud clutching at her skin.

Chin pressed into the ground, she dug in her hands and tried to yank herself free, but the icy water wouldn't let go.

She wiped mud from her face and stared back towards The Guesthouse.

It was a sharp silhouette against the grey sky. Flames bloomed from its roof and illuminated patches of marsh across the hillside. For a moment she remembered how the building had first appeared to her. Pale, stately and beautiful, surrounded by green, and framed by trees and the distant blue hills. As her breathing began to slow, she recalled her excitement when she first clicked on the web page and saw pictures of The Guesthouse online. Its sweeping rooms full of dark-wood bookcases and roaring fires. Artistic shots taken on summer days of ivy-covered stone walls, windows glowing a welcome to visitors.

The windows were lit up now too, but with sparks of red and orange. With fire.

Was it her imagination or could she really feel the heat of the flames on her face? Hear them crackling as white smoke and black embers billowed into the sky? She watched, hypnotized: too exhausted to keep struggling.

Then the fire illuminated another, smaller silhouette. A dark figure. Moving away from the open front door and down the slope towards her. A shadow walking calmly through the rain. As if it knew she wouldn't get far, knew she would be waiting here in the mud.

Waiting to die.

Chapter One

Six days earlier

A shriek of sound cut through the silence. Buzzing and whirring. Hannah forced her eyes open, fumbled for her phone on the bedside table, then on the floor. Finally she had it, dropped it, groped for it again. *Shut up. For God's sake shut up.*

A croak. 'Hello.'

'Han, at last. I've been ringing and ringing.' It was Lori.

Hannah pressed the phone to her ear and lay back with her eyes closed.

'Where are you?' Lori's voice was harsh.

Where was she? Her eyes blurred as she tried to focus. Sunlight cut through the drawn curtains and fell across the bed. She looked at the clothes strewn around the room. Her own room.

'I'm at home. Why? What's wrong?'

There was a pause. 'So you made it back all right.' Lori sighed. 'I feel like shit today – probably those cheap cocktails. How are you coping?' She didn't wait for a reply. 'Look, I was really worried about you last night, and then you just disappeared. Who was that guy you went off with?'

A sudden flash of memory, of nausea and hot shame. Sweaty plastic seats in a taxi somewhere in London, hands groping. The stranger's lips on her mouth, on her neck, his hands down her top and up her skirt. The taste of cheap booze and cigarettes, the taxi spinning with something like desire. Not thinking for once, not feeling bad for once.

Then the world had tilted further, her hand had gone to her mouth and she'd had to push him away. 'Stop . . . I'm going to be sick.' Swearing from the driver as he braked to a halt. The door opening and her stumbling out onto the street. Vomiting cocktail after cocktail, shot after shot. Down her skirt and her bare legs, onto her shoes.

Then the shameful walk back to the taxi that seemed to last a lifetime. Strangers in the street pointing and laughing. The desperate urge to get warm, to swallow some water, to be back home.

She'd pulled at the door handle of the taxi, but nothing happened. She tugged at it again. The driver wouldn't even look her in the eye as he started the engine and began to pull away. Her bag flew out the window and onto the street, its contents spilling into the gutter. The guy, whose hands had groped her just moments ago, had sat dead still in the back seat, staring ahead as they drove into the distance.

Hannah swallowed and stared at the ceiling of her bedroom. Her mouth dry as she sat up and looked around for a glass of water. 'Yeah, just some wanker. I told him to drop me off and get lost.' She coughed into the phone. 'Sorry I left you like that.'

Silence on the end of the line. Then Lori began to talk, starting off gently, but quickly getting into her stride. The nagging tone, one thing after another about all that Hannah had done wrong. She tuned it out after a while and pulled the covers over her cold shoulders. When she stretched her leg over the side of the bed she saw the red, angry scrape on her knee, and remembered weaving and stumbling her way home. She'd fallen through the garden gate, her knee smacking onto the path. Terrified her mum would hear. Twenty-five years old and back living with her mother. Back getting shit from her school friends.

Lori was still speaking, the words blending into one. 'I know you've had a hard time, but I'm sick of it. Just sort yourself out. You can't keep fucking up your life.'

Then, finally, a long silence that Hannah couldn't face trying to fill. The phone felt sticky with sweat in her palm.

Lori spoke again, her voice softer now. 'Look . . . you're my best friend. We've known each other for years.' Another pause. 'But . . . I'm tired, Han, really *really* tired. I didn't want to say this, but I'm starting to get why Ben and you broke up . . . why he was so angry with you.'

Hannah tried to speak but Lori drowned her out, loud again, firm. 'Listen, until you sort yourself out, I'm done with you. I don't want to hear from you. Don't bother calling me. Texting me. Just leave me alone!'

Then the phone went dead. Hannah stared at it for a moment, then let it fall from her hands to the floor and watched it thump into a pile of dirty clothes. Some peace and quiet at last. Her head fell back onto the pillow and she closed her eyes.

When she woke again, all she could think about was water. And something to still the hammering in her head. In the bathroom she put her mouth under the tap and washed down a couple of paracetamol. Her knees shook as she sat on the edge of the bath, the floor swaying beneath her, thinking back over her conversation with Lori. *Why Ben and you broke up . . . why he was so angry with you.*

The bathroom door rattled. 'Hannah. Are you all right?' Her mum.

'Yeah, I'm fine. Just an upset stomach.'

Footsteps in the corridor as her mum walked away. In the mirror Hannah saw last night's make-up smeared around her mouth and eyes. Her stiff and unwashed hair hadn't been trimmed or coloured for ages. It looked yellow rather than blonde, the roots dark. No wonder the job interview yesterday had been such a disaster. It was a surprise she'd even got as far as an interview this time.

She stepped into the shower and turned the power on full. Stood in the hot water for as long as she could, letting it numb her throbbing head, then dressed and went downstairs. Better go and face it.

Her mum, Ruby, was sitting at the kitchen table with a coffee pot in front of her. As always there were papers and a laptop open next to her. Hannah poured herself some coffee and sat opposite, pulled out her phone and began to scroll.

'Morning.' Ruby took off her reading glasses and pushed back her dark hair. It was streaked with grey now, but to Hannah she looked the same as always. Except those tiny new creases around her mouth and eyes, the ones that Hannah had caused. There was no denying it: Hannah's lifestyle over the past weeks and months had aged her mother.

Ruby reached for her hand and it felt so warm and familiar that Hannah had to look away. 'How did the interview go?'

Her throat felt raw. 'It was all right. They'll let me know in a week or so.' She remembered the way the panel had looked at her as she stammered through their questions. The silence while she muttered her thanks and stumbled towards the door. She still couldn't meet Ruby's eye. 'I didn't really fancy it though.'

Ruby sighed. 'Have you seen anything that you *do* fancy?' Hannah gritted her teeth, but her mum continued speaking. 'And what time did you get in last night?'

'*Mum*.' A deep breath, trying not to let it turn into a sigh. 'About one, I think.'

Ruby shifted, closed the laptop and began loading papers into her bag. Hannah stood up and walked to the sink, staring out at the immaculate lawn and the freshly painted brown fence. Her mother had probably been lying awake last night, listening for the key in the lock, thinking about all the things that could have happened to her daughter. Even though Ruby had worked right through Hannah's childhood, she had always been there. Always came to school plays, sports days, parents' events. Took time off when Hannah was sick and read to her every single night.

The years of hard work had all paid off and her mum was now a successful financial consultant, working long hours, but still finding the time to keep this house spotless – and to worry about her daughter's life. Hannah knew she could still rely on her; she just didn't want to. Because Ruby couldn't help her now. There are some things that even your mum can't cure.

'Hannah, are you listening to me?' Ruby was fiddling with the handle of her bag. 'I don't think you're ready to start a new job yet. It's too soon. Why not have a couple of weeks off?' A stiff little smile. 'Take a holiday. I can help out if you can't afford it.'

There was a pause and eventually Ruby sighed. 'After what happened with Ben . . . you're probably still in shock. That's why you're behaving like this.'

Hannah turned back to the garden and took a few cautious sips of her coffee. She felt her stomach begin to churn and tipped her mug out into the sink. Watched the brown liquid swill down the drain, then moved towards the door. 'I'd better dry my hair.'

'I'll make some food,' Ruby called after her. Hannah wanted to say she couldn't eat anything, wanted to look her in the eye and tell her how she really felt: how guilt was eating away at her insides, making her drink more and more. How she wished she could have kept the flat that she and Ben had shared. How she still cried herself to sleep thinking about him.

Instead she went slowly upstairs, feeling a hundred years old. Ruby was right: she couldn't face the thought of a new job. She'd lost the last one because she'd been arriving later and later, hungover most of the time: making mistakes. And because she didn't care enough to try. Didn't care about anything.

The next day, Hannah tried ringing Lori four times and left messages, but there was no response. By evening, she felt abandoned, like she was back in the playground at school and all the popular girls were whispering about her. But Lori wasn't like everyone else, she was always there. Hannah locked her bedroom door and sat on the bed, her hand shaking as she held the phone, dialled the number she knew by heart, listened to the ringing until it went to voicemail.

'Lori . . . it's me again. Listen, I'm sorry. I'm going to fix this . . . I just need some time to get my head together.' She swallowed. 'You're my best friend.'

The only one she had left. Everyone else hated her almost as much as she hated herself. She ended the call and wiped her eyes on her sleeve.

Her phone vibrated in her hand and for one second she thought it was Lori, calling her back to say sorry and to tell her it was all going to be all right. Or maybe it was another hate-filled message from one of Ben's friends. But she had turned off notifications for Facebook, Instagram, and Twitter, so it couldn't be that. She unlocked her screen and found the tiny red notification next to the image of a house on her screen, an app she hardly ever used: Cloud BNB.

Of course: the holiday to County Mayo in Ireland. Ben had persuaded her to book a room at The Guesthouse, a beautiful country home, and she had forgotten all about it. They were supposed to go together.

Hannah clicked on the message from the host: Henry Laughton. His photo showed a solid-looking man wearing a Barbour jacket, standing at the foot of a green hill with a muddy dog at his side.

Hi Hannah and Ben,

I hope you're looking forward to your stay at The Guesthouse. As promised the kitchen will be stocked with enough food and drink to last the whole of your stay. Fallon village has a small local store for any other essentials and there is a supermarket fifteen miles away if you need anything unusual or exotic.

As this is self-check-in, I may not be there to meet you. Entry is by key code – a second code will let you into your own room – and you may arrive any time after 2pm. Please make yourselves at home.

Other rooms for use by guests are the large eat-in kitchen, the drawing room and the library. So plenty of space to spread out and be solitary or sociable as you prefer.

She finished reading and closed her eyes. Couldn't stop herself remembering when the offer email had first arrived. Sitting at her desk with Ben beside her and her life intact.

She had pointed at the email from Cloud BNB on her

screen. He looked over her shoulder, his head close to hers. Hannah clicked through to the website and they both read the description. The Guesthouse was owned by Preserve the Past: a charity dedicated to restoring historic Irish buildings.

They moved on to the photographs. The luxurious bedrooms with large windows facing sweeping countryside views. Roaring fires and stone floors. Wide-angled shots that made the rooms seem enormous. The building itself had classical lines and some original architectural features inside.

Ben leaned over her shoulder and clicked back to the offer email. 'Wow, so cool – and cheap. We should go. Can we go? It's perfect, and a great area for walking too.'

She laughed. 'OK, well you've managed to put me off completely now.'

'The offer is for the opening week. We'd be the first visitors, so they're throwing in all sorts of extras. Food and drink in the fridge, logs for the open fires, free run of the house.' He kissed the back of her neck and slid his hands down to her breasts, whispering in her ear. 'We might be the only guests. Imagine cuddling up in front of a roaring fire miles from anywhere.'

Hannah continued to look through the photos. 'I love the building, but it's kind of . . . outdoorsy. And . . .' She touched the screen. 'There are five visitor bedrooms, so it could be packed.'

'We'll just take a bottle to our room and lock ourselves in for the week.' Ben kissed her again and again. Short sharp kisses on her neck on her face, her lips, and then everywhere and they were soon making love on the sofa.

An hour later they booked the best bedroom on offer and organized their flights.

*

Hannah bit her lip and killed the app. She was due to arrive in Ireland in two days' time. She couldn't go – there was no way – she should reply to the host and cancel. Pulling on a jumper and leggings, she forced herself to go downstairs.

Her mum had gone to do some work in the study and a pot of pasta simmered on the stove. At the kitchen window Hannah poured herself a glass of water with a shaking hand. Outside in the garden, autumn had crept up without her noticing, the trees heavy with red, orange, and golden leaves, their colours glinting in the evening sun.

There was a reason she had chosen County Mayo. It was probably why the offer email had been sent to her in the first place, after she had spent long nights trawling through Cloud BNB, zooming in on Fallon village, refreshing the page, waiting for a sign to appear there like a beacon. It was a reason she didn't want to think about now, something that she had only ever told Ben.

What would Ben say if he could see her now? She could remember the smell of his aftershave, the way he held her at night when she awoke screaming from a nightmare.

The way he looked at her when he found out that she was cheating on him.

She took a sip of water, trying to ignore her shaking hand. When Ben realized what Hannah had done, their argument had spiralled into a fight that ended their relationship. She'd tried to make him understand, promised it would never happen again, but it had been no good. He'd stormed out into the night, and that had been the last time she would ever see him.

Hannah looked around the kitchen at the immaculate surfaces. Her mother's constant, almost oppressive worry, this house like a pristine cage. Maybe she *should* go to Ireland, to get away from it all. She watched a magpie hop down onto the lawn and begin to peck at something dead in the grass. Her mum and Lori would certainly be relieved to see the back of her.

Everyone would.

Because Ben was dead, and it was her fault.

Chapter Two

She regretted it as soon as her plane landed. She'd left London in sparkling sunshine and arrived at Ireland West Airport to drizzle that turned to rain. And it got worse as the taxi headed for Fallon. Water flooded down the cab windows, the frantic *swish, swish* of the wipers failing to drown out the driver's annoying country music.

At least he didn't speak to her and he held his thick red neck so stiffly it was obvious he wouldn't welcome any chatty comments from the back seat. She tried to relax as green mile after green mile sped by, distorted by the streams of grey water. It didn't matter what the weather was like: she wasn't here to enjoy herself, just to get some respite, to get away from social media and from London's clubs and bars. Ben had encouraged her to make this trip and had paid half the cost. At least this was one tiny way in which she wasn't going to let him down.

She must have dozed off, because the cab door suddenly opened, and the driver was standing staring in at her. The rain had eased to a thin colourless veil, as if a net curtain hung in front of the fields.

The fields that stretched out for miles on both sides.

She sat up in her seat and looked around. They were

parked in a layby in the middle of nowhere. 'Sorry, excuse me, I think there's been a mistake. I asked for The Guesthouse.'

The man nodded.

'It's on an app called Cloud BNB. It's where I'm staying.' She pulled out her phone. 'I can show you a picture.'

He said nothing. His wide, ruddy face expressionless as he gave the screen one fleeting glance.

'It used to be called Fallon House.'

He pulled the door wider, not looking at her. 'This is as far as I go.'

It must be a joke, probably some sort of local prank. She swallowed. 'I want *The Guesthouse*.'

He turned away so that, with his accent, she struggled to make out the words. 'Take the path over the fields. Ye can see it there.' He pointed along a muddy track towards a low range of hills. 'Keep going straight.'

'But where's the village?'

He gestured ahead. 'Along this road. 'Bout five or six miles.'

'The website said the house was near the village,' she said weakly.

He ignored her and walked back, opened the boot and slung her case down onto the roadside. She had no choice. She and Ben hadn't intended to bring a car, so neither of them had thought to check whether the place was accessible by road.

Cold rain dripped down the neck of her parka as she shrugged on her rucksack and pulled up her hood, staring at her trainers and wishing she had brought water-resistant footwear. It was only afternoon but felt like a gloomy winter evening. Bleak, nothing like the sunlit hills and glittering streams the website had promised.

The driver closed his door, impatient now. He pointed again. 'That's the way.'

The track led off through puddles and muddy ridges towards the hills. She looked at her stupid wheeled suitcase. How the hell was she going to drag it through all that?

She fumbled for her purse. 'Could you carry my case for me?'

He laughed, but there was a flash of sympathy in his pale eyes. 'Sorry, love, I've got another fare in the village.'

And then he was gone. She stared at the taxi as it drove into the distance, its wheels kicking up wet spray from the road.

Shivering in the cold, she walked across to the footpath. As she trudged through the mud, half-pulling, half-carrying her case, she thought about the bottle of vodka she'd bought at the airport. A nice vodka and Coke: that would be her reward when she got to the house. If she ever did.

At the end of the first field, she stopped under the shelter of a tree for a breather. It couldn't be far from here. She dumped her case on the floor and pulled out her phone to call up a map. One bar of signal. Her finger hovered over the Facebook icon on her screen. This was exactly what she had told herself not to do on her holiday. Why she had turned off all her notifications and promised herself to stay away from social media. But after a moment, she opened the app and sat down on her case with a sigh. Just one final look.

She deleted two friend requests from random guys she vaguely remembered chatting to in a bar. Then felt the familiar stab of pain as she navigated her way to Ben's wall. Before she could stop herself, she'd clicked on his profile pictures, scrolled through his albums. She knew them all in perfect detail.

Her favourite picture of Ben filled the screen, but when she went to reload the page, it froze. His eyes were replaced by a slowly buffering circle, then he disappeared. She sat there for a moment, watching the whirling circle, thinking back to the exact moment when she had found out that Ben had died.

It was just two days after the argument that had ended their relationship. She had been on her laptop at home, scrolling through Facebook, when a direct message had flashed up at the bottom of her screen:

Check out Ben's wall. Hope you're pleased with yourself. Bitch.

She had shrugged and told herself it would be pictures of Ben with another woman. Some sort of sick pay-back to make her jealous.

But it had been something far worse. A memorial wall, hundreds of posts about Ben's death. Endless messages of grief and anger. Her boyfriend was gone and everyone was blaming her.

She had read message after message, choking on her tears. Ben had been knocked off his bike two days after he found out she'd cheated on him. Two days during which he'd stayed at his mate, Charlie's, ignored her messages and refused to talk. Then he'd just stood up from the table, went out for a bike ride and never came back.

Hannah swallowed and wiped the rain from her phone's screen. Couldn't stop herself from reloading Ben's Facebook page and trawling down through the messages. There it was, the comment Charlie had left on the day Ben died:

After what happened he was so upset. Said he needed to clear his head and went out on his bike. I never saw him again.

Seven people had liked the comment and someone had added a reply:

If it wasn't for his so-called girlfriend he would still be alive. He wanted to die because of what she did.

The page buffered again. Hannah clenched her phone until her knuckles went white. After the accident, the car driver said he hadn't seen Ben until he rode right out in front of him. And the police found that his bike lights were switched off. Charlie gave evidence about Ben's mood, his drinking, the breakup, and the police believed it.

Believed that Ben had wanted to die.

Lori and Ruby – the only people still talking to Hannah – kept telling her she needed to stop looking at social media altogether. Stop torturing herself. Well, this holiday might be her opportunity.

Because the Facebook page had whirled to a halt and then died again. And at the top of the screen a red cross cut through the signal bar. Perfect – no reception. She turned the phone off and on again, stood up and waved it around above her head. Still nothing. And nothing for it, but to start trudging again.

It seemed like hours later when, soaked and exhausted and cradling her case in her arms because one of its wheels had broken, she spotted a wonky signpost stuck into the mud at the side of the path.

THE GUESTHOUSE.

At least it existed. It wasn't all some grand joke dreamed up by the taxi driver. She put down her case and looked back the way she had come. Mist had settled on the fields and the slope above her, shrouding the road from view.

A movement, something grey, flitting across the edge of her vision. She turned a hundred and eighty degrees, her phone clutched in her hand. Nothing but mist and silent hills. She listened hard for the sound of footsteps, for any indication that she was no longer alone. There was a tiny noise from the bank of fog on the hill above her, as if someone had kicked loose a scattering of stones.

Shit. She turned on her torch app with shaking fingers and waited, totally still. Blood rushing in her ears. Could you still phone 999, even with no signal? Was it 999 in Ireland?

She shone the pathetic beam of light into the fog and walked carefully towards the noise. It was all going to be fine. This was just her overactive imagination, all the stress of the past few weeks catching up with her. There was nobody for miles, for God's sake, nothing to worry about.

Another sound stopped her dead.

There *was* something. A rustle in the grass, some dark shape moving along the ridge, the same flicker of movement in the corner of her eye. This time she spun fast, phone raised, and gasped.

Chapter Three

A blur of grey flew towards her and she choked on a yell, tripped and landed heavily in the mud.

The animal stopped to look at her.

It was a cat. Just a cat. She picked herself up and tried to brush the mud off her jeans, glaring at the cat as it ran in front of her, a strip of muscle and fur heading the way she was going: along the rutted track and up the hill.

'Great – my own guide.' Her voice sounded thin in the silence.

She picked up her bag and started walking again, following a rutted track through the hills. A few minutes later, the mist cleared enough for her to make out a distant shape in the gloom, a dark shadow hemmed in by trees. Thank God, this had to be the place.

The first thing she was going to do when she arrived was log into the wifi and give the host a piece of her mind. What sort of website doesn't mention that the house is miles from anywhere? Inaccessible by road? And surely it was supposed to be *near* the village.

Perhaps it wasn't all bad, though. It would be peaceful, which was what she needed, and Henry Laughton's message had mentioned a kitchen fully stocked with food and drink.

So there was likely to be wine. And tomorrow she'd walk to the village, start to build a picture of the area, try to find someone who might be able to help her. Might have answers to the burning questions that had drawn her to this godforsaken area in the first place.

As she drew nearer, the building rose up from the middle of a cluster of trees, just as beautiful as its photographs online, even shrouded in fog and drizzle. She knew about architecture, used to love it, and this was a perfect example of classical Georgian, with massive wrought iron gates and a wide gravel path leading up to the huge door. She guessed this path had once carried on all the way back to the road.

She knew one thing for sure: Henry Laughton would have to improve access if he wanted to get any decent five-star reviews. He certainly wasn't going to get one from her, no matter how good the house was inside.

Standing at the gate, she stared up at the perfectly symmetrical building, its front door flanked by tall windows set into pale walls. Lights glowed inside and she could just make out a figure looking down from one of the top windows. Someone there to greet her.

But as she walked up the drive, still clutching her broken case, she noticed that the front door was pitted with dents and marred by patches of flaking black paint. The window frames were peeling, too, and a slimy green stain ran down the wall.

The figure still loomed in the window, as if it had been standing there forever.

Hannah shivered, suddenly aware of the silence and space all around her. She squinted back along the muddy track that wound its way down the slope, overlooked by nothing but bare peaks, and felt suddenly tiny and insignificant, lost in a sea of hills. For a moment she thought about turning around, calling a taxi and driving back to the comfort of a city, crawling into her mother's arms, but she was too cold and it would be dark soon.

She remembered her entry code and spotted the keypad on the wall beside the door. Dragged out her phone and tapped in the number. A buzz and a click. The keypad lit up, a greeting flashing in green across the screen:

Welcome to The Guesthouse. You have checked in. Enjoy your stay.

The great black door opened onto a spacious hall full of warmth and light. A marble floor stretched away towards a sweeping staircase in the middle of the room, with landings branching off to either side. A row of paintings hung along one wall. Strange dark pictures that seemed to be of shadowy figures that might have been animals or people, she couldn't tell. Underneath sat a small leather sofa that looked fairly new.

The website had mentioned that Preserve the Past was still renovating a number of their properties, but she'd assumed work on the interior of The Guesthouse was finished. The slightly rundown exterior wouldn't matter if the rest of the place was like this. And if the picture of her guest room wasn't fake, then she would have no complaints about that. Just about the horrible trek from the road.

The second key code would get her into her room. And she was tempted to head straight there, but she should first meet the host, the caretaker, or whoever it was she'd seen waiting for her at the window.

'Hello?' Her voice sounded hollow in the cavernous hallway. She walked to the bottom of the stairs. 'Hello, anybody there?'

The sound echoed. Silence seemed to settle into every dark corner of the house, and a cold bead of sweat trickled down her spine. The building was empty. That shape at the window must have been a curtain or just a shadow.

With another quick glance around she kicked off her white New Balance trainers. At least they *had* been white. Now they were covered in slimy mud, bits of grass, and soaked through with water. Ben would probably have suggested she buy hiking boots, but Ben wasn't here any more.

She hurried upstairs, her trainers in one hand, not wanting to ruin the soft new carpet. Here were the bedroom doors, each with a brass number plate and a neat keypad, all freshly painted in gleaming white. The two rooms at the top of the stairs were numbers five and six. The website had only offered five rooms to rent, but it looked as if there were at least ten.

Her room was number one, right at the far end of what should probably be called the west wing. There was another door next to it, but it was narrow and unnumbered. A storeroom or something similar perhaps. And right at the end of the corridor a tall window. She peered out of it and saw that it faced the gates. This could be the window she imagined she'd seen the figure standing at, but there was no one here now.

Looking through the glass she could see that muddy track snaking away through the rough green grass, a pale sun low in the sky, peeking through the clouds. She had got here just in time. Wouldn't like to navigate that in the dark.

Outside her own room she tapped in the second code, the floorboards creaking under her feet. With a final glance back along the corridor, she told herself to ignore the feeling that she was being watched. Even if there *were* no other guests, a week alone would do her good. Make her less jumpy. She could exercise, stay off the booze. She'd soon get used to the isolation, to the high ceilings and the long, silent corridors.

But as soon as she was inside, she locked the door behind her, trying to calm the heavy beat of her heart.

The room was spacious and light. A bed stood against one wall with the bathroom next to it. Opposite, a wardrobe and an enlarged photograph of a bay with a stormy sea. Close to the door stood a chest of drawers with a kettle and drinks on top.

Through the huge window she could look down on what once must have been a pretty rose garden at the side of the house. Now it was just a mass of bare stems and tangled undergrowth. The ground rose then dipped away into the distance towards grey-blue hills on the horizon and, beyond them, a strip of the Atlantic Ocean.

It would all have been so different if Ben was with her. She swallowed and dumped her case by the window. Threw her rucksack onto the floor, then remembered the vodka and pulled out the bottle, staring at the label. She deserved all of this: the mud, the loneliness, the miserable walk through the fog and rain. The shittier the better. Keep it coming. The thing to remember was: stop thinking about Ben. He was gone and she had to carry on with her life.

The en-suite bathroom was spacious with a row of expensive-looking toiletries and a pile of soft white towels on a shelf behind the door. She took a glass from beside the sink and poured in a slug of vodka. Topped it up with Coke, swallowed a long gulp and sighed.

Once she had changed out of her muddy clothes and spread out on the comfortable double bed, she began to relax. This wasn't too bad. A few more gulps. She checked her phone, watched the buffering circle slowly rotate on her screen. Still no signal. Then she spotted a white card on the bedside table with the wifi code.

When WhatsApp loaded up, she sent a message to her mum and Lori.

I made it! The place is perfect. No phone reception, but that suits me. Looking forward to lots of long walks and feeling better already.

Obviously neither of them wanted to speak to her anyway, but at least they couldn't complain that she'd left them worrying.

Her phone dinged with a message. Henry Laughton.

I hope you have arrived safely at The Guesthouse and had a good journey. A hearty welcome from all of us at Preserve the Past.

Do contact me with any problems or queries and I'll arrange for someone to deal with them.

You should find toiletries and tea/coffee etc in your room, but there are further supplies in the kitchen. Take whatever you need.

Enjoy your stay.

She swallowed the rest of her vodka and tapped out a reply. Aimed for the right passive-aggressive tone. She had been *very* surprised about the lack of road access to the property and felt this should have been made clearer on the website. Her clothes and shoes were ruined. There was nothing to be done about it, of course, but she thought it might help to have some feedback for future guests. She hit send.

For the first time in ages she was hungry, so she pulled on thick socks and looked out into the corridor. Hesitated for a minute or two, listening. Not a sound, except her own breathing and the gentle ticking of a clock somewhere. Then she forced herself along to the top of the stairs and leaned over the balustrade to peer into the hall below. Next to the main door someone had left some wellies and a pair of walking boots. Other guests must have arrived, because she could hear the comforting hum of voices downstairs.

She padded down. Put a smile on her face, pulled out a stick of gum from her pocket to mask the smell of booze. She had chewed a lot of the stuff recently, whenever she was at home. The voices were coming from a big door at the back and to the right of the stairs. A dark tapestry, showing some kind of hunting scene, hung on the wall beside it. Pushing it open she found herself in a huge country kitchen.

Seated at the massive oak table, fiddling with a phone, was a guy who looked about her own age. Behind his black-rimmed glasses, his eyes gleamed as he flashed a white smile.

'Hello. Good to see you. Come in, come in.' He stood and held out his hand. 'I'm Mohammad – Mo – and that's my dad, Sandeep.'

He nodded to an elderly man standing in the corner. Hannah took Mo's hand and tried not to think about the awkward handshake at the end of her most recent disaster of an interview.

When Sandeep also stretched out his hand she could see the likeness. But while Mo was smiling, his father looked unhappy, angry even. He was holding a cloth and seemed to be cleaning the warm Aga.

'So, you're not the hosts?' Hannah asked.

Mo laughed. 'I wish. No, my dad's just a cleaning fanatic.' He turned to Sandeep. 'Come on, Dad, give it a rest. This is meant to be a holiday.' But his father ignored him.

'How long have you been here?' Hannah thought of the shadow at the window when she first arrived.

'About half an hour. And you?'

'An hour or so I think.' So it couldn't have been them. 'Had a proper nightmare walking all the way from the road.'

Hannah went to the fridge. Milk, cheese, butter. Some cold meats, lots of vegetables, orange and apple juice. But no wine. She sighed. 'I'm surprised the host didn't warn us about the trek across that bog. My new trainers are ruined.'

Mo looked down at her socks. 'Me and Dad like to walk, but yeah, it was a long way.'

An old-fashioned coffee maker started to steam on the Aga. Sandeep filled two mugs with coffee and pushed them towards her without a word. His eyes were clouded. With annoyance, anger, or something else, she couldn't guess. She sat beside Mo and passed him a coffee, all the time aware of Sandeep stooped in the corner, wiping the worktops, fussing with the Aga again.

Mo blew on the mug and took a sip. 'For a while we thought we might be the only guests, stuck out here on our own. It's nice to have company.'

He smiled at her across the table. It was a shy smile, but very warm. 'So what brings you all the way out here?'

It was too direct, although he couldn't possibly know that. She paused, not wanting to mention Ben, but struggling to think of a plausible lie. In the end the truth just seemed to come out.

'My father . . .' She swallowed. 'He used to live in this part of Ireland. He died five years ago.' Hannah could feel her jaw tightening. She never talked about him. What was she doing telling a complete stranger?

'So you've been here before?' Sandeep had turned to face her, his voice loud in the silence.

'Dad?' Mo glanced at Sandeep then leaned across the table. 'Don't mind him, he doesn't want to be here.' Mo had a strange accent that Hannah couldn't place. London certainly, but something else too.

She glanced at Sandeep and sipped her coffee. 'No, my parents separated when I was young and then my dad died. I never had a chance to get to know him properly.' She turned the mug around in her hands. 'When I saw this place on

Cloud BNB, I thought it would be nice to see where he lived. I guess I wanted to find out a bit more about him.' It was the truth as far as it went.

Sandeep turned towards her. 'You came on your own?' Once more that disapproving tone. And Hannah saw a flash of Ben laughing, shaking back his fair hair and leaning in to kiss her. *Come on, you know you want to go. Can't keep putting it off. We'll have a great time.*

She heard Mo mutter something under his breath. It could have been, 'Sorry,' but she was damned if she was going to let a moody old man get to her.

She looked at Sandeep. 'I'm interested in the house. I studied architecture and used to work at an architectural practice.' That was all he was going to get. 'What about you guys? Why did you decide to come here?'

'I didn't. It was *his* idea.' Sandeep turned away and continued to scrub the kitchen surfaces. 'This place is filthy. It's going to take me all evening to get it clean. And my clothes are still soaking wet from the walk.'

Hannah looked away and wondered why someone would be so unhappy about their holiday. Mo moved around the table to sit beside her and put his phone between them, pushing his glasses further up his nose with one finger. 'I'm interested in the house too, but the history. I've just finished my master's in history. Have you read about this place? There's some cool stuff on Preserve the Past website.'

Without waiting for an answer, he tapped his phone and held it up for her to read.

This property was originally called Fallon House after the local village of Fallon. Built in 1763 for the Anglo-Irish Lord Fallon, it remained in the family until the death of the most recent Lady Fallon. Preserve the Past then acquired it and changed the name from Fallon House to

29

The Guesthouse. Preserve the Past is a registered charity and all the proceeds from guest rentals go towards continued renovations.

Mo frowned. He flicked back and forth between pages. 'Weird. I swear there was more here when I looked before, some fascinating background about the area.' After a few seconds, he gave up and put down his phone. 'Apparently some bits of the house are closed off to visitors, because they're still being renovated. When there's enough money, I guess. These things cost a fortune.'

Sandeep scrubbed harder at the Aga.

'Well the outside's a bit rundown, but it looks pretty good in here. The entrance hall is beautiful.' Hannah smiled at Mo.

'It's incredible. Have you seen—'

One of the cupboard doors slammed shut with a bang. They both jumped and turned to look at Sandeep.

He flung down his cloth and stared at them, his eyes bright. 'Stop it. Stop it.' He coughed and put a hand to his mouth. 'This place . . . it's not right. There's something about it . . . It isn't safe.' There was a stunned silence. 'I know you think I'm an idiot, Mo, but you need to listen to me.' He stabbed a finger at his son. 'I'm leaving tomorrow, and you should too.'

Hannah blinked. She tried to think of something to say, as Sandeep paced back and forth across the kitchen. After a moment he pulled up a chair and sat down heavily. There was a pause before he began to speak, softly but with an intensity that kept Hannah rooted to her seat.

'I'm not joking.' He glanced between them. 'There's just . . . It's a horrible building. It just feels all wrong somehow, dark and cold . . . I don't know, like something bad happened here.' His knuckles were white on the edge of the table.

'Come on, Dad,' Mo tried to smile. 'It's fine. No one has lived here for years. It's been completely done up and—'

'I don't care! I don't care what *renovations* have been done. I don't care about its architecture. We should never have come.'

Chapter Four

Hannah stared at Mo as Sandeep stormed from the room and the door slammed behind him. Mo looked down at his phone, unable to meet her eye.

After a pause, she said, 'Is he all right?'

Mo didn't answer, and Hannah found herself glancing out of the kitchen window towards a small brick-built outhouse that crouched in the darkness under the trees. She swallowed.

When Mo finally spoke, his voice was croaky. 'I'm sorry about him.' He took off his glasses and rubbed them on his shirt. 'He's just tired after that long walk, and he hasn't been sleeping. He's got this cough and his doctor said he needs a rest, so I booked the holiday. Thought he'd love it.' A little laugh. 'He used to live in the area, you know. Came here from Pakistan, married Mum and they stayed for years. I was born near here too, lived in Ireland until I was fifteen.'

Hannah tried to smile. 'That explains the accent.'

'Yeah, I had a full-on Irish brogue when I arrived in London. Got bullied at school and managed to get rid of most of it. But I've never been as happy as I was when we lived here. Still feel Irish, I guess.'

He glanced at the closed door. 'Since Mum's death my dad has been really low. Hasn't bothered about anything. I've been popping in to check his post and emails and I spotted this offer from Cloud BNB. Guessed he must have been thinking about visiting. So I decided to book it as a surprise.'

Then his smile faded. 'It was a mistake to come. At first he refused, didn't want to go to Ireland at all, but I kept on until he finally agreed. It was all going fine until we arrived and started walking down that bloody track. He was confused, kept saying we were going the wrong way. We carried on, him silent the whole time, and when he saw the house, he just lost it. Flipped out. Said this wasn't The Guesthouse; it was all some kind of joke. They'd changed the name just to fool people.'

'Does he know this place then?'

'Apparently, but he wouldn't talk about it. Wouldn't say why he hates it so much. Just kept going on and on about its bad reputation, how it feels *all wrong*.' Mo tried to smile.

Hannah thought about the figure at the window when she first arrived. They lapsed into silence and listened to the wind tapping against the kitchen window.

Something tickled at her ankle and she jerked away, her leg hitting the table with a bang. The grey cat stepped out from underneath and Hannah laughed nervously. 'Stupid thing.' But when she picked it up and tried to put it on her lap, the cat leapt down and went to lie by the Aga.

'Knows its own mind,' Mo said. 'It was crying at the window when we came in here. I tried to open the back door.' He gestured behind them. 'But it's locked and I couldn't find a key. Had to let it in through the front.'

They lapsed into silence and watched the cat lick each of its back legs in turn.

Then there was a loud buzz and a click from the hall, and the front door swung open letting in a gust of wind.

'I hope this is our host.' Hannah pulled back her chair and they both stood. 'He's got some explaining to do.'

They walked into the hall and stood awkwardly by the stairs. But the figure who stepped through the door was nothing like the burly man from the website.

A stunning young woman walked in – tall, dressed all in black, her short hair almost white. A long strand hanging over one eye. Like Hannah, this girl had dark roots and streaks, but they were blue and purple: a fashion statement rather than laziness.

The new guest stood at the door looking at them. For a brief moment an expression of something like distress passed over her face, before it was replaced by an irritated frown.

She slung a rucksack onto the floor by the door and pulled off her black Doc Martens. Left them by the walking boots and wiped a muddy hand on her trousers.

'Hi, I'm Lucy.'

Her fingers were covered in rings, her ears crowded with studs. A sapphire-coloured stone glittered on the side of her nose, highlighting her high cheekbones and huge blue eyes.

Mo seemed to recover himself and stepped forward. 'I'm Mo and this is Hannah.' His Irish twang came on stronger. 'I'm here with my dad and Hannah's on her own like you.' Making sure Lucy knew they weren't a couple, Hannah guessed. 'We were having some coffee in the kitchen.' They all headed through, sitting at the table again.

Lucy stretched out her long legs. 'Bit of a walk, eh. I thought it was supposed to be near the village.' She stood up and went to the fridge. Then looked in the freezer and opened a couple of cupboards. 'No booze either. That's a bummer.'

Hannah felt her spirits rise: someone she could get along with. She considered mentioning her vodka upstairs but thought better of it. 'I'm going to walk to the village in the morning and find a shop.'

'Good idea, I'll come with you.' Lucy smiled, but when the buzzer sounded again, she flashed an anxious glance at the door.

Raised voices drifted out from the hallway and, after a moment, three people entered the kitchen. A little family, bringing with them gusts of ice-cold air. The woman, arms crossed over her fancy white top, gave them a stony look. 'I hope one of you is the host.'

Hannah sighed. ''Fraid not. There's no sign of him. Looks like he's avoiding us. The website did say it was self-check-in, though, so the host doesn't have to be here. That's why we have the electronic keypad—'

'It's ridiculous,' the woman interrupted. 'We've had to park miles away on the main road and stumble down a dirt track – in the dark – and with a child too.'

The teenage girl went red and turned away from them. The poor kid was probably around fourteen.

Her father gave them a warm smile. 'Yes, well. I'm Liam and this is my wife, Rosa, and daughter, Chloe.' His smile got bigger. 'Excuse Rosa, it's been a long walk.'

Rosa's voice was still sharp. 'And I don't like the thought of our car out there in the middle of nowhere.'

'Ours is too,' Mo said. 'They should be all right in a place like this. Not much crime around.' He gestured to the Aga. 'There's coffee on the stove.'

'None for us.' Rosa looked at Chloe and Liam. 'We should find our room and have a shower. Come on.'

But Liam stepped towards the Aga. 'You go on. I could do with a hot drink.'

Rosa stared at him for a moment, then strode out, Chloe trailing after her. The girl glanced back at Lucy as she reached the door.

Liam poured himself some coffee and held up the pot. 'Anyone else?' Hannah and Mo shook their heads.

'I'll just have some juice, thanks.' Lucy went to the fridge.

Hannah concentrated on her own mug but noticed Liam and Mo sneaking glances at Lucy.

Liam was tall and strong-looking with sandy hair thinning at the front. He had a warm Scottish lilt to match his warm smile. He sat at the end of the table, leaned back and took a gulp of coffee.

'So, what brings you all here?' His eyes flicked along Lucy's legs.

Lucy raised her glass of orange juice and laughed. 'You first, Liam.'

'We don't live far away, actually, but we're in the middle of a house move and having some problems. Sold our place and bought a new-build. But the work has been delayed – it's been a complete nightmare to be honest – so we're marking time here. Rosa found this place and I negotiated us a deal. A pretty good one, too.' He flashed a white-toothed smile at Lucy. 'I don't know how much you lot are paying, but apparently we can stay as long as we like.'

There was an awkward pause, then Lucy put her glass down on the worktop. 'Moving house is always a bloody nightmare.' She looked out the window. 'I'm dying for a cigarette. Might head out for one in the garden.'

Hannah had given up a few years ago, but over the past few months the old craving had crept back into her life and now she felt its familiar stirring. 'Can I steal one? I'll get some more tomorrow.'

Lucy nodded, and they walked out the front door.

The rain had stopped and the dark starless sky stretched away towards the horizon. Still and black, darker than any night Hannah had known in England. Lucy flicked a switch by the front door and a dim lamp buzzed on, illuminating the grey cat as it snaked past them and ran along the patio into the night.

They sat on a big iron bench, and Lucy lit her cigarette. 'How long you staying?'

She raised her lighter to the cigarette in Hannah's lips and clicked, the flame flickering in Lucy's eyes as Hannah sucked in a lungful of smoke. She tried not to cough. 'Just a week. You?'

'Maybe two,' she laughed. 'But I'm not so sure now.'

Hannah took another drag and laughed. 'I'm sure *Liam* would like you to stay.'

Lucy grimaced. 'Great, he's just what I need.'

'You did seem kind of surprised to find us all here, though. Were you expecting to be alone?'

Lucy turned to face her. She really was gorgeous. 'Was it that obvious? I make music. Just broke up with my band and got an offer for a solo contract. I wanted somewhere quiet, you know, somewhere to write and think. Thought this place would be empty, that no one else would arrive until at least next week.'

'You make music, cool.' She might have known. 'What kind of stuff?'

'A mix of things to be honest. Punk, death metal, you know.' Hannah nodded vaguely as Lucy continued, 'I need to make my mark before I get past it. Twenty-five isn't young in the music industry.'

So they were the same age. Hannah settled into sullen

silence and continued smoking. Thought about everything Lucy had already accomplished, about what it must be like to stand on stage as a sea of people cheered your name. Then she pictured her own messy bedroom back in her mum's house, her own messy life. She took a final drag and stabbed the fag out on the bench.

Mo and Liam had managed to make a meal, with Sandeep's assistance. They'd used a huge frying pan to knock up what Mo called 'a kind of ratatouille'. Everyone sat together at the kitchen table, but only Rosa was talking.

'I just don't understand why they didn't mention the lack of road access.' A wave of her fork for emphasis. 'Needless to say, I've left a complaint on the website and sent our host several messages.' She looked down at her dish and gave it a poke, as if noticing it for the first time. 'This looks lovely, but isn't there any meat in the fridge?'

Liam touched her other hand. 'Mo and Sandeep are vegetarian, love.'

Rosa went to say something, but Lucy got there first. 'Me too. There's a big chorizo sausage in one of the cupboards, though. You could fry that up and add it in.'

Rosa smiled tightly and took a drink of water. 'No, it's fine. I'll do something with meat tomorrow.' Hannah had been trying to place her Scottish accent and realized it was just like Maggie Smith's in that movie her mum was always watching, *The Prime of Miss Jean Brodie*. Posh Edinburgh.

Chloe gave Mo a shy smile. 'I like it, thank you.'

During the meal Hannah stayed quiet. It seemed that they all, except Lucy, had some kind of connection to the area. Liam obviously loved the sound of his own voice, even more so than his wife. He told them all that he was a very successful GP who'd recently retired from a local practice and was moving back to Scotland with his family as soon as their house was ready.

Lucy wasn't Irish, but she'd been living in Dublin. She'd been attracted by Preserve the Past website and its promise of comfortable historic houses in quiet locations.

'But this was the only one I could afford. I also think self-check-in is a cool idea – it just makes sense. I mean, who actually wants to meet the host?' When nobody responded, Lucy went on. 'I've stayed in B&Bs before where they never leave you alone.'

Hannah couldn't sit still. She picked at her food and her eyes kept returning to the drinks cupboard in the corner of the room that by rights should have contained wine, at least a few bottles of Henry Laughton's expensive vintage stuff. Hannah's hands felt clammy and her top kept sticking to her back. She wanted to open a window, but it was freezing outside. When Mo stood up and suggested cheese and biscuits or ice cream, Hannah made her excuses and went to leave the room without meeting anyone's eye.

'Chocolate ice cream for me. What about you, Chloe?' Mo said.

'She'll have some fruit or a plain yogurt,' Rosa replied.

Hannah slipped out the door. Wouldn't fancy being Chloe and putting up with Rosa The Dictator for a mother. But by the time Hannah was halfway up the stairs, she was thinking of nothing but the vodka waiting in her room.

But something made her stop, a prickling along her spine like a feather touching skin. She turned and stared around the hallway, expecting to see someone watching her. But it was empty, just the strange paintings across one wall and the tapestry hanging beside the kitchen door.

Then a huge bang echoed around the space, and Hannah let out a gasp. She dropped to her knees.

Another crash, this time even louder, from somewhere in the house above her. Then silence.

Heart thumping, one hand on the bannister, Hannah stared up the stairs and waited for the ceiling to fall down on top of her.

Chapter Five

The kitchen door burst open and the others piled out into the hallway and peered up at her. She stood and turned to them.

'What the fuck was that?' Liam pressed his fingers to his mouth. 'Sorry, no excuse for bad language. Sorry, Chloe.'

Rosa held her daughter closer, and Mo put a hand on his father's arm. Only Lucy looked calm.

Mo ran up the stairs to Hannah and put his hand on her back, eyes concerned. 'Are you all right?'

For a moment she was aware of how good his touch felt. Then she thought of Ben, thought of the random guy from the other night, the random guys on so many recent nights, and stepped away.

'I'm OK. I think it came from upstairs.'

Mo looked down at the others. 'I'll check it out.'

Liam started up the stairs. 'I'll come with you. It's probably a window crashing down. If the cords rot on these old sashes, they break in the wind. I opened a couple of dodgy ones in our room.' He ran up past them, his eyes lingering on Hannah for a second too long.

Mo followed. 'We should all be careful.'

Hannah waited on the stairs as her heart rate returned to

normal. Liam entered the family room at the top and emerged moments later holding up a piece of white cord.

'Yes, that's it. I knew it. The damn thing's broken: worn out.' He grinned and headed back down the stairs. 'I'm surprised they didn't replace them all when they did the renovations. Maybe just missed that one. Anyway, be careful with them and we'll let the host know.'

Sandeep's voice cut through the hall. He had been silent for so long Hannah had almost forgotten he was there. 'That didn't sound like a window banging in the wind. It was too loud, and the wind isn't even that strong. It could have been a problem with the roof. Something could come crashing through on us.'

Rosa looked up at the high ceiling with a frown, but Liam just laughed. He bounded down and put his arm around her. 'Don't worry about it. The roof's completely sound – I had a good look around earlier.'

Hannah couldn't remember him exploring the house, but she was too tired to care. Let him blow his own trumpet for a bit. She said nothing and carried on upstairs. The vodka was calling her.

When she got to her room she poured herself a large glass, topped it up with Coke, and swallowed it down with a sigh. She'd left her phone charging but the lead had come loose and was lying on the floor. When she plugged it in again she saw a reply from Henry Laughton.

Apologies about the road access. We had hoped to have a metalled approach lane installed before your arrival, but planning permission was delayed. I did message you about this a few weeks ago and a notice was added to the website. I hope it doesn't interfere with your holiday too much.

I'm sorry I wasn't there to greet you, but I'm held up at
one of our other properties.
Regards Henry.

Hannah knew it was possible she had missed his message.
She hadn't been taking much notice of anything recently,
except all the trolls on social media.

But surely one of the other guests would have seen the
message. No doubt old Henry, in his fancy Barbour jacket,
was chuckling to himself, assuming he'd get away with it.
She couldn't be bothered to reply; Rosa would probably give
him an earful anyway.

Sitting on the bed she realized that for a short while today,
surrounded by people who knew nothing about her, listening
to the chatter over dinner, she hadn't once thought about
Ben. And as she took another sip of vodka, she tried to keep
those dark memories at bay, tried to ignore the familiar pain
beginning to settle around her heart.

A small chest of drawers with a kettle and an array of
white china containers filled with posh teabags, instant
coffee and chocolate stood by the corridor wall. She made
herself a mug of chocolate, undressed and climbed into bed.
Took a soothing sip of the drink, then added a slug of vodka
and left the bottle on the bedside table, close to hand.

The bright lamp made her dry eyes throb. But when she
switched it off, the images she dreaded began to swirl around
her in the blackness.

She tossed and turned in the bed, clutching at her duvet,
unable to stop herself from reliving the same dark memories.
Thinking back to Ben's funeral.

She remembered getting out of the cab on the side of the
road and walking all alone towards the church through
crowds of people. His friends and family turned to face her
– whispering – then moved away.

She sat alone at the very back of the church as Ben's family filed towards the coffin, his younger brother following behind with bloodshot eyes. He had always been friendly to her, and when he came to sit next to her after the service, she thought for one tiny moment that he was going to tell her it would be all right. That everyone knew she wasn't to blame.

Instead he hissed, his voice low and bitter, 'Mum and Dad asked me to say: don't come to the grave or the house afterwards.' He swallowed. 'Just stay away from us.'

She sat there, alone in her seat, as the crowds filed out. Her head bowed, staring at the floor.

She must have drifted off to sleep then, because suddenly she knew she was dreaming. Thoughts of Ben and his family gradually vanished, but Hannah felt no relief – just a sense of absolute terror.

She was still in bed, the sound of her breathing low and steady in her ears. A curtain moved softly in the breeze from the window, fluttering gently across the floor. A floorboard creaked somewhere nearby and she knew with terrible certainty that she was no longer alone. There was someone else in here, in the room with her, watching her sleep.

A musky smell that she couldn't place, a feeling of helplessness when she tried to sit up. She couldn't move.

There was a rustling sound and a shadow stepped out from the darkness at the corner of the room. Silhouetted in the grey light that fell through the curtains, it shuffled and then stopped. Moved slowly closer to the bed. Hannah's heart thudded louder, her palms clammy. Her neck throbbed, but still she couldn't move.

The sickly-sweet smell was overpowering now. Somehow familiar, it crawled its way down her throat, choking her.

Another creak from a floorboard, closer now. The shadow

loomed above her, but she couldn't turn her head to face it, couldn't even breathe. It was human, it must be, yet it seemed to slide like water over ice as it reached the edge of her bed. A cold chill settled in the room. She was shivering, yet her legs were blocks of stone anchored to the bed. *Get up. Get out.* She tried to scream, but there was only silence.

And then the dip and creak of the bed. The mattress sinking under a groaning weight as something pressed it down. Huge and dark, so close to her that she could almost feel it through the duvet. Almost imagine it reaching out to touch her.

She was suddenly wide awake, completely alert. Sitting upright in bed, drenched in sweat.

She gasped and threw off the damp duvet. Flicked on the light and scanned the empty room. Her heartbeat gradually slowed as she listened to the quiet house. Her throat was so dry, it ached. In the bathroom she gulped down a glass of water and filled it again. Stared at the pale face in the mirror. Her hand shook as she downed the second glass.

She checked that her door was still locked and the window secure, then poured a shot of vodka and drank it down. Drew the curtains, got back into bed and huddled under the duvet, shivering, just like in her dream. And it *was* just a dream, some stupid dream.

Nightmares were nothing new. She remembered waking up terrified beside Ben in the middle of the night, so scared she refused to go back to sleep again. Ben would gently hold her and whisper that it was all right and she was safe and everything was going to be OK. He would stroke her hair and kiss her neck and tell her she was safe, until she finally dozed off.

But this had been different: it had felt real.

She couldn't sleep for hours. Her mind wouldn't stop

raking back over the dream, reliving it in vivid detail. The drip and the creak of the mattress, the feel of that heavy weight pressing down. And just when she had finally exhausted herself, when sleep reached out to claim her, she heard something else. A murmuring noise, somewhere nearby. Low and persistent.

She lay there listening in the pitch-black, until all she could hear were the small creaks of the old house, the gurgling of pipes, the call of an owl outside. She pulled the duvet up over her head. Had she been dreaming again? Tomorrow, she was going to lay off the alcohol; Lori was right, it was starting to mess with her head. How many days since she had last been sober? She rolled over and tried to sleep once more.

It was then that she first heard it. The sound of a child crying.

Chapter Six

A sobbing child somewhere inside the house.

Chloe must have had a fight with her mum. Hannah rolled over in her warm and comfortable bed and closed her eyes. Tried to shut out the sound, but it went on and on, quiet but insistent, until she could think of nothing else. Chloe was in a family room with her parents, so wouldn't they have woken up to look after her?

There was something so disturbing about the sound – so desperate and sad – that Hannah eventually threw off the covers and went to the door. A very low light was coming from the other end of the corridor, oozing out a pale glow. The family room was right at the top of the stairs. Pulling a sweater over her pyjamas, she put her head outside. The sound – a gentle heart-rending sobbing – seemed to be louder out here. Hannah told herself to calm down.

Afraid she wouldn't remember her door code, she wedged it open with one of her shoes and headed along the corridor to the top of the staircase. The weak light of a lamp filtered down into the dark hall below. She paused outside each of the guest rooms in case the noise was actually coming from one of them, maybe a radio or TV. But they were silent. As she came close to the family room, the noise suddenly stopped. She paused, listening hard, expecting to hear hushed voices inside.

Silence. If they had heard her footsteps perhaps they were keeping quiet. Embarrassed, maybe. Hannah stood for a moment wondering what to do. She didn't want to disturb them, reminded herself not to get involved. The light at the end of the corridor flickered and buzzed, then went out, enveloping her in darkness. The only sound was her heart thudding loudly in her chest.

And then, with a click, the light came back on. Hannah swallowed. She glanced around, her neck tingling with unease. She was alone, nothing had changed.

She hurried back to her room.

The next day, Hannah woke to early morning light filtering across the room. She groaned and rolled over, opened one eye and looked at her phone on the floor. Nine o'clock. Why was the room still so dim?

Pulling the curtains wide, she looked out into a wall of white. Thick mist smothered everything, even covering the bare little rose garden below. There was no way she could navigate that rutted track in this fog, so her plan to visit the village would have to wait.

When she got downstairs, Liam, Rosa, and Chloe were in the kitchen, the remnants of a full English breakfast on the table in front of them. Chloe's plate looked untouched, her eyes red and swollen.

'Chloe, eat up,' Rosa said. 'You need a good breakfast.' And Chloe bowed her head and shovelled a few baked beans into her mouth.

Liam gave Hannah an easy smile. 'Morning there, sleep well?' His eyes flickered over her.

Her face burned as she looked away. 'Not really.' This

was the moment when someone should explain why Chloe had been crying, but the only sound was the scraping of a fork against a plate.

'Stop playing with your food.' Rosa's voice was loud. 'What on earth is wrong with you this morning?'

Chloe looked like she was on the verge of tears. Liam reached for a piece of toast and began buttering it. 'Try this with some scrambled egg.'

As Hannah was pouring herself tea, Mo came in. He met her eyes with a warm smile and she felt her heart beat a little faster. A feeling inside that she didn't deserve to experience again.

'Guess what . . . I've found something.' Mo nodded towards the door. 'Come and have a look.'

Holding her warm mug she followed him to the opposite side of the hall, through a set of double doors, and into a beautiful high-ceilinged room. A large fire roared away in the grand fireplace in a corner.

'I found a stack of logs out the back. Got the fire going first thing.'

'Amazing. It's so warm in here.' The grey cat was curled up on a fireside armchair and Hannah, not wanting to disturb it, settled into one of the others.

Mo took a poker from a fancy metal stand and moved a log in the grate with a flourish. 'I've never lit a proper fire before, but I'm getting the hang of it now.' He used his phone to snap a picture. 'I'm pretty sure this is an Adam fireplace – a nice one, too.' Hannah couldn't help smiling. Mo paused to frown at his phone. 'Still can't get a signal.'

Hannah dug out her iPhone and glanced at the screen. There wasn't even wifi any more. No way was she going to walk all the way to the village without Google Maps, even if this fog cleared. They needed to find the router.

Mo wiped his hands on his trousers and flopped into the

sofa. 'Shame about the weather. Could be a good excuse to explore the rest of the house, though. What do you reckon?'

'Yeah, I'd like that.'

Liam appeared at the door. He rubbed his hands together in what she was beginning to recognize was a habitual gesture. 'A fire! Terrific, just what we need.' He crouched by the fireplace and held his palms up to the flames. 'Makes me almost glad of the fog.'

They all looked towards the wide French windows and to the white wall of mist that pressed against the glass. Hannah turned back to Mo. 'How's your dad this morning?'

'Complaining as usual.' Mo smiled. 'He's having a lie-in. Didn't sleep well again.' Someone else who'd been kept awake by the crying, Hannah guessed. Mo went on, 'He's pretty annoyed that we're gonna have to stay another day.'

Liam threw another log on the fire. 'If it clears up, I thought I'd go into the village and buy some wine for anyone who wants it. Can't have a dry holiday now, can we? I don't drink when I'm at work, too busy you know, so I like to indulge a little when I'm away.' He grinned up at Hannah. 'Maybe we could find some board games and have a few drinks together later on.'

Mo poked at the fire again, his back turned to them. As much as Hannah couldn't stand Liam, she needed to get to the shop. 'If you're going, I need to get a packet of fags for Lucy. Reckon you could give me a lift?'

'No, no, don't worry about it. You stay and enjoy yourself.' Liam turned back to the fire. 'I'll get cigarettes, plenty of wine and whatever spirits they have in the shop.'

Hannah tried to protest, but he was adamant. She thanked him and felt her stomach rumble, reminding her she hadn't eaten breakfast.

Back in the kitchen Rosa stood at the sink, washing up, and Chloe sat at the table, still scowling at her plate. She'd probably been told to stay here until her food was finished. Hannah took a plate from the cupboard and made herself a couple of pieces of toast. Pulled up a chair next to Chloe and whispered, 'Can I help you with that?'

Chloe gave a tiny smile, a glance at her mother, and then nodded. Hannah scraped most of Chloe's food onto her own plate and started to eat. 'You look pretty tired. Did you have trouble sleeping, like me and Sandeep?'

The girl nodded.

'We all slept like logs,' Rosa said, turning from the sink.

They all fell silent and Hannah continued to eat. What had really happened last night? And why didn't Rosa want to talk about it?

She was clearing away their plates when Mo appeared at the door. 'Who's up for a tour?' He smiled at Chloe. 'I'm hoping for a secret passage.'

'Come on, let's go explore,' Hannah said as she shepherded Chloe through the door.

Rosa turned from the sink, a tea cloth in her hand. 'Be careful.'

'It's all right. I'll keep an eye on her.' Hannah held Rosa's gaze for a moment, then they all filed out into the hall.

In the drawing room, Lucy sat curled in the leather armchair beside the fireplace, an open book on her lap. Her tiny shorts, fluffy socks and huge sweatshirt only made her look more beautiful. When she noticed them at the door, she put down her book and gave them a tired smile.

'Nice fire, Mo. I'll be snuggled up in here until this weather improves.' A yawn. 'I'm shattered. Need a duvet day, I think.' She stretched out a slender leg, revealing an intricate tattoo on the side of her thigh. Mo seemed to be finding it hard to speak.

Chloe was also staring and, when she spoke, it was in a quiet voice that made her sound younger than her years.

'We're going to look around the house, if you want to come too?'

Lucy smiled and put down her book. 'You know, I might just do that. An explore would be fun.' She stood up and stretched. 'Give me a minute to get changed.'

'We'll meet you outside your room,' Mo said. 'Might as well start upstairs.'

When Lucy left the room, Mo, Chloe, and Hannah lapsed into silence, watching the fire crackling in the grate. Then the door banged open and Rosa burst in, making them jump.

'For God's sake, there you all are. Couldn't you hear me calling?' She didn't wait for a response, but stood framed in the doorway, pointing out the window at the fog. 'I tried to stop him, but Liam is insisting on going to the village. It's madness. Completely stupid. He'll get himself killed. Can someone please try and talk some sense into him?'

Mo stepped forward. 'I can try, but I doubt he'll listen. Maybe we should see if Dad's awake. He'd be able to do it.' He noticed Hannah and Rosa exchange looks. 'He doesn't talk about it, but my dad was a copper for thirty years.' A smile. 'Knows how to talk someone round.'

There was a pause and Hannah tried to imagine Sandeep as a policeman. He certainly knew the difference between right and wrong.

Rosa too looked doubtful, but eventually she sighed. 'OK, but please be quick.' Chloe and Mo followed her from the room.

Hannah picked up the book Lucy had left on the chair. *Wild Swimming: The Best Hidden Dips in Ireland*. She imagined Lucy hiking through the wilderness in her Doc Martens, tackling lakes and rivers, no doubt emerging from the water looking as gorgeous as ever.

Just the thought of swimming was enough to make Hannah squirm. She couldn't swim and had no desire to learn. Ben had tried several times to bring her along to the pool or tempt her into the water at the beach. She bit the inside of her mouth and forced thoughts of Ben from her mind.

The fire flickered as a gust of cold air blew into the room from the hallway, and Hannah heard Mo running down the stairs. She poked her head out and saw Rosa standing at the open front door, pecking away at her phone with Chloe at her side.

Mo reached the bottom of the stairs and ran a hand through his hair. He looked suddenly older. 'Sorry, Rosa. I can't get him up. He's still not feeling well – it's his cough.'

'Too late.' Rosa didn't even bother to look up from the screen. 'The selfish bastard wouldn't listen.' There was a surprising bitterness in her voice, as if the trip to the village was a personal attack. Chloe stood very still, her hands clenched. After a moment, Rosa caught Hannah's eye and sighed. 'I'm just worried about him. He can be incredibly stubborn.'

'I'm sure he'll be all right. It looks like it's clearing up out there,' Hannah said, her eyes on Chloe who – despite her obvious anxiety and embarrassment – hadn't shown even a flicker of surprise at her mother's outburst. The cracks were starting to show in Rosa's perfect family, and Hannah couldn't help but think that she might deserve it.

Rosa closed the front door with a slam and stomped back into the kitchen. 'I'm going to try Liam again. The signal's terrible, but it sometimes works in here.'

There was a moment of silence, then Mo pointed up the stairs. 'Come on, Chloe, race you to the top.' She was staring after her mother, a deep frown on her face.

'OK, I'll be the starter.' Hannah stood at the bottom of the stairs, one arm raised.

Mo took up a runner's pose beside her. With a final look towards the kitchen, Chloe joined him with a small smile.

Hannah shouted, 'On your marks, get set, go.' She dropped her arm and Mo ran halfway up the stairs, his long legs covering two steps at a time.

Before the top he slammed to a stop and sprawled face first on the steps, clutching his side and panting. 'Oh no. My side, my side. I've got a stitch.'

Chloe thundered past him, laughing and whooping, and almost collided with Lucy on the landing.

When Mo had limped his way up and reached them, Chloe slapped his arm. 'You cheated. It wasn't fair. You let me win.'

Lucy laid her palm on Mo's side and frowned. 'Nope, that's genuine. A nasty stitch.'

As their laughter reached Hannah down in the hallway below them, she suddenly felt very alone. Her mind drifted back to the playground, when she had watched from a distance as everyone else had fun together.

She was about to turn back to the drawing room, when Chloe shouted down from above. 'Come on, Hannah.' And when she ran up to join them, Chloe grabbed her hand and pulled her along with her.

It didn't take long to explore the top floor. Their five occupied rooms made up the west wing: Hannah's number one at the far end of the corridor, Sandeep next to her, then Mo. Lucy's room, and the family room, were near the top of the stairs.

The east wing had five doors, then a narrow one right at the end: another storage room, the twin of the one next to Hannah's room, she guessed. A matching window overlooked the front of the house from this side too. When they got to it, Chloe stood for a moment looking down, her fingers pressed to the glass.

All the large rooms had brass door numbers and keypads. Hannah pointed out the beautifully carved wooden rails and cornices, the two ceiling roses in the corridors, each with a sparkling crystal chandelier, and talked about their design.

Mo headed towards the stairs. 'There must be a cellar down here somewhere.'

'I'm not sure I can face looking at any more chandeliers,' said Lucy with a glance at Chloe. 'Anyone up for trying to find a board game downstairs?'

But Chloe stopped and stared across the hall, through one of the tall windows, her expression dark. 'It's Dad.'

Hannah moved to her side and saw Liam trudging up the gravel drive out of the mist, a scowl on his face, no shopping bags in his hands. He couldn't have been to the village and back already. Hannah bit back her disappointment.

The front door opened and he came in, pushing off the hood of his anorak and shaking rain across the floor. Chloe ran downstairs to him and he bent to give her a hug and a stiff smile.

He shook his head. 'Sorry, no luck. I made it about halfway. Slow going, I can tell you, bloody treacherous. I met a local idiot on the path, too, and guess what: the village shop is closed for the week because of some stupid annual holiday.'

With Chloe clinging to his arm he went into the kitchen. Hannah felt herself lean against the wall for support.

Mo let out a sigh. 'Well, that's that then.' He turned to Hannah and then his face changed. He frowned and stepped towards her. 'Are you all right?'

Lucy touched her shoulder and Hannah tried to smile. Her legs felt weak and her brow prickled with sweat, but she was going to be all right. There would be a pub in the village that would sell her a bottle of wine tomorrow.

'I'm fine, just a bit tired.' She brushed them away with a weak smile. 'Didn't sleep well last night, probably all the excitement. I'll just go for a lie-down.' Mo and Lucy watched her as she walked carefully back up the stairs, her trembling hands stuffed into her pockets.

In her room, she sat on the bed and told herself to be calm. It was nothing to worry about, just the stress of everything she'd been going through, the fallout from her disturbed sleep. A nice vodka and Coke would help to steady her nerves.

Her mouth felt dry as she looked around the room. The glass sat on the bedside table, where she'd left it, and so did the Coke. But the vodka had gone.

She looked in the bathroom, on all the surfaces. Checked under the bed, shook out the duvet and threw it on the floor. Dug under the mattress, opened her bag and rifled through her clothes.

Then she slumped on the bed and a horrible thought began to creep its way into her mind. Confused memories of last night came back, that awful dream and her reaching for the bottle in the dark moments between waking and sleep. Could she have drunk the whole thing? If she couldn't remember finishing a whole bloody bottle in one day and disposing of the evidence, there was something seriously wrong.

She began to pace back and forth across the room. But there *had* been some left, she was sure of it. And if she was right there was only one possible explanation. Time seemed to slow as she stared at her bed. Looked towards the door.

Someone had been in her room.

Chapter Seven

She glared at the clothes and bedding strewn all around her. Someone, some creep, must have been in here, tampering with her things. Her skin crawled. She checked her bag again, but everything seemed to be there: purse, credit cards, keys. Were Mo and Lucy taking the piss? She wouldn't even put it past Liam. He looked the sort to enjoy practical jokes, and he obviously liked a drink.

Or maybe someone was so uptight that they couldn't bear to have alcohol anywhere near them. But how had they known it was here? And how had they known her key code?

Only Preserve the Past knew that. The website had mentioned a cleaner who came just once a week, but they weren't due for another four days. Henry wasn't around, so Hannah was the only one with a record of her booking.

She thought back over the past few hours.

There seemed to be only one short period when someone could have got in. She had wedged her door open and gone to see why Chloe was crying. That ruled out the family and Lucy, because she had listened outside their doors. Even Mo was unlikely, so that left Sandeep.

His room was close to hers and he had been acting

strangely, hadn't talked much over dinner. Maybe he didn't approve of alcohol.

But he was just a harmless old guy who didn't seem all that steady on his feet. She would have heard him shuffling down the corridor, too. Unless.

In the bathroom she splashed her face with water. Stared at the mirror and thought about what was on the other side of her wall. She wouldn't have heard Sandeep if he had hidden in the little storage room, waiting in the dark for his chance.

She crept out into the empty corridor and stared at the keypad beside the mysterious door. *Think, think*. What was the code? But when she slapped the door in frustration, she felt the latch open and the door give way. She pushed harder and fell inside, the door shutting behind her.

The room was gloomy, just the sort of place where someone could hide. If this door had been on the latch last night, it would have been easy to wait in here and slip into her room.

She could make out a desk and on it a small lamp. When she hit the switch, the bulb cast just enough light to illuminate dusty surfaces and spider webs. She was in some kind of office, one that hadn't been used in a very long time. A few rotten floorboards had fallen through, leaving splintered holes. There was no way Henry Laughton did his paperwork in here.

The desk was clear of everything but dust. Hannah brushed off the chair, sat down cautiously in case it gave way, and opened one of the drawers. A pile of small hardback books in various dark colours: red, blue, black. Picking one up she read the first few pages and then did the same to the next one. She counted ten diaries altogether, ranging from twenty to ten years ago. These must belong to the previous owners: the Fallons. She remembered Mo talking animatedly about them over dinner, about stuff he'd seen on Preserve the Past website. The family had died out some years ago, their house falling into disrepair, then the Trust had taken over.

It seemed wrong to look, but she carried on flicking through the pages. There were no scandalous confessions, just occasional initials and times on various pages, for what were obviously appointments. *O.H. 3pm, Doc L. 9am*, etc. There wasn't even a name in the front or any phone numbers and addresses. On one page she spotted a star beside a word in capitals: *MADDIE*. Checking the other books, she saw it appeared in them all. Someone's birthday perhaps.

The second drawer contained only a notepad and a couple of pens. As she piled the diaries back in, a piece of torn paper fluttered to the ground, with a sentence scrawled on one side.

She's been fed so DO NOT give her any more. Just some water. J.

Must be about a pet. She slipped the paper into the notepad and moved towards the window. When she pulled back the threadbare curtains she got a faceful of dust. Coughing and waving her hand around, she looked out through the dirty glass into the mist. It was beginning to clear and she could see partway up the hill at the back of the house. Her heart skipped a beat and she tightened her grip on the windowsill.

There was something else down there now, something moving. It was too big to be an animal. She watched as a figure emerged from the fog – a man walking slowly along the rise at the back of the house. She couldn't make out his features, but it didn't look like Liam, Mo, or Sandeep. Shrouded in dark, heavy clothes, it reminded her of the figure from her dream. Her heart thudded in her chest.

The man stopped for a moment. He was totally still, but he would see her if he turned towards the house. Hannah's hand shook as she stretched out for the lamp and switched it off, shrouding herself in darkness. But she couldn't step away, couldn't stop staring at the shape of his shoulders. The horribly familiar way that he moved. He was strolling along the ridge again, so smoothly he seemed to slide, just as the figure in her dream had done.

Her eyes followed him on up the hill until the mist swallowed him and he was gone. As if he'd never been there.

She pulled the curtains shut and collapsed onto the chair. Was she finally losing it? Was it all in her head? It must be. But it was nothing to worry about. She needed a drink, that was all. This was the first day without one in a long time. The man was probably just a hiker. But whoever he was, she had to go out and find him, to talk to him, because she needed to know for sure.

Needed to know that he was real.

Walking back to the door, avoiding the broken floorboards, she realized something else had been bothering her all this time. And now she knew what it was: that smell from her dream last night, it was in here too.

The room spun and suddenly all she could smell was that cloying stink. She needed to get out, needed fresh air.

She waited, listening for anyone outside in the corridor, because she didn't want them to find her here.

When she turned the handle, it wobbled but the door didn't move. She tried again, this time putting her weight behind it.

The latch. The fucking latch. Why had she let it close behind her?

She wrenched at the door handle, twisted and turned it, pushed and pulled. *Come on, come on.* Rattled and shook it. *Move.*

At last the handle began to shift and she pushed down harder, shifted her weight backwards. And the handle came off in her hand.

Chapter Eight

She made herself count to ten, then pushed the handle back into the hole. It clicked and turned, then kept on turning uselessly, until she let it fall back out onto the floor.

A wave of nausea almost overpowered her and she leaned her head against the door. It was the dust and that fucking smell, the thick stink that seemed to be everywhere.

And then with her face pressed to the wood, she heard something. Breathing, someone standing in the hallway, inches from the door.

She stopped herself from calling out. What if they had hidden in here last night? She listened to the silence, then to the breathing, heavier now.

'Who's in there? Who is it?' Lucy, a hint of fear in her voice.

Hannah gasped with relief. 'Thank God, Lucy. It's me, Hannah. I got locked in.'

'I can't open it. Did you use a code?'

'It was on the latch, but it's stuck now.'

Lucy tapped away at the keypad for a moment. 'It's not working. I'll have to break in.'

A sudden thought, a memory of a name scrawled in black: *MADDIE*. Hannah grabbed one of the diaries, skimmed through the pages, and returned to the door.

'Lucy, hang on, I've got something. Try the number 1701.'
No response. 'Lucy? Are you still there?'

After a pause, Lucy answered. 'I'm here. What did you say?'

Hannah called out the number again and listened as Lucy keyed it in. There was a click and a buzz, then the door opened and Hannah almost fell through it.

Lucy stood there, white-faced. Hannah took a moment to steady herself, to try a laugh. 'Thank you. Jesus, this bloody house is a nightmare.' Her mouth felt dry.

Lucy's eyes narrowed. 'How did you know the code?'

'Just a guess. I found some old diaries in there. One of the Fallons was born on January 17th, so I thought it was worth a try. Maybe all the codes are important dates from the house's history – Mo would be into that.'

Lucy's smile looked forced as she opened the door and peered around the room. 'God, what a dump. Look at those boards – you could fall through the floor.' She shut the door and sighed. 'I don't want to be boring, but we should probably keep an eye on Chloe. If something happens to her in one of these rundown old rooms, Rosa really will lose her shit.'

Hannah smiled.

'Fancy a coffee?' Lucy asked as they walked towards the stairs. 'It always helps after a shock.'

'Sounds good.' Hannah followed her down. It was too late to catch the hiker on the ridge and she couldn't face going back to her alcohol-free room. She realized she still had the diary in her hand and shoved it into the back pocket of her jeans.

Mo and his dad were sitting in the kitchen eating sandwiches, Sandeep hunched over his plate, his eyes half-closed, wrinkles criss-crossing his face. As they entered, he glanced up and smiled at them both, his expression warmer today.

What possible reason could an elderly ex-policeman have for going into her room? But if not him then who else?

Mo pointed to the Aga. 'Coffee's made.'

Hannah poured herself a mug and stood close to the heat of the Aga, feeling the cold sweat on her back beginning to dry. She looked out the window at the thick wall of fog and tried to work out how long it would take to clear. She would head back to London as soon as it did, no matter what her mother or Lori said. Mo glanced at her, and she realized her hands were shaking.

'Are you all right?' he asked.

Hannah stayed silent and Lucy exchanged a glance with Mo. 'Hannah's had a bit of a shock,' she said. 'She got trapped in one of the rooms upstairs – the door handle came off – and she almost fell through the rotten floorboards. It's pretty dangerous, so we should probably try to stay out of anywhere that isn't open to guests.'

Mo raised an eyebrow, and Hannah wondered why carefree Lucy was suddenly so uptight about health and safety. Pushing away his plate, Sandeep turned to Mo. 'Didn't I tell you? The place isn't safe. It's falling apart, everything is covered in dust and it hasn't even been properly renovated.'

Hannah took her chance and sat down opposite him. She needed to get him talking, find out what it was about this house that scared him so much. And see whether he'd been into her room.

'Sandeep, Mo said you used to be a policeman.'

Sandeep frowned at his son. Then took a sip from his mug, scratched the wooden table with his fingernail for a moment, and nodded. 'I did, joined up when I arrived in Ireland – the first Pakistani copper in the area.'

Mo began to clear away the plates. 'The first *Pakistani* in the area.'

'But we had no problems fitting in,' said Sandeep. 'Not at

first anyway.' A shadow flickered across his face and he sighed. 'It's all so long ago now.'

'Only ten years since we left Ireland,' said Mo. 'I didn't even know this place existed until a few months ago, but it must have been amazing back in the day.'

Sandeep stared through the window at the outhouse. 'It was past its best by the time I moved here. But my older colleagues used to talk about Lady Fallon's parents and their grand house parties. Important people from all over the world would come, as well as everyone from the village. Marquees in the grounds, immaculate gardens, servants and all that.'

Hannah sipped her coffee. 'I bet they had a proper driveway then.'

'They did but, by the time I came, you needed an all-terrain vehicle to get here. Everyone used to say Lady Fallon was a recluse.' His voice went up a notch when he mentioned her name. Lucy filled her glass in the sink and turned to face them, looking bored.

'Were there any staff here in your day?' Hannah continued, thinking of something Sandeep had said. 'To look after the house and the grounds? Only it looks like someone still tends the garden.'

Sandeep shook his head and pushed his chair back. Stood up slowly with a frown. 'No staff, just a half-witted gardener called Robert, but I could never get much sense out of him.'

Hannah shifted in her seat. 'So you did visit.' There was an awkward silence, then she continued. 'When was that?'

Sandeep coughed, raised a hand to his mouth, and suddenly looked very old. 'I did, but it was a long time ago now.' He picked up his plate and shuffled to the sink. 'Damn this cold. And these chairs are no good for my arthritis.'

Mo called after him as he headed to the door. 'The fire's going in the living room and Liam's got the TV on. Do you want me to bring you a blanket?'

'A blanket?' His chuckle turned into another racking cough. 'I'm not an invalid, not yet at least. I'm going back to my room.'

Mo gave them a tight-lipped smile and followed him out.

'Fancy a smoke, Hannah?' Lucy gestured to the door. 'You look like you could do with one.'

Outside the fog had lifted slightly, as if a layer of condensation had been wiped away from the world, and they lit up and walked along the side of the house.

'Let's have a wander. I can't stand being inside all the time,' said Hannah. She looked up the slope and remembered the way the hiker had seemed to glide, drifts of fog clinging to his coat, and then just disappear. She shivered and reminded herself that he would be long gone by now.

They went through the rose garden and up towards the rise at the back of the house. A patch of sun cut through the mist and for a brief moment they could see for miles, across empty rolling hills to the narrow strip of sea. There was no sign of life, not even a bird. Then the fog settled again and they were suddenly alone.

Lucy finished her fag and stubbed it out under her boot. 'You hit a touchy subject back there.' She fixed her with a stare. 'Mo told me his dad left the force under a bit of a cloud, went through a pretty rough patch.' She paused. 'He said it's probably best not to talk about it around him.'

Lucy and Mo had obviously been spending time together and Hannah couldn't suppress a spike of resentment. She flicked her cigarette butt into the grass and told herself it was none of her business.

As they skirted the house, Lucy began to open up about her background. She was the only child of two successful lawyers, neither of whom had been too pleased when Lucy joined a band instead of going to university. Whenever she mentioned music, she grew animated, her hand gestures more pronounced. Hannah could see how she'd be able to hold a crowd under her spell.

'It's been brilliant, really amazing. And now I have this one chance to branch out on my own, to play the sort of music I love.'

They fell silent and Hannah couldn't help dwelling on her wreckage of a life back in London. On the way she had left her job as an architect, burned all her bridges and ruined her chances. As they walked on through the mud, she found herself telling Lucy; not about Ben, but about the person she'd been, the dreams she'd had, before it all fell apart.

'Cool,' Lucy said. 'I love architecture, but I could never do anything like that. You have to be so skilled, and inventive too. I bet you'll be a huge success one day.' She put an arm around Hannah, giving her a little squeeze, and it was so comforting that Hannah had to resist the urge to rest her head on Lucy's shoulder.

Patting her pockets, Lucy broke away. 'Shit, my cigarettes. I left them on the garden bench.' She turned and walked away. 'Back in a second.'

Hannah watched her go and stood alone, waiting, clutching herself against the cool breeze. A minute or so passed, she stamped her feet to keep warm, and then she thought she heard a sound coming from the other side of the house: a rhythmic rattling that seemed to be getting louder. Maybe a window banging in the wind.

Clank, clank, clank.

She turned her back to the wind that was starting to build, clearing away the remaining fog and cutting through her jacket. Maybe she could make it to the village soon.

The sound carried on, rattling and banging, a horrible lonely sound that made her want to turn and run. Lucy was nowhere to be seen, but it could be one of the others, Mo collecting logs perhaps. The wind howled along the wall and the clanking grew louder. Every time she thought it had finished, it would begin again. *Thunk, clank, thunk.* Where was Lucy? Hannah pulled up her hood and edged towards the corner of the building, thinking of the man she'd seen from the window. The shadow that had been in her room last night.

She stood with her back to the wall of the house and listened to the rhythmic sound, not daring to look, her heart thudding in her chest. She closed her eyes for a moment, but knew she had to face it.

Took a step closer, rounded the corner, and there he was. Just as she knew deep down he would be.

Chapter Nine

The man she'd seen from the window, dressed all in black, shuffling towards her. She almost turned to run, but he didn't seem to register her at all. He hunched over and put down his shovel, then walked slowly towards a wheelbarrow, as if she wasn't even there. He picked up a few logs and threw them inside. They thunked against the metal barrow, making the sound she had been so frightened by just moments ago. Hannah bit down a laugh, knowing she was on the verge of hysterical giggles.

The hunched man was old, too old to be the man in her dream. He wore a thick black duffel coat and a woollen hat that covered straggly grey hair. His heavy beard framed a face worn down by years spent in the wind. She gathered herself and walked towards him.

'Hello.' After a moment, she tried again. 'Hi, there.'

He carried on moving slowly forward, as if he hadn't heard. Then he straightened, a hand went to the small of his back and he squinted at her.

'Hi, I'm Hannah.'

He grunted and muttered something in a thick Irish accent. 'Rob – gardener.'

She tried a smile. 'Nice to meet you.' There was an

awkward silence. 'Shame about the weather. Are you here every day?'

'Once a week.' He rubbed his back with a gloved hand and pushed the wheelbarrow forward, cutting off their conversation. Hannah could see that his other gloved hand was oddly twisted, like the root of an old tree, and he kept it clenched under the handle of the barrow – he used his wrist to hold on rather than his fingers. This must be the Robert that Sandeep remembered; he might even have the key codes for the rooms. She had a sudden vision of him lying in wait in the storage room, only metres from her bed, running his twisted hand down the wall, listening to her every move. Maybe her dream *had* been real? She swallowed and hurried after him, determined to get him talking, to find out as much as she could.

'So, Rob, I'm one of the guests. This place is amazing by the way. Were you here with the previous owners?'

He nodded but shuffled onwards, the wheelbarrow bumping over the ground.

'Look,' Hannah said. 'It's cold and the wind is picking up. You won't be able to work much longer. Why don't you come in for a cup of tea?'

He shook his head and chuckled, an unnerving sound in the silence. 'No, thank ye, not for me. I don't go in there. Never did, never will.'

Hannah forced herself to continue. 'There's chocolate cake in the kitchen. What about a piece of that?'

'Thank you, sure, but I don't go inside,' he said.

'Why not? Surely you're allowed into the house?' Hannah frowned at him, but when he didn't reply, she tried another smile. 'I've been reading about this place online and the history is fascinating. I was really hoping – and I know some of the other guests are just as keen as me – that you could tell us something about the previous owners, about what the house used to be like.'

He stopped the barrow, but still wouldn't meet her eye. A knot of his dirty grey hair moved in the wind. Was he about to say something? But then he turned back to loading logs into the wheelbarrow.

Hannah was about to give up when a window opened at the side of the house and Liam's head poked out.

'Hannah, do you want some cake?' He glanced warily at Rob.

'Yes, please. Bring out a slice for Rob here too. He's the gardener.'

The window shut and a minute passed in silence – Rob steadily picking up logs and Hannah trying to think how to get more out of him – then Liam emerged around the corner of the house, balancing three pieces of cake on a large plate. He paused to rest them on the low wall that surrounded a wood stack, wiped a hand and held it out to Rob.

'I'm Liam, another guest, we met on the path earlier. Thanks for the heads-up about the village shop.' He grinned, but Rob ignored his proffered hand and turned back to the log pile.

Liam's smile faltered and he took a piece of cake from the plate. Turned to Hannah. 'Glad this bloody mist has cleared a bit. Chloe was getting restless, so she and Rosa have gone for a walk around the grounds.'

Rob pulled off a glove with his teeth and shuffled over, picked up a piece of cake and took a huge bite. It was ridiculous to think that this poor old man could be dangerous, but all the same Hannah was glad to have Liam with her. She wondered where Lucy had got to.

'I was just asking Rob about the history of the house,' Hannah said. 'He's worked here for years.'

Liam looked down at the gardener's twisted hand, which he kept at his side, and Hannah suddenly remembered Liam was a doctor. He talked through a mouthful of cake.

'I've heard the Fallons were nice people.' He wiped a finger over his lips. 'They must have been good to work for.'

Rob nodded.

Hannah smiled at Liam. 'Rob was saying that he never goes into the house, but he won't tell me why.'

Liam gave a hearty laugh that sounded fake. 'Doesn't want to get mud everywhere, I guess.'

He patted Rob on the shoulder, but the man flinched and stepped away as if he had been stung. His piece of cake fell to the floor and landed in a muddy puddle. They all stared at it for a moment, before Liam said, 'Bad luck. Good for the foxes though.'

But Rob wasn't listening; he was shuffling away from them. 'I should be gettin' back home. That fog's closing in.'

And sure enough, without them realizing, the wind had died and the mist had begun to gather again along the hills. Hannah tried not to stare as Rob struggled to put his glove back on, wondering if she should offer to help.

'Do you live nearby?' she asked.

''Bout a mile off, down there in a cottage.' He pointed at a distant valley, towards a rolling wall of white mist. 'It'll be a rough night,' he said. 'You folks stay inside.'

They couldn't hold him up any longer.

At that moment, Rosa and Chloe emerged from the fog at the top of the rise, Rosa's loud voice unmistakable. 'The wind's died and it's really settling in again. What a nuisance.'

As Hannah and Liam turned to look up at them, Chloe stopped walking, still some distance away. Her eyes focused on Rob.

The gardener stared back at her, a look close to horror on his face. He shuffled away, muttering, arms clutched around himself.

Chloe burst into tears and ran to her father's side, Rosa

hurrying behind her. She put her arm around her daughter's waist.

'Who the hell is that? What's wrong with him?'

Rob stopped moving, his eyes still fixed on Chloe, his chest heaving. Then he muttered to himself, shook his head and turned towards the outhouse.

'It's my damn eyes again, playin' tricks. Stupid old fool. There's no way it's her, it couldn't be feckin her. She's gone, been gone for years.' The wheelbarrow squeaked as he pushed it down the hill, and no one spoke.

They stood in stunned silence for a moment, then Rosa and Liam led a tearful Chloe back inside: Liam with his arm around her, occasionally scowling back at Rob, and Rosa whispering something under her breath.

Hannah waited until they had gone inside, then followed Rob, catching him up as he opened the outhouse door and shoved the wheelbarrow inside.

She stepped in behind him. 'Rob, are you all right? That girl, she's . . . she's Chloe, Liam's daughter. Did you think she was someone else?'

'Don't mind me,' he muttered as he pushed the barrow into a corner. 'I've been here too long, thought it was her.'

In the dark of the outhouse, Hannah could barely see his face, but she thought he might be smiling. He stepped towards her, and she shrank backwards.

'The little girl,' he said.

'What? Who are you talking about?'

He came so close that she could hear his chest wheezing. Then he walked past her and opened the door, and Hannah let out a breath she didn't know she'd been holding. He waited for her to step outside, then closed the door behind them.

'Which little girl?' Hannah asked.

He sighed and, for the first time that day, he looked directly into her eyes. Hannah stepped back involuntarily and bumped into the shed, but he didn't notice. He was pointing up at a window on the top floor of the house.

'The girl at the window. The crying girl.'

Chapter Ten

Hannah felt a quiver go through her as her eyes followed his pointing finger. She thought about the figure she had seen when she first arrived, about the crying she had heard in the night. But this was stupid, ghosts didn't exist. It could all very easily be explained.

'You heard a girl crying? When was that?'

'She . . . she used to stand at that window there.' He jabbed his finger at the house again. 'First saw her when I was out there in the field, diggin'. Heard this odd little sound and looked up there.' He paused. 'It was strange. This tiny girl, with her hand pressed against the glass. Her face . . .'

But he must have seen Hannah's expression because he sighed and turned away. 'Forget it. I better be goin' before this fog gets any worse.'

Then he started along the gravel path towards the gate.

Hannah went after him, her heart racing, and reached out for the damp arm of his coat. 'Wait. Who are you talking about? Who was she?'

He pulled away. 'No one, don't you worry. It doesn't matter, just an old tale, like. Won't harm you none.' He lumbered away through the gate and into the mist. She stood for a long time looking after him, picturing a little girl with her hand pressed against glass, tears running down her face.

'Hannah!' a voice called from the house. She shook away her thoughts and turned to see Sandeep standing at the front door. 'Are you all right?' He had his arms wrapped around himself. 'I saw you from the window, talking to that man. It was Robert, wasn't it? The gardener, the one from all those years ago.'

She went up to join him, taking off her boots to leave them by the door, pausing for a moment to collect her thoughts. 'Yeah, that was him. I tried to get him to tell me more about the house, but the weather's getting worse and he had to head home.'

Sandeep pulled his cardigan tighter and shivered. 'Well, come in and close the door. It's bloody freezing. I hope that drawing room fire's still going.'

She followed him through to the hall, her mind still on what Rob had said.

A girl at the window.

It was probably just one of those stupid myths that got passed around in small villages. She had never been one for ghost stories and she wasn't about to start believing in them now. But she couldn't stop herself from remembering the desperate sobbing from last night, the figure at the window when she first arrived. When the house had been empty.

Liam, Rosa, and a pale-looking Chloe walked down the stairs towards her, and she realized she was still standing in the hall on her own. Liam touched her shoulder. 'Are you all right? That man didn't frighten you, did he?'

Hannah brushed him away. 'No, I'm fine. He seems harmless.'

'Well,' Rosa sighed. 'You do look a little pale, and he scared Chloe. Did you see the way he stared at her? I think we should report him to the host, make sure he doesn't come back again.'

Liam saw Chloe's worried look and put his arm around her. 'Hannah's right, he's just an old man. He won't come near you again, I'll look after you.' He ran a hand through his hair. 'Come on, I'm starving, let's go and make some food.'

Hannah watched them enter the kitchen, then went into the drawing room. She found Lucy curled up in one of the fireside chairs, Sandeep in the other. Hannah flopped onto the sofa with a sigh.

'There you are, Lucy. What happened? I thought you were looking for cigarettes.'

A sleepy smile. 'I looked everywhere but couldn't find them. When I went back round the house, you'd gone.'

So something else had gone missing, vodka and now cigarettes. The packet had probably just blown away in the wind, though. Or maybe Rob had picked them up by mistake.

Hannah turned to Sandeep. 'It was funny talking to Rob out there. He seems to have been through a lot over the years.' She put on a casual tone. 'When you first met him, was it at this house?'

He closed his eyes and she thought he looked sad and suddenly very tired, as if the very mention of this house had sent him off to sleep. But after a few moments, he answered her, his voice frail.

'When I was in the guards, I was called to the house, that's all.'

Lucy gave Hannah a look that said *leave the poor old man alone*.

Then the door opened. 'Dad?' Mo walked into the room.

Sandeep sighed, glanced from Hannah to Lucy and back again. 'It's all right,' he said without turning to his son. 'Maybe it's time I talked about it.'

He coughed weakly and huddled forward, reached his hands out towards the flames. 'I used to love my job. Worked in Dublin first, but when I married Mo's mum, I transferred here. A quiet country area, perfect for bringing up a child.' He snorted. 'Or so I thought.'

Mo dragged a chair next to his dad, sat down and looked at him, put a hand on his shoulder. 'It's all right, Dad. No need to do this.'

A log shifted in the fire and no one spoke.

'The truth is,' Sandeep turned to his son, 'I should have told you years ago. You and Mum. She was so angry with me for giving up my career, and you hated having to start again in London.'

Mo swallowed. 'You told us the new station sergeant didn't like you, that he was a racist and he was trying to fire you.'

'There was some truth in that, but I could have stuck it out.' Sandeep coughed again. 'It wasn't the racism, not really, it was this place – this damn house. It all started when I first came here, first set eyes on this horrible building. It ruined my career – ruined my life.'

Chapter Eleven

Fifteen years ago
The Policeman

It's probably just another nuisance call, some kids playing games in a phone box. But he gets out of the car anyway and locks the door, then stares along the muddy track towards a row of clouds scudding over distant hills. Checks his watch. It's near the end of his shift, and his dinner will be ready soon. Meera will be cooking, her hair tied up in a tight bun at the top of her head, her clothes sweet with the smell of food.

At the start of the path he stops and sighs. This is why the new sergeant smirked when he gave him the job and promised it wouldn't take long. There was no way to the house by road, so you had to walk bloody miles through muddy fields. Meera's going to be furious.

Close to an hour later, he finally reaches the top of a hill and catches his first glimpse of the house. An imposing Regency structure that rises like a rock face from the land-scape. It's every bit as impressive as he has been told. He passes through the well-maintained gardens and admires a few of the plants. A row of white magnolias seems somehow out of place here, as if it's been taken a long way from home and forced to adapt. He remembers seeing plants like these in Pakistan, lining the banks of rivers and streams. As his hand brushes against the thick petals, he wonders how people can prize these flowers but shun him and his family. Perhaps the gardener would give him some cuttings for Meera, to remind her of home.

When he reaches the entrance, he pauses for a moment and stares at the huge black front door, a foreboding slice of darkness in a wall of wind-beaten stone.

The bell rings and, after a moment, the door opens. A tall handsome man steps out to shake his hand, and Sandeep puts on his official smile. 'Mr Fallon?'

The man's handshake is firm. 'Just call me John.' He doesn't have much of an Irish accent, but then the posh people round here often don't. It's the same back home: the rich have the best British accents. It's why his parents made sure he learned to speak that way too.

'Sorry to bother you, sir.'

The man gestures him inside. 'Not at all. Come in, come in. What can I do for you?'

They stand in the hallway and Sandeep takes a moment to glance around, taking in the line of portraits in heavy gold frames on the wall. His whole house would probably fit in here.

'Would you like to see the drawing room?' the man asks.

'Oh, no, this won't take a moment. It's just an enquiry about your little one, your daughter, is it? We've had a report about a child in distress.'

The man takes a step back and frowns, then a smile flashes across his face. 'I'm sorry, I'm afraid there's been a mistake.'

'Well, it's soon cleared up. If I could just make sure she's all right . . .'

The man's laugh echoes in the empty hallway. 'That's not possible.' A pause as he looks at Sandeep, as if expecting him to start laughing too, and then his tiny smile dies. 'I'm afraid someone has been having a little joke at your expense. The locals, or maybe your colleagues.' Their eyes met. 'My wife and I don't have any children.'

A grandfather clock ticks quietly by the stairs, and Sandeep frowns at him. 'But we've had a report. I wouldn't be doing my job properly if I didn't look around.'

'Any other time, I'd be happy to give you a tour, but we're expecting guests and I really must get ready for them.' His smile now is kindly, sympathetic. 'The fact is, someone's wasting your time with the old ghost story about this house. Ask your colleagues about it when you get back to the station – they'll fill you in.'

Sandeep thinks of Meera's warm smile turning to a worried frown as she waits for him back home. He has no warrant and no reason to doubt the man.

'Thank you then, sir. Sorry to have disturbed you.'

On his way through the garden, he stops and looks back at the beautiful house for a few moments. There's something about it that makes him want to walk all the way to the road without looking back. Makes him want to wash his clothes and shower, to rid himself of that strange smell in the hall.

As he turns to leave, the wind whistles against the magnolia plants and he tells himself that it always makes that moaning, whining, noise. But as he walks on, a tiny part of him thinks it sounds just like a child crying.

Chapter Twelve

The fire crackled but no one spoke. Hannah wondered whether Sandeep had heard the child last night, but she couldn't bring herself to ask, didn't want her drunken nightmares laughed at by a room full of strangers.

Something else had bothered her about the story: the mention of a strange smell. It brought back thoughts of being trapped in the little office and of her dream.

The sound of scraping cut through her thoughts. She looked up to see Mo crouched by the fire, raking out ash with the poker. He turned to Sandeep, with a strange glint in his eyes. 'I still don't understand. You didn't leave the force until five years later, so what does the house have to do with it?'

Hannah frowned and glanced from Sandeep's aged face to his frail hands. He seemed very old to have been in the police ten years ago, but then he wasn't particularly healthy.

'When I got back to the station,' Sandeep went on, ignoring his son. 'I explained what had happened and I watched them all trying not to laugh. They told me about the ghost story, as if the whole thing was a joke that I was too stupid to understand. It turned out I wasn't the only one who had heard the child – there had been plenty of reports over the years – but they'd all been ignored.' He coughed and his hand went to his chest. 'There was a lot of superstition back then. I wasn't happy, but I let it go.'

He took a sip of water, his eyes glassy. 'A couple of years later I came here again after another of those damn phone calls. That's when I met the gardener, Robert.' Another cough racked through him and his chest began to heave. 'Sure it was him who'd made the call.'

'Dad.' Mo stood up as the coughing worsened.

Sandeep sucked in a rattle of air and rested his head back on the chair, his hand over his heart, his face pale.

'Shit.' Mo started to pace up and down. He looked at the others, ran a hand through his hair, then went to the door and shouted for Liam.

A few moments later, Liam entered and knelt beside Sandeep.

'Dad had a heart attack last year.' Mo was pacing again. 'Keeps forgetting to take his pills.'

Liam took Sandeep's wrist and frowned. 'Your pulse is racing. Come on, let's get you upstairs and you can have a lie-down.'

Sandeep nodded weakly, letting Mo and Liam gently help him to the door. Hannah followed them out and watched them navigate the stairs: Sandeep clung to his son, his face gleaming with sweat. He glanced around the hall as if the very walls were after him.

In the kitchen, Rosa stood frying something at the Aga, while Chloe chopped vegetables.

'We're making a beef casserole and a vegetable one for the people who don't eat meat,' Chloe said.

Rosa muttered something about it being a lot of extra work, and Hannah took a seat at the table. When Mo came in, he gave them all a weak smile and slumped down beside her.

'How is he?' Hannah said.

He blew out a sigh. 'All right, I think. Liam says it was probably just a panic attack, but he should stay in bed and shouldn't travel for a couple of days. Don't know whether I'll be able to persuade him, though.'

Lucy entered the kitchen and went to fill a glass with water. 'Perhaps you should call an ambulance and get him looked at in hospital. Best not to take a chance.'

Mo laughed. 'Dad would never forgive me. Can't stand a fuss and Liam doesn't think it's that serious, so long as he keeps quiet for a few days and takes his pills.'

Rosa turned from the sink. 'And Liam is a brilliant doctor, you know. Worked in hospitals in the casualty department for years before he became a GP. If anyone can deal with a medical emergency, it's him.' It was the first time Hannah had seen her really smile.

Mo stared hard at the table.

After a moment, Lucy sat beside him and took his hand. 'I'm sure he'll be all right.'

Mo tightened his grip and looked into her eyes, sending a pang of something like loneliness into Hannah's chest.

Coming in, Liam sat down with a sigh. 'He's going to be fine, just fine. I've made sure he's taken his pills – and I don't think it's anything serious – but with his medical history it's best not to take any chances. He needs a proper rest, that's all, so I've given him a sleeping pill and we can see how he is in the morning.'

There was a long silence. Hannah couldn't stop fidgeting and thinking of the evening ahead with nothing to drink, wondering how long it would take for the weather to clear. The only thing to do was to keep occupied, so she turned to Mo.

'If Sandeep's resting and we're trapped inside, do you fancy carrying on exploring the house?'

Chloe grinned. 'Yes, please.'

Mo stood up and stretched. 'Sounds good. I can't face sitting around doing nothing.'

'Just be careful,' Rosa said, as Chloe ran to Hannah and grabbed her hand.

'We won't go anywhere dodgy,' Hannah said with a smile, suddenly realizing how long it had been since she had last thought of Ben, last logged into social media. Even if this place creeped her out, she had to admit the break was doing her good.

Lucy came with them as they headed towards a closed door along from the kitchen, which they hadn't been through before. Hannah expected it to be locked, but the door swung open to reveal a smaller version of the drawing room. A soot-stained little fireplace crouched in one corner, empty bookshelves lined the walls, and the scuffed and dusty parquet flooring smelled of wet paint. Hadn't the website said this was a room guests could use?

Hannah walked towards the grimy window and rubbed it with her sleeve, but outside the thick fog smothered everything in a wall of darkness. She rubbed her arms and tried to pull across one of the long red velvet curtains, showering herself in dust. The fabric at the top was threadbare.

'This must have been the library. What a shame.' Mo picked up one of the few remaining books scattered on the shelves and ran his hand over the cover. The only other bit of furniture was a set of wooden steps designed to access the top shelves.

As they left the room and closed the door behind them, there was a depressed silence. Hannah wasn't sure what she or any of them had expected, but not this dull and rundown room.

Then Chloe pointed along the hall. 'Look.' She hurried

over to a dark heavy-looking door, and Lucy called out for her to wait.

But Chloe held it open for the others with a smile. 'Ooh, this looks better. A whole other section.'

The door led into a corridor that stretched away into darkness. Hannah groped on the wall and found an old-fashioned light switch. When she pressed it, the bulb buzzed and a faint glow flickered against the green paint on the walls, giving the place a strange watery shine. They walked cautiously along to the end and found another solid-oak door secured with a heavy padlock. Chloe held up her iPhone and used the torch to illuminate a sign:

Danger. Closed to Guests.

'Maybe it's where they store the paints and stuff for the renovation,' said Lucy.

Mo pointed at another door to the left. 'No sign here.' He opened it to reveal a bare wooden staircase that wound steeply up into the house. 'Aha, the back stairs, I read about these. They lead to the old servants' bedrooms, I think.' And without looking back he bounded into the dark.

They followed him up the steep stairs, Chloe's iPhone illuminating the narrow passage's rough whitewashed walls. Hannah held out her hand, but Chloe just smiled at her and shook her head.

'I'm OK. This is so cool.' They paused on the little landing halfway up beside a small window. There was no sign of Lucy coming behind them.

'The stairs must go right up to the third floor,' Hannah said. 'This landing seems to be on the same level as our bedrooms.'

They both looked out the window through the mist to the garden below, and Hannah felt Chloe's cold arm tremble against her. Mo's footsteps creaked on the floorboards above them.

They walked up the stairs and entered a labyrinth of empty rooms. There was no carpet here, just worn bare boards, no heating either. This was probably the way it had always been for the servants, bleak and unforgiving.

Stepping into one room, they went over to a tiny window in the corner, barely big enough to see through. These rooms would be dark even in the daytime, oppressive even in the summer.

'I don't like it up here,' Chloe said.

'Nor me.' They both jumped as Mo poked his head round the doorway and grinned.

'Don't do that!' Chloe said, half-laughing, but half-scared.

'Imagine these rooms furnished.' Mo came to join them at the window. 'They would have been pretty nasty even then: hard single beds, a wardrobe, and a couple of chests for clothes if you're lucky.'

There was a long pause as they stood lost in their own thoughts. A floorboard creaked nearby. And, without a word, they headed together for the stairs.

After dinner Hannah went straight to her room. She took a chair and wedged it against the door, with her suitcase in front of it. Anyone who managed to move the chair would fall over the case. She checked and double-checked that the window was locked, the curtains closed. Then she made herself a cup of hot chocolate and tried to read.

She was heavy with exhaustion, but her mind wouldn't relax. A long soak in the bath might help, so she went to the bathroom, turned on the hot tap, selected one of the scented bath oils and poured it into the tub.

Once it was full, she undressed and stepped into the fragrant water, easing herself down into the bubbles and wedging a thick towel behind her head. The fidgeting she'd been struggling with all day gradually subsided. She smiled and thought back to her last glass of vodka: a whole twenty-four hours ago.

She closed her eyes and the warm suds began to soothe her mind as well as her body. Her thoughts wandered to all the strange things that had happened since she checked into The Guesthouse. Once she had been to the village to ask about her dad, she could head straight back to London, she decided. A flicker of guilt as she realized how far away Ben now seemed. But her mother and Lori were right: to function properly again, she needed to let him rest.

She closed her eyes and tried to clear her mind, focusing on the delicate smell of the bath oil, enjoying the silence. Until darkness enveloped her and she drifted into sleep.

A creak from the bathroom door and she was suddenly alert. The door swung gently open, letting in a wall of cold air. She tried to turn her head, but couldn't move.

It was happening again. She had to wake up, had to get out.

Above her pulse racing in her ears, she could make out another sound. Shuffling, something shuffling through the door and into the room. The dark figure again, its breathing loud in the quiet room. She tried to turn, but couldn't move. The door closed and they were alone together.

And that suffocating smell seemed to wash over her in waves, making her sick.

She tried to whimper, but nothing came out. A floorboard creaked right beside the bath and she tried to scream.

Complete silence.

And then a great weight pressed down on her from above. She sank deeper into the water, her head submerged, and she slipped quietly to the bottom of the bath. A sudden thought came to her as she lay there, perfectly still: suck in great lungfuls of hot soapy water, end it all before it's too late. But it was already too late, because there was something in the water with her.

About to touch her.

Chapter Thirteen

She jolted upright, her arms slipping on the sides of the bath. Coughed soapy water out of her lungs, gasped in air. Her head had been underwater – she had nearly drowned – and the water was now cold. The harsh taste of soap burned her lungs as she spat into the bath. Climbed out of the tub, shivering as she wrapped herself in one of the towels. The bathroom door was open. Had she left it like that?

Out in the bedroom, everything was the same, nothing had been disturbed. She dressed quickly, trying to get warm. It had only been a bad dream.

And bad dreams were her oldest friends. She'd been having them for years, for as long as she could remember, long before she checked into this bloody guesthouse. They had just never been so vivid, so detailed.

And she couldn't remember anything like that smell. It made her want to be sick, made her want to drink vodka after vodka to burn it away.

She huddled in bed, grabbed her phone and earbuds, and called up some peaceful, relaxing music. After a while her eyelids began to droop, so she plugged in her phone and switched off the lamp. Maybe now she would be able to sleep without dreams.

A loud bang woke her, and she sat up quickly. The heavy darkness of midnight settled all around her.

It would be a window crashing down again, or something thudding to the floor in one of the other guest rooms, some piece of this ancient house crumbling and falling apart. Whatever it was she wasn't going to let it keep her awake.

She rolled over and lay there, listening, until she heard something else. This time it was a sound she couldn't identify. A scratching, like nails on bathroom tiles, or rat's claws on wood. Then it seemed to be rattling, wood tapping against wood, a window frame shaking in the wind.

She remembered the way Rob had pointed up at the window. The image of a little girl, hand pressed to the glass, tears running down her face.

She sat up and turned the light on. This was all in her head, probably just the first day or so without alcohol taking its toll. But she had to find out for sure, had to prove to herself that those noises weren't real, or she would never get back to sleep.

This time she pulled on her trainers and her parka over her pyjamas. She reached for her iPhone: it was dead, out of battery. Somehow the cable had fallen out again, so it hadn't charged. *Shit*. She threw the phone on her bed, then thought better of it, and plugged it back in. Stepped out into the corridor and listened to the silence.

But as she tiptoed towards the stairs, a tiny noise came along the corridor. Faint and distant, but definitely there, an insistent sound.

The sound of a little girl crying.

This time she was in no doubt. There was no sound like it; the sobbing of someone in desperate need of help. She listened at each of the occupied guest rooms, considered waking up the others, but decided against it. What if they couldn't hear it? What if they thought she was losing her mind? The low light at the end of the corridor wasn't on, but the wind had picked up outside, clearing the fog and leaving just enough moonlight for her to see in the dark. It didn't seem to be coming from the family room, so it wasn't Chloe. Could it be a woman rather than a child? Surely not the calm and collected Lucy?

She walked to the end of the other wing, her body shaking with cold and with fear. And for a few moments she was almost certain she would trace it to the little room right at the end. But as she got closer, the sound grew fainter.

There was only one place left to look: downstairs. Darkness enveloped the hall, but a thin grey light trickled through the tall windows. She stared down from the railing into the eerie shadows below and thought about the walk across that bare echoing hall. She pulled her parka closer round her.

Even as she decided to head back to her room, she found her feet taking her across the landing and down the stairs. Drawn onwards by the sound of a child in distress, by a little one who needed her.

And as soon as she was in the hall, she knew with terrible certainty where the sound was coming from: the narrow corridor with the padlocked door at the end.

She opened the heavy oak door and peered into the pitch-black tunnel. There were no windows and she groped for the light switch, the bare bulb flickering on but hardly penetrating the darkness. As she slowly crept along the corridor towards the sound, she felt like a diver feeling her way along a deep undersea tunnel.

She reached the end, her breathing loud in the confined space, and pressed her ear to the padlocked door. Tried pulling and shaking the padlock, but it was no good.

She stood there, panting, wondering what else to do.

And then the crying stopped.

Feeling suddenly exposed, alone in that greenish light, she spun around to stare back down the corridor.

Silence – a deafening silence all around her. Nothing except her own respiration and the pounding of blood in her ears.

But maybe there *was* something else. It was the flickering greenish light that did it, of course, but she almost imagined she could hear water. Not running, but swirling behind the door. As if there was a lake or a river back there, as if behind this door was a whirlpool where her nightmares were born.

Her insides lurched as something tugged at the edges of her memory. Something terrifying hovered, not behind the door in front of her, but behind a door in her own mind.

She had no idea how long she stayed like that – frozen – pressed against the dark wood, listening to the swirl and whisper of whatever was on the other side, fighting the urge to remember. But eventually she found herself stumbling back along the corridor and out into the hall.

Panting heavily, she shut the door and leaned against it, wishing she had a padlock to keep it secure. To keep a lock on her own mind. Because if it opened, what other nightmares would crawl out into the light?

Still shaking, she crept across the hall. Something had happened back there, some ancient memory had stirred and all she knew was that it had nothing – and everything – to do with her life with Ben. She had loved him so much and yet she had sabotaged their relationship, pulled it apart from the inside. She couldn't remember when those bad dreams had first started, but she knew when they had begun to get worse: when she began to distance herself from her friends; when the drinking had started too. Started so she could pretend she wasn't haunted, haunted by something she couldn't name because that would mean confronting it.

Ben had tried to help, tried to talk it through with her, which had only made her more frightened. Until, finally, she had driven him away. That's what she had done, sought out an escape route.

She paused at the bottom of the stairs. No, none of this was real. It was brought on by withdrawal symptoms, her craving for alcohol – she'd heard about this happening – vivid hallucinations after going cold turkey.

Then a tiny sound made her look up.

And there, at the top of the stairs, stood a tall dark figure.

Chapter Fourteen

She grabbed the bannister to steady herself.

Lucy came running down to her. 'Hannah, is that you? What's wrong?'

Colours and shapes blurred around her, the whole house seemed to bend and buckle. She sat heavily on the stairs and Lucy crouched beside her. 'Shit, what happened? Are you OK?'

Her voice felt raw. 'I heard a noise . . . it woke me up. I thought it was . . . a child crying.'

Lucy touched her arm. 'You're freezing. Let's get you warm.' She helped her up and into the kitchen. 'Sit here by the Aga.'

They pulled hard chairs close to the warmth, Hannah hugging herself, still shivering, Lucy sitting beside her, elbows on her knees. Hannah felt herself starting to calm down. Nothing had happened, it was just her mind playing tricks.

Eventually she was able to look at Lucy in the light of the kitchen. She realized how pale she was, how frightened. She seemed so young without her earrings and her make-up, so exposed.

'Did you hear it?' Hannah's voice shook, almost praying the answer would be *yes*.

There was a pause, then Lucy shook her head. 'I only heard you downstairs. Where did you go?'

Hannah looked away. 'That padlocked door down the corridor.'

'I came out when I heard a door opening and closing downstairs,' Lucy said. 'No lights were on and I thought someone had broken in. Fucking terrified me.' She looked thoughtful for a moment. 'I did hear a fox scream a couple of times in the night. It's a seriously creepy noise – maybe that's what you thought was crying.'

She was trying to reassure her, just as Ben used to do, but it was no good. Hannah shook her head. 'It wasn't a fox.'

'Well, let's stay here for a while and listen. If there *is* anything, we'll find it together.' Lucy put a hand on Hannah's shoulder.

They listened in silence for a while, but the house was quiet, no sounds even from the pipes or creaking wood. Eventually Lucy stretched her arms above her head, her legs out in front of her, and yawned.

'I'm shattered, think I'm going to fall asleep, even on this bloody uncomfortable chair.' Another yawn. 'So – let's talk – to keep ourselves awake. I've told you why I'm here on my own, but what about you?'

And in the low light of the kitchen, by the warmth of the Aga, Hannah found herself spilling out most of the story, the bits about Ben at least. Lucy listened patiently and when it was over she reached out and held Hannah close for a long moment. A great weight fell from Hannah's shoulders and she felt tears begin to fall. She cried as she had never cried before, not even when Ben was holding her tight. Not even when Ben died.

Lucy tore off a piece of kitchen paper for her. 'It's all right. You've had a bad time – been through a lot – and, to be honest, I'm not sure this is the best place for you to be at the moment. It gives me the creeps.' She brushed a strand of hair from Hannah's damp cheek.

'I know, you're right. But there's something I need to do here first.'

Lucy frowned and leaned back in her chair. 'Really? What do you need to do in a rundown old guesthouse?'

'Well, not so much the house – it's the area.' She took a moment. 'My father used to live near here. My parents broke up when I was four or five and I don't remember much about my dad.'

'Are you planning to visit him?' Lucy's voice was soft.

'I can't do that. He died five years ago.'

'But you know where he lived?'

Hannah shook her head. 'Just that it was in the Fallon area.'

Lucy yawned again and a shadow passed across her face. 'Why don't you head to the village tomorrow? Find people who knew him, get it – whatever it is – out of your system, then we can all leave. I don't fancy another night here to be honest.'

She stood and stretched, her black silk dressing gown falling open to reveal a sliver of pale, perfectly toned stomach.

Hannah wiped her eyes. Her nose had been running and her hair was probably bent into weird contortions. She was pathetic, confiding in this cool stranger. For a few minutes she'd imagined they had a real connection, thought they could be great friends. She shook her head.

'I'm sorry, forget about it, I'm a mess. We should go back to bed.'

They walked together to the bottom of the stairs, then Lucy paused and turned, the faint light from above glinting in her eyes. 'Your father? Did you love him?'

The question hung in the quiet air and Hannah knew for sure that the sense of connection she'd felt with this stranger had been an illusion. 'I suppose. In a way, yes, I think I must have done.'

At the top of the stairs Lucy turned to her, a hand on her arm. 'Try to sleep for the rest of the night. You need it,' she whispered. And at the door to her own room, she gave Hannah a smile that wasn't quite a smile.

Back in bed Hannah tossed and turned. Lucy thought the crying noise had been a fox and maybe she was right. Physically Hannah felt better than she had in a long time, the low-level headache behind her eyes now just a dull throb, nothing like her usual hangovers. But mentally she was exhausted.

She gave up trying to sleep and threw off the duvet, then groped in the drawer of her bedside table for some painkillers to help her sleep. Swallowing the pills down with water she made a decision. When she was back home she would go to see Ben's parents and his brother. They might not forgive her, but it could help with their recovery, could help with her own. And she deserved to feel their anger, to face whatever they wanted to say to her.

But while she was here, she would try to give herself a break from guilt – if that were possible. Ben had wanted her to go, to help come to terms with her turmoil about her dad. Lucy was right too: it would help to find someone who had known him. And that shouldn't be too difficult, because only five years had passed since his death.

All Hannah knew about him was that his name was Jack Roper. He had remarried after her parents' divorce, when she was four or five, then moved to Fallon in Ireland.

She also knew that her mother hated him. His death caused the biggest argument she had ever had with her mum, when Ruby delayed telling Hannah about it for nearly three months. Finally admitting that she'd had a letter from the executor of his estate, some friend of his called Declan O'Hare. The letter said that Jack's second wife was already dead and the couple had racked up a lot of debts, so there would be no property or money left.

Although her mother was reluctant, Hannah insisted on reading the letter. It mentioned the village of Fallon and said Jack Roper had died from a heart attack.

But what maddened Hannah was the final sentence.

I know he loved his daughter very much. Often spoke about his little girl and how he wished he'd been able to see her grow up. So if she would like to come over I'm sure we could let her choose one or two small keepsakes before everything is sold. It will have to be before the end of the month.

Hannah switched on the light and got out of bed, walked over to the window and back to the door: paced miserably to and fro. Just as she had after the argument with her mum.

She had written back to the executor, to this Declan O'Hare at his Dublin address, but he hadn't responded to any of her letters. It was too late now, but there might be people in the village who knew Declan, if not her father. There was always Sandeep, too, with his memories and knowledge of the area. He might recall Jack Roper or his second wife.

The old diary from next door lay in the open bedside drawer, so she picked it up and flicked through it. The only interesting thing was that date, January 17th, marked every year with the name: *MADDIE*. She picked up her phone, which now had some charge, and managed to get online using wifi. A quick search revealed that the Fallons were land-owners with houses in Hertfordshire and Ireland. The English estates had been lost in the early years of the twentieth century, but they'd held onto the Irish house until the final member of the family died ten years ago.

The most recent Lady Fallon was called Jane, not Maddie. Hannah remembered the note that had fallen out of the diary about leaving food out for the dog. The initial had been J, so Jane Fallon would fit.

Another website revealed that Jane's aunt was called Madeleine. There were no dates for her, so perhaps she was the Maddie in the diary, still alive five or ten years ago when the diaries had been written. She pulled a pen from her rucksack and noted down the names and dates of the last few owners on a picture postcard from the bedside table.

The darkness outside her windows had turned to grey, the faint light of dawn filtering through the curtains. With no one around, this would be a good time to double-check the rest of those diaries.

She stepped out into the corridor and turned back to the little office. The key code worked and this time she pulled the chair over to hold the door ajar. Avoiding the holes in the floorboards, she opened the desk drawer and rummaged inside. Grabbed all the diaries and the notebook.

She couldn't bear to stay here long, so headed back to her room, that awful lingering smell seeming to follow her out into the corridor.

Stuffing the diaries into her suitcase, she felt a wave of tiredness sweep over her, but knew she still wouldn't be able to sleep. A decent coffee from the kitchen was what she needed. She was about to go downstairs when she noticed the scrap of paper, with the scribbled instructions and the initial J, lying at the bottom of her open bag. Crouching down, she picked up one of the diaries at random and flicked through it, in case there was anything similar. Did the same with a couple more but found nothing. On a page near the back of the last one, however, she came across a short list of email addresses.

And the final address in the list made her stop, sit back on her heels and drop the book.

jack.roper@oneworld.com

Her father's email address.

Chapter Fifteen

On her way downstairs Hannah saw the glow of the kitchen light and hesitated. It would probably be Lucy, unable to sleep again, like her. Hannah couldn't face seeing her so soon after last night's embarrassment, but the thought of strong coffee pushed her onwards.

It was Sandeep, sitting at the table in a heavy tartan dressing gown, sipping what looked like green tea. He gave her a weary smile. 'Morning.'

She sat opposite. 'Morning. How are you feeling?'

He shook his head and frowned. 'I'm OK. Don't know what got into me last night, but I feel fine now. After that so-called doctor made me take a sleeping pill, I missed dinner and woke at the crack of dawn. I'm starving and now I can't even go back to sleep.' He rubbed his face. 'I bloody hate early mornings.'

Hannah smiled. He could be a moody bastard, but she liked him. Smothering a yawn she started to make coffee, holding up the packet to him. 'You want some?'

'Not for me. Don't touch the stuff,' he said.

Hannah wasn't going to miss her chance. 'I suppose you don't drink alcohol either?'

He stirred his mug. 'When I was a copper, I saw alcohol

do some nasty things to people, but in moderation I can't see the harm.' A little chuckle. 'I used to have the odd pint when I was in the force. My excuse was that it helped me bond with my colleagues, but I enjoyed it.'

So he was hardly likely to have tipped away her vodka.

Once she had sat down and taken a sip of her coffee, she continued. 'I've been meaning to ask you about Fallon village. You must have visited it a lot when you were a policeman.'

He gave a little grunt and she ploughed on. 'You know my father lived around here, until five years ago or so, and I just wondered if you ever came across him? Heard about him maybe. His name was Jack Roper.'

He sipped his tea meditatively for a moment, then shook his head. 'Unless he was a thieving bastard . . .' One of his rare smiles. '. . . I probably wouldn't have met him. Fallon's not that small. Where exactly did he live?'

She twisted her lips. 'The truth is, I don't actually know. We lost touch.'

He patted her hand and she asked about Declan O'Hare, but he shook his head.

'What you said yesterday about your visits here as a policeman was fascinating. Do *you* believe the place is haunted?'

His dark eyes looked quickly into hers. 'Of course not.'

'But, you know.' She took a breath. 'Each night I've heard . . . noises. Weird stuff, what sounds like crying, coming from down in the closed-off section of the house.'

Sandeep took another sip. 'I haven't heard anything, but then I'm pretty deaf and last night I was drugged by that bloody doctor.'

'What about all those years ago? You heard something then.'

'It was just the wind.' But he wouldn't meet her eye.

'Are you still planning to leave today?' she asked, taking another sip.

He stood up and went to switch on the kettle. Hannah waited while he made himself more tea, certain he was going to open up to her, hoping for some piece of the jigsaw that would prove she wasn't losing her mind. When he sat down again, he leaned back in his chair.

'Mo wants me to stay for another couple of days. He's worried that the journey will be too much for me and he may well be right.'

Blowing on his mug, he looked around the kitchen. 'You know, this place has haunted me for years – wherever I've been living – and now that I'm back, it might finally be time to put an end to it.'

Chapter Sixteen

Thirteen years ago
The Policeman

Here again, standing in the lonely road at the end of the track, staring up into the hills. There had been another garbled anonymous call mentioning Fallon House. The crackle of static, sobbing down the line.

Sergeant Murdoch had roared with laughter. 'Sandeep! Where is he? Sandeep's your man for that. He's the feckin ghostbuster.' And when Sandeep walked up to his desk, Murdoch had clapped him on the back with a grin. 'Off you go, old fella. It'll be good craic.' As Sandeep left the station, laughter rang out behind him.

Once again the walk had been long. A bitter wind howling across the bog, stinging his face. Bent double, he had trudged up the slope along the muddy track. Trying not to think of Murdoch's smirking face, of his leering colleagues laughing as he left the station. Of the real reason he'd been sent here.

Now he's standing at the edge of the garden, staring at the bare magnolia shrubs that litter the flower beds like forgotten corpses. The house is in shadow, all the curtains drawn. It's probably locked up for the winter and he's come all this way for nothing. Maybe one of the other officers made the prank call, just for *the craic*. He shrugs and moves closer to the house. Might as well check it out, wouldn't want to ruin their joke. The wind picks up and he has to bend even further forward, as he moves through the garden's twisted bushes and shrubs. He rings the bell and bangs on the front door, but the sound echoes into silence and nobody answers.

The sun creeps lower over the hill and, by the time he's knocked on all the doors and peered through the windows, it's nearly dark.

He stands at the back of the house and looks up at one of the tiny windows on the third floor, thinking he spots a movement, a flash of white against glass. But he blinks and looks again, struggling to see properly in the gloom. No, there's nobody here, the place is deserted. He turns to leave and begins to walk back through the garden.

That's when he sees something else, a shape in the corner of his eye. Something huddled near the back door: a dark lump, slumped and totally still.

His heart thumps in his ears and time seems to slow down. He sees a magpie flying slowly away over the trees, hears it screech, feels the wind against his face. A trickle of sweat crawling down his neck.

It's a body.

He runs over and crouches down beside the figure.

A man, curled up on the ground. One gloved hand stretched out as if reaching for something.

And the glove and the sleeve are soaked through with blood.

Chapter Seventeen

Sandeep sipped his tea and gave her a weak smile. 'It was Robert, the gardener, still alive but badly hurt. It was pretty nasty – I've never seen so much blood. When I tried to remove the glove, he came round and started screaming.'

'What had he done?'

'As far as I could see it was just his hand, but it was a real mess. I made a tourniquet and called an ambulance. It had started to rain by the time they arrived and they had to stretcher him along that muddy path, slipping and sliding down the slope. And his hand was so badly smashed up they needed to remove two fingers.'

She remembered the glove Rob never took off and the way he held his twisted hand. Sandeep coughed for a moment and then continued. 'He told them he'd dropped a pile of logs on it.' A small laugh.

'You didn't believe him?'

'The doctors didn't either, but there seemed to be no other explanation. He was alone, miles from anywhere with no witnesses, but a few logs couldn't have done that much damage. The surgeon reckoned his hand had been struck multiple times by something metal and they found traces of blood on a shovel nearby. Trouble was – as my sergeant was only too happy to remind me – I was the only person anywhere near him that day.'

The door opened and Mo came in and frowned, then went to his dad. 'There you are. I've been knocking on your door – I thought something bad had happened. Lucky I know your key code.'

Sandeep coughed and waved him away. 'Stop fussing. I just couldn't sleep.'

Mo looked at Hannah. 'He can never remember to take his pills.' Then back to Sandeep. 'They're still beside your bed. I thought we agreed you'd take them when you woke up.'

Sandeep stood suddenly and held his chair for balance. 'For God's sake, I'm not a child.' Then he swayed slightly and his voice quietened. 'I'll take them now.'

When he had shuffled out, Mo poured himself some orange juice and took a carton of eggs from the fridge. 'Much as I love him, he can be a nightmare.'

Hannah was still thinking about what Sandeep had said. She needed to ask him a few more questions, knew there was more to his story, but didn't want to annoy Mo by pestering his dad. She took a sip of her cold coffee and grimaced. 'How did you sleep?'

'Not that well to be honest. Worrying about Dad.' He gave a weak smile.

At that moment, Lucy appeared. She somehow managed to look stylish even this early in the morning in her black puffa jacket and blue bobble hat. Her face was flushed from being outside in the wind, but she looked as if she'd had eight good hours of sleep.

'Morning.' She went to the Aga to warm her hands, and there was an awkward silence. 'So, what's the plan for today, Mo? Are you still going to take your dad home?'

'I don't think he's well enough to do the walk yet, so he's

going to rest for another day. Actually, in some ways I think being here is helping him. Getting rid of all those bad memories.' He took off his glasses, rubbed them on his sweatshirt and put them carefully back on again. 'Having friendly company is good too.'

They were finishing breakfast when Liam, Rosa, and Chloe arrived and Rosa set about making a fry-up. Liam rubbed his hands together. 'The weather looks better today.'

Rosa stabbed at a rasher of bacon in the pan. 'It's not raining, if that's what you mean.'

There was silence for a moment and Chloe looked at the ground.

'Liam?' Hannah forced herself to smile. 'I was thinking of heading to the village later. Any chance of a lift?'

'Sure, no bother,' Liam said. 'We're going for a walk first, but afterwards, I can take you.' He pulled out a map. 'I checked out some good trails around here. Always loved map reading, you know. Did a couple of orienteering courses last year and got pretty good at it. We're off for a stroll after breakfast, if anyone fancies it?'

'I'm up for a walk.' Lucy rose from the table. 'I need a smoke, but after that I'm game.'

'Yeah, me too,' Mo said, with a side-on glance at her.

She waved a cigarette packet at Hannah. 'Managed to find another packet in my bag. Want one?'

As they went to leave the room, Lucy rubbed Mo's shoulder. 'Don't wash up. We'll do it later.'

Outside they sat on the bench by the front door and silently lit their cigarettes. Hannah couldn't think what to say, couldn't make up her mind about Lucy. At times she felt really close to her, was in awe of her, but then those odd surges of envy and resentment would return. She reminded herself what happened to her last relationship. If Mo and Lucy hit it off, she should be happy for them.

'Did you get to sleep in the end?' Lucy blew out a cloud of smoke.

'Not really.' Hannah drew on her own cigarette. 'I'm sorry if I freaked you out.'

Lucy smiled. 'I wasn't scared, just concerned.'

Another stab of dislike. Hannah was tempted to tell Lucy that she was a condescending bitch, but instead she finished her cigarette and stubbed it out in a flower pot. 'I owe you for these.'

'Don't worry about it. I'm trying to quit.'

'Nice. I can never give anything up when I've got loads of work to do.'

Lucy flicked her butt into the wind. 'I've done it before. My boyfriend, Damian, always says I've got the strongest will of anyone he's ever met.' She laughed.

An hour later, everyone except Sandeep set out through the wide gates. Hannah couldn't help feeling sorry for him; she wouldn't want to stay in that house on her own. Liam marched off at the front with his map, Chloe beside him. From time to time he touched her back to help her along, as if she were a small child who could barely walk. Rosa kept her distance from them, hands stuffed into her pockets.

Then came Lucy and Mo, chatting and laughing together. *Get a room.* And finally Hannah, bringing up the rear, billy no mates. Trying to avoid getting even more mud on her new trainers. She didn't blame Lucy and Mo; nobody wants to walk with the loser at the back.

As they trudged onwards it was impossible not to think about Ben. He would have loved this. To take her mind off him, she forced herself to focus on the mystery of her father. The fact that his email address – it had to be his – was in a diary at the house proved that he lived locally. He had been an architect, so maybe he did some work for the Fallons or met them socially. She hadn't got anything useful from Sandeep, but it might be worth asking Liam about Jack and his friend, Declan. A doctor in the area – even if he hadn't worked that close to Fallon – would come across a lot of people. This afternoon, she would go into the village to ask around, and tomorrow she would head back to London.

Chloe came running over and grabbed her arm. 'Can I walk with you for a bit?'

Hannah smiled and they walked on in companionable silence. After a while Hannah broke it. 'Are you having a good holiday?'

A sigh. 'It's not really a holiday, just somewhere to stay until we can move to our new house.'

'You're not looking forward to it then?'

Chloe glanced at her parents up ahead. Their intense discussion seemed to be on the verge of becoming an argument. 'It's tiny, and I don't want to live in Scotland.'

'Have you told your mum and dad?'

'They won't listen. And anyway, we have to get away from Ireland and we can't afford anything else.' She fell silent, looking down and kicking a stone into a ditch full of water at the side of the path.

Up ahead Liam stopped to consult his map and Hannah wondered if he was lost. Iron grey clouds piled up over the strip of sea on the horizon, a storm rolling in from the Atlantic.

They walked on for a bit without speaking, before Hannah decided this was too good an opportunity to miss. 'You know, I thought I'd sleep better in the country, but I keep waking up in the night. Haven't been able to sleep properly at all since I arrived.'

Chloe looked away but didn't speak.

'What about you?' Hannah pushed. 'Only I noticed you seemed tired yesterday. And the weird thing is.' She lowered her voice. 'In the middle of the night, I swear I keep hearing a child crying.'

Chloe stopped walking and glanced at her parents. Her voice was so quiet that Hannah had to lean in to hear her over the wind.

'I've heard it too. Mum and Dad said I was dreaming, told me to stop being silly, not to mention it or everyone would get into a panic.' She was speaking quickly now. 'Dad said telling stories like that would ruin the holiday and scare you and Lucy, because you were just girls on your own. And I mustn't tell Sandeep either, because he's ill.'

Hannah bit her lip and leaned closer. 'Well, I heard the noise and I wasn't frightened. If you hear it again, come and find me and we can investigate together.'

Chloe nodded and they carried on walking, beginning to catch up with the others.

Rosa's loud voice cut through the wind. 'Darling, walk with me for a bit.' Chloe grimaced and shrugged, nodded to Hannah, then ran to join her mother.

Hannah fell into step with Mo and Lucy. Mo zipped up his coat. 'Looks like there's a storm coming in.' Heavy black clouds gathered over the sea, closer to land now. 'Hannah,' Mo continued. 'I've bored Lucy with my life story and my job at the university library – in return she's impressed me with her amazing adventures – so now it's your turn.'

As they walked along the ridge, Hannah told them about her university days and about the kind of architecture she loved. As she spoke, she watched Chloe run on ahead and reach a grove of trees, their branches bent almost horizontal by the sea wind.

Lucy looked at her watch. 'Shit, it's getting late. I need to head back, get some work done.' She sighed and gave them both a smile. 'See you guys back at the house. Enjoy the rest of the walk.'

'I'll come with you.' Mo dug his hands in his pockets. 'Can't leave Dad on his own for too long.'

Hannah said goodbye and watched Lucy take Mo's arm as they walked off over the hill and down towards The Guesthouse. When they had disappeared from view, she turned and ran to catch up with the others.

Rosa waited for her and the two of them trudged up the final slope towards the cluster of trees in silence.

Halfway up, they heard a shout. A sudden cry from the top of the hill that carried down to them in the wind. It was Liam. Hannah ran forward, scrambling up the slope, and saw Chloe emerge from the trees, waving her arms in the air, screaming.

Then she dived back into the woods and Hannah and Rosa sprinted up the final ridge, slipping on wet stones, almost falling over on the boggy grass. As they got to the trees, Hannah saw Chloe standing in the gloom of a clearing, a blank look of terror on her face. Hannah felt a sick lurch of fear and ran faster, thundering through twisted branches to join her.

Chloe stood there, a hand to her mouth, staring towards a deep ditch just a few yards away. Liam's voice shouted up to them from the trench. 'All right, I'm all right. Just stay back everyone.'

Rosa pulled Chloe into her arms. She sobbed and struggled to reach her dad, but Rosa dragged her away from the ditch and into the trees. Hannah stepped cautiously to the edge and looked down. At the bottom of the sheer drop, she could see Liam, unharmed, crouching down. She squinted to see through the gloom as fat raindrops began to fall, bouncing on the grass around them.

Her stomach clenched and she felt suddenly very cold.

Liam hunkered down next to a dark shape, a black crumpled heap of soaking wet clothes. The rain fell faster, hammering into the undergrowth.

But it wasn't just a pile of clothes; it was a man. Face down, arms splayed out, one hand stretched in front of him, as if reaching for someone. Grey hair splattered in mud.

It was Rob.

Chapter Eighteen

Liam stared up at Hannah, his breath clouding around him. 'He must have been here since yesterday,' he shouted. 'Got lost in that damn fog and fell.'

Her mouth was so dry she could only stammer. 'Is, is he dead?'

'No, but we need to get him to hospital.'

She pulled out her phone and stared at the screen, heart racing. 'I've got no signal. Hang on, put this over him . . . keep him warm.' Pulling off her parka, she passed it down to him, letting cold rain trickle along her neck.

Liam's own phone was in his hand. 'It's faint, but I have a signal.' He wiped the rain off his screen. 'You need to get back. It's too cold out here without a coat. And make sure Chloe and Rosa get home too, will you? I'll stay here with him until help comes.'

Rosa and Chloe argued but, as the wind and the rain intensified, they finally agreed. Chloe clutched her mother's arm, crying softly. Hannah shook uncontrollably as they walked fast through the dark, slithering down the hills. All she could think about was the last time she had seen Rob. How she had chatted to him for too long, kept him from going home as the fog descended. How it was her fault if he died.

She imagined him stumbling through the mist. Missing his footing on the edge of that ridge and slipping down into the void, tumbling to the bottom. He probably hit his head and lay there all night, eventually succumbing to hypothermia. Hannah thought of a child crying, of a fox screaming into the night. Of a gardener lying there with his twisted hand stretched out across the ground.

As they approached the house, they could see the kitchen lights glowing. Hannah's soaked clothes clung to her skin and her teeth chattered.

She stumbled into the kitchen, ignored Mo and went straight for the Aga, stretching out her hands for warmth. Their wet clothes dripped onto the tiled floor, as Rosa explained what had happened. Hannah felt herself sway and Mo caught her, held her close, rubbed life back into her arms. She stayed still for a few moments, remembering how Ben used to hold her like this, then she stepped away.

'Thanks,' she said. 'I'm all right. Had to leave my parka to cover him.'

Rosa held up her phone. 'A message from Liam. Help is on its way.' She stopped and looked at Chloe. 'Go and change your muddy shoes.'

But Chloe stared at her. 'I'm not going until you read the rest. I'm not a baby.'

Rosa sighed, then read on. Her voice sounded unnaturally loud.

'The ambulance is going to be too late, though.' She paused and glanced up at them. 'Rob didn't make it and Liam's staying with the . . . with him. The police are on their way, and we all need to wait here in case they want to speak to us.'

Chloe began to sob and Mo started to say something, but then stopped. Hannah had to turn away, feeling suddenly very tired. She muttered something about a sweater and went to her room.

Closing the door, she lay on the bed and stared at the ceiling.

It was her fault.

Another man was dead, and it was her fault.

She was woken by the windows rattling and the sound of rain beating down outside. She opened her eyes and saw water streaming across the glass, heard the whole house creaking under the strain. She grabbed her phone to check the time. She'd been asleep for about an hour. Crawling out of bed, she washed her face and got dressed, tried not to think about the way Rob had looked, sprawled across the mud in the dark.

Heading for the stairs, she noticed a light shining underneath Lucy's door. Maybe she would be up for a smoke. A talk, it would be good to talk.

She paused to listen and from inside Lucy's room came a muffled groan and then a sob.

Hannah went up to her door and stopped. Silence, then another sob.

She knocked lightly. 'Lucy, are you all right?' Nothing. 'It's Hannah.' Another, louder knock. The silence seemed to grow, but she stood waiting, almost sure she could hear Lucy breathing on the other side of the door.

It opened a crack and Lucy peered out. She wore headphones and looked surprisingly young. Her voice sounded rough. 'Hi, what is it?'

'I was worried, thought I heard you crying.'

A headshake. 'I'm working, trying to finish something off.'

Lucy opened the door wider and pointed to her laptop and a keyboard by the window, pieces of paper scattered around them. 'You must have heard me singing.' She pulled off the headphones and smiled briskly. 'Sorry if it was loud. I get a bit snappy when I'm writing.'

Hannah tried to smile back. 'No, it's fine. And I'm sorry too.'

When Lucy closed the door, Hannah headed for the kitchen. Lucy's eyes had been red, as if she'd been crying and had removed black tracks of mascara in a hurry – Hannah knew all about that.

It was difficult to understand why Lucy would be crying, but the longer Hannah spent with her, the stranger she became. Surely Rob's death couldn't be the cause, because she didn't know him, hadn't even seen his body. But maybe it had brought back memories of a recent family death.

Downstairs in the kitchen, Rosa stood violently stirring something on the Aga, while Mo and Chloe played a board game at the table, their faces pale and strained.

Rosa spun round when Hannah entered and brandished her phone. 'Can you believe it? Liam just messaged me again. The ambulance has arrived, but he couldn't leave them to get on with their job. Oh, no. He's following them to the hospital.' She waved the phone again. 'In case they need to *speak* to him. And he's taken the car, so Chloe and I are trapped here.'

'We weren't going out anyway.' Chloe's voice shook and Hannah wanted to cheer her on.

'The police will have to check what happened,' Mo said. 'They generally interview whoever discovers a body. Maybe Liam has gone to sort it all out, so they won't have to come here and talk to us. If anyone needs to go anywhere, I can drive them.'

Rosa scrubbed at the stove with a damp cloth.

Hannah sat down opposite Mo. 'How's Sandeep?'

He took off his glasses and rubbed the lenses on his shirt. 'Not good, I'm afraid. He knew the guy, not well, but they met a few times. He's in the drawing room, but I think he wants to be alone.'

'I hope he's OK.' Her questions for him would have to wait. But there was still Lucy and she couldn't leave that alone. 'Lucy seems upset. Did she say anything to you about it?'

Rosa let out a laugh. 'A bit of a drama queen, if you ask me, making it all about her. For attention, of course, as if the rest of us aren't shocked too.'

Chloe stood up, her eyes flashing. 'And it's not all about you, either.' She marched from the room and they listened to her footsteps on the stairs.

Rosa dropped her wooden spoon onto the Aga, and Hannah and Mo shared a look. Rosa picked it up again, gave the pan one more stir, turned down the heat and faced them with her arms folded tight across her chest.

'You think it's funny, don't you? You have no idea what it's like, what I have to put up with.' And before either of them could speak she stomped from the room.

Hannah collected Chloe's scattered counters and dropped them into a little plastic pot. 'I don't reckon Lucy wants attention.'

'No.' Mo frowned. 'She gets enough of that already.' Hannah ran her finger over the grain of the wooden table as Mo went on. 'It was really weird, though. When Rosa told her what happened, Lucy looked as if she'd seen a ghost. She practically ran out of the room.'

They sat for a few seconds, then Mo stood. 'Better go and check on the old man.' He made a mug of tea and headed for the drawing room, with Hannah following him.

Sandeep was lying back in the leather chair by the fire with his eyes closed and a blanket over his knees. As they entered, he sat up and smiled. 'A nice hot cuppa, just what I need.' Hannah could see the veins standing out on his shaking hand as he took the mug.

She sat in the leather armchair opposite him. 'How are you feeling? How's the cough?' she asked.

'Fine, fine. Don't worry about me.'

Mo hovered by the door. 'We'll leave you in peace then, shall we?'

Sandeep frowned and waved a hand at them. 'Stay, please. I'd rather have company if you can bear it.'

Mo turned away. 'I'll just check on Rosa's soup.'

Hannah waited, sensing Sandeep was in a mood to talk.

He rubbed a hand over his face and stared into the fire. 'I've been thinking about poor Robert, you know.' A log shifted in the grate. 'He'd been with the Fallon family all his life and his father was head gardener before him. Rob was born in that cottage when it was still within the grounds of the estate. He would have been with the last Lady Fallon all her life.'

'Did you ever meet her?'

His hand shook as he put down his mug and stared into the fire. 'Just the once, but I'll never forget it. It's what finished my career.'

Chapter Nineteen

Eleven years ago
The Policeman

It's been a couple of years since the last call-out to Fallon House, but Sandeep has never entirely forgotten it. Some days at work he finds himself staring out of the window at the distant hills and thinking about Rob – about how he looked when he found him – about him curled up outside the back door in the wind, like a dog that had crawled home to die beside his master. When Sandeep last tried to persuade his boss to investigate the gardener's accident, he had been laughed out of the room, the *Ghostbusters* theme tune ringing in his ears.

Unable to leave it alone, he had gone back to the doctor who had treated Rob's injuries and who had initially agreed with him – that the wounds were no accident. But he now seemed to have changed his mind. The police had done a cursory check to confirm that the Fallons had been out that day and that nobody else had been seen in the house or the grounds. They had ticked the boxes and closed the case.

But here he is once more, standing by his parked car looking along the muddy track over the green fields towards the hills.

A new phone call had come in and apparently no one else had been free, so the buck had been passed down the line to his desk. Some jokes never get old.

This time Sandeep had heard the recording himself, listened through static and patchy signal to the tone of panic in the caller's voice:

Help! ... *crrrrrrr* ... *someone's hurt* ... *crrrrrrr* ... *they're bleeding.*

And then the line had gone dead.

He locks his car door and starts the long walk up the hill. It's a lovely spring day, the first time he's ever been warm on this walk. When he reaches the ridge he gets his first glimpse of the building, its windows open, lights shining out. At least he might get some answers this time. He walks past the blooming magnolias and knocks on the door.

It's opened by a very thin lady, her blonde hair caught up at one side. She gives him a pinched smile, but he knows immediately that something's wrong. 'Could I speak to Lady Fallon please?'

She glances back into the house. 'I'm Lady Fallon.' Her voice is frail, her shoulders hunched; she's nothing like the glamorous lady of the manor he has always imagined.

The door is still barely open, and her eyes keep flitting back and forth. He tries a smile. 'I wonder if I could step inside for a moment?'

She moves back carefully, making sure he can't get far into the grand hallway. He smiles again. 'I had the pleasure of meeting your husband a few years ago. Is he home today?'

A headshake. 'No, he's in Dublin on business.'

He feels a prickle down his spine, the sense of being watched, that someone else is here.

'The thing is.' He coughs. 'We've had a report that someone has been hurt at this property. Do you know anything about that?'

She blinks. 'Sorry, I've no idea what that could be. I'm here on my own.' A tight-lipped smile. 'And I'm not hurt, as you can see.'

She certainly doesn't look well, but he has no choice but to take her word for it.

'Perhaps I could have a quick look around, just so I can keep my boss happy?' It's worth a try, and she might loosen up after a while.

Her face is pale, her eyes strangely blank. 'No, sorry, I—'

She stops and looks back into the house. 'I have to get on. You'll—'

It's then he hears the cry.

Chapter Twenty

'You heard it *inside* the house?' Hannah leaned forward.

'I did, just that one time. A single cry, but enough for me to know I had to do something.'

Hannah stared at him, willing him to go on, as if the harder she looked, the better she could see into his memories. Eventually he continued.

'Lady Fallon insisted I had no right to look around and legally she was correct. I didn't hear another sound inside that house and she kept saying it had been a fox screaming outside. That they had a litter of cubs up on the bank and a vixen who was always making a racket. That I had been listening to those ridiculous old stories about a ghost.'

'What did you do?' Hannah asked.

Sandeep coughed for a moment. Then lay back in his armchair, letting out little gasps and rubbing the back of his neck.

The door opened. 'Soup's ready.' Mo's face fell, and he went to his dad, crouched beside the armchair. 'Are you all right?'

Sandeep shook his head. 'I'm fine. For God's sake, stop fussing. I'm just fine.'

Mo looked down for a moment then stood again. 'Well,

there's food in the kitchen if you want it.' When neither of them replied, he walked out, closing the door behind him.

Sandeep spoke gruffly, as if berating himself. 'He means well, my son. Caught me at a bad time as usual.'

When Hannah said nothing, he brushed his hands over his knees and stared into the fire. 'Where was I? Oh yes, I made a fuss, of course I did. Tried to get a warrant for a search – all the outhouses and so on. But I was refused, told to stop.'

'And you did?'

He glared at her. 'What do you take me for? I thought a child was in danger, so I used to go over there whenever I could. Talked to Rob too, but he just kept on saying the same thing.'

'What?'

'Well I could barely understand him most of the time. He'd just mutter away to himself about this and that. Kept saying stuff about a face at the window. Completely crazed if you ask me. Could never tell whether he thought there was a ghost. I got him to let me look in his cottage, the greenhouse and the potting sheds, but found nothing. He refused to come to the station to give a statement and, after a while, he just started avoiding me.'

'What about your boss?'

'He did send someone else over, apparently, but he found nothing. In the end I was told they'd had a complaint about me – I could be charged with harassment and conducting a search without a warrant.' He coughed and his hand clenched into a fist. 'Lady Fallon said I had searched the whole house without permission. Complete rubbish, but everyone knew how obsessed I was with the place, so they were inclined to believe her. The lady of the manor could do no wrong.'

He pulled up his blanket with a trembling hand. 'And that wasn't the end of it either; the accusations only got worse.

One day I was called into a meeting, sat down in front of a row of sergeants and told that Lady Fallon had made a serious accusation. She said I'd assaulted her, made inappropriate advances.' His lips twisted. 'Can you imagine? She didn't pursue it, thank God, but that was it – the end of my career.'

There was a long silence as they both stared into the fire. Sandeep sighed and continued. 'My wife didn't believe it, but she still blamed me. Blamed my obsession with this place.'

'What happened?'

'I gave up and left the area. We went over to London. I took an office job that paid half what I'd been earning, and Meera never really forgave me. And Mo – well, it was years until he settled.'

They sat for a while and listened to the flames crackling in the hearth. And then, a piercing sound cut through the house.

Close by and very loud.

Someone screamed.

Chapter Twenty-One

Hannah rushed out into the hall and found Rosa sitting on the bottom stair, staring at her phone, her eyes brimming with tears. Sandeep stumbled behind, gripped the doorframe. 'What is it? What happened? Are you all right?'

Rosa's screwed-up face burned red. 'Bloody man. Stupid bloody man.' Hannah sat next to her and Sandeep limped to a small sofa at the side of the hall.

'He says it's the weather,' Rosa sobbed. 'It's too bad to drive back, so he's staying overnight – with a friend.' A sharp laugh. '*A friend.*'

Hannah tried to think of something to say, as the rain whipped against the windows and Rosa stared bitterly at her phone. 'Apparently the police will be over to see us tomorrow, so we can't even leave.' She wiped a tear from her face and stood with a shrug. Back to the normal Rosa. 'Better tell my daughter her father has abandoned us.'

She stomped up the stairs and Sandeep watched her go, shook his head, then shuffled back into the drawing room. Hannah stayed where she was for a moment, until she heard shouting from the family room.

Your precious father! You have no idea. It's always me that has to deal with it.

There was a pause. Then Chloe, her voice shrill and angry: *Shut up! Just shut up!*

Hannah jumped as the door at the top of the stairs banged open, and Chloe raced down, passed her, and out the front door.

After a few seconds Hannah followed. The rain was even heavier now, the wind stronger, but Chloe had only got as far as the garden bench under the porch. She huddled in one corner, clutching herself against the cold, her eyes wet with tears. Hannah stood beside her, watching the rain pound against the grass. A drip trickled down her neck and a fine spray, blown in under the porch, settled on her face.

After a while Chloe pulled out a tissue and wiped her nose. 'I'm all right. It's just my mum . . .' She shook her head, and Hannah knew that frustrated feeling well.

'It's freezing. Why don't you come in and watch some TV in my room for a bit?'

Chloe nodded and wiped her eyes.

Upstairs, Hannah made them hot chocolate and they sat next to each other on her bed.

Chloe took a sip. 'Thanks. I've used all the chocolate in our room.' She laughed bitterly. 'Mum says I've had enough.' She leaned back against the wall and drained the last of her mug. 'She's really worried about Dad and I'm not helping, but she's so . . .' She shook her head again.

'Mums and daughters are always a difficult combination.' Hannah took the empty mug from her and put it on the bedside table. 'I used to have endless fights with mine when I was a teenager.'

'And your dad? Did you get on with him?'

'He's dead.'

Chloe swallowed. 'Oh. Sorry, I didn't—'

'But I never really knew him. They broke up when I was five.'

Chloe sat very still for a couple of seconds. 'My parents might be getting a divorce.'

Hannah leaned over and gave her a hug.

'It's all an act.' Chloe's voice shook. 'Them being together, all of us one happy family. Has been for ages. He's been cheating on her, you know.' She broke away and looked up at Hannah. 'And the house in Scotland . . . well, I think it's just for me and Mum. He'll be living here with *her*. That's why we're staying in this fucking place.'

Hannah went to speak, but Chloe carried on. 'My mum wanted to rent somewhere in Scotland, but he said this was better. It just happened to be near his girlfriend. That's probably where he is now.' She swung her legs over the side of the bed and shoved her feet into her trainers.

Hannah remembered Liam saying that Rosa had been the one who had found The Guesthouse. Another lie to cover his tracks.

'I'm sorry, Chloe.' Hannah put an arm around her again. 'Look, you're nearly old enough to do your own thing. A couple more years and you'll be off to work or university. You can make your own—'

'I'm starting a new school . . . away from all my friends,' Chloe went on. 'We've got no money now and it's all because of Dad.' A tear ran down her cheek. Hannah passed her a tissue and wondered why Liam had retired if he was poor. Surely doctors of his age were well paid.

'His girlfriend, she was one of his patients. Mum says he's done it all before, that's why he got the sack.' She sobbed again, blew her nose with the tissue. 'Please don't tell anyone. I shouldn't have said anything.'

Hannah took her hand. 'Of course. Don't worry.' They

lapsed into an awkward silence, Chloe clearly cringing with embarrassment.

In the end she got up and went over to the window, to watch the rain beating down against the glass. 'It was sad about that man who died, wasn't it?' She stared down into the rose garden. 'He was pretty scary, though.'

'Yes, he was, but completely harmless. He just wasn't used to talking to strangers.'

'I didn't like the way he stared at me, you remember? But it wasn't just that, it was when I saw him from my window, lurking around out there in the fog. That really scared me.'

Hannah went to stand next to her. 'Me too.'

'He was there one minute and then gone the next.'

Hannah spoke as gently as she could. 'It's the way the ground is out there, all the dips and rises.'

They watched the rain for a moment and then Chloe sighed. 'I wonder how Lucy knew him?' she said.

Hannah wiped condensation off the glass. 'I don't think she did, at least she didn't meet him in the garden with me.'

There was a little smile on Chloe's face now, a secret smile that said she knew something Hannah didn't.

'I heard her calling him.' Chloe lowered her voice. 'My bed is by the window, you see.' She gestured to the space they were standing in. 'I couldn't sleep, so I played a game on my phone until it started to get light. You know *Candy Crush*? It's pretty good.'

When Hannah didn't respond she carried on. 'Anyway the room was stuffy so I pushed open the window to get some fresh air and that's when I saw him. He was just a black shadow and at first I thought he was a ghost. But when he moved I could see it was a man. A big man like the gardener. I knew it had to be him even though I couldn't see his face.' She leaned back, her eyes glowing.

'Then I heard it – a noise from next door, from Lucy's room.'

'What was it?'

'A creaking noise, Lucy's window opening, I think. And her voice, calling to him, all faint and soft like she didn't want anyone to hear.' She grinned. 'But I heard. I had my ear pressed right up to the open window.'

'That doesn't mean she knew him,' Hannah said. 'She might have been wondering who he was, telling him to go away.'

Chloe smiled. 'She knew him all right. Or thought she did. Like me she guessed it was the gardener and she called him by his name to make sure. *Rob? Is that you Rob?* That's what she said. Said it a few times.'

'And what did he do?'

'Nothing, I don't think he could hear her. He just walked off into the mist.'

Their eyes locked for a moment and the rain drummed into the glass.

'What was that?' Chloe turned and put a finger to her lips. 'Shhh!'

A crackling sound, then the lights flickered and buzzed. Chloe shut her eyes tight. And – with a bang – all the lights went out.

Chapter Twenty-Two

Chloe whimpered and Hannah could only just make out her face in the gloom. She reached for her, willing her voice to sound calm.

'It's all right. Don't worry, it's just a power cut, probably all this wind.'

There was a clatter outside on the landing and a shout from Rosa. 'Chloe, are you in there?'

'Let's go,' Hannah said.

Chloe grabbed her hand like a frightened child. As soon as they opened the door, Rosa clutched her daughter to her. 'There you are. *Thank God.*'

Lucy's door opened and she called out. 'Sorry. It might be me. I turned on my light and, with all the other stuff I'm using, it might have overloaded a circuit.'

'Great,' Rosa said. 'Just great. What are we supposed to do now?'

'It'll be fine.' Hannah spoke firmly. 'There'll be a fuse box somewhere downstairs.'

She took out her mobile and switched on the torch, noticed the low battery symbol flash up again. She left Chloe and Rosa on the stairs and Lucy on the landing and padded down to the hall, as Mo emerged from the kitchen with a torch.

'I thought the fuse box might be in that storeroom.' He pointed the beam back the way he had come. 'It isn't, but I did find this.' A wave of the torch.

She went with him to look into all the downstairs rooms, their beams of light illuminating paths through shadows and cobwebs as the sun fell from the sky. The house felt like a shipwreck full of abandoned empty rooms, its secrets hidden forever under layers of grime. When they came back into the hall for the last time, Hannah's phone abruptly died. She could just make out Rosa and Chloe sitting huddled on the stairs, but Lucy seemed to have disappeared.

The beam of Mo's torch shook a little as it settled on the door that led to the green corridor, the only place they hadn't looked. They made for it, their footsteps loud in the darkness. Mo passed the torch to Hannah as he opened the door and she was glad of its weight in her hands. She stood back and shone the light along the green walls for him. Let out a sigh of relief when he whooped and shouted that he'd found it. The fuse box was just inside the door.

A couple of clicks, a buzz, and the lights flickered back on. Rosa and Chloe came downstairs, Rosa muttering something under her breath.

Lucy opened her door and began to come down too. 'My lightbulb's gone. That must be what did it.'

'Give me a minute,' Mo said. He went back into the kitchen and emerged moments later with a metal stepladder. 'These were in the storeroom too. I'll fix your light.' How long had he spent exploring this house on his own? Hannah hadn't even noticed a storeroom.

Lucy tried to take the ladder from Mo, but he carried it past her and up the stairs. 'It's OK, I've got this.' When he reached her door, he stood awkwardly with the steps and pulled a bulb from his pocket.

Lucy walked slowly up towards him. 'Thanks. I'll do it.'

And she took the bulb, put it in her own pocket and reached for the ladder. Mo passed it over reluctantly, and she dragged it inside. Before he could say anything else, she closed her door, leaving him on the landing, his forehead creased as if he had failed a particularly easy exam.

As Hannah walked back to her room, she wondered what had happened to Lucy's usual charm. Mo must have thought he was in with a chance, and she had humiliated him.

She flung herself on her bed and plugged her phone back in, waited for it to glow back into life. There was no wifi or signal. Switching it off, she lay back on the bed, letting her mind wander.

Maybe Chloe was right and Lucy *had* known Rob. The fact that she had called his name from the window didn't prove she knew him; there were any number of ways she could have found out what he was called. There might even have been a mention on Preserve the Past website, but that didn't explain her tears after the discovery of his body.

Needing a distraction, Hannah jumped up and walked across the room. Even without wifi, she had an idea where she might find some answers about this house.

She raked in the bedside drawer for the postcard, on which she had recorded the names and dates of the last few Fallons. Then she opened her bedroom door a crack and peeped out. The dark corridor stretched away towards the stairs, the only sound the pounding rain against the windows.

Once she had crept past all the occupied guest rooms and along the opposite corridor, she moved faster. There it was – the little room at the end – the twin of the office next to her bedroom.

The door was locked, but she pulled the postcard from her pocket and thought for a moment. Tapped in the most obvious date to try, the last Lady Fallon's birthday. The keypad beeped and she threw a fist into the air as the door clicked open.

Inside, the dingy room looked just like its twin: the same rough curtains covering the window, the same layer of dust coating everything. She clicked on the light and a bare bulb in the centre of the ceiling flickered on. Remembering last time, she used a chair to prop the door ajar and stepped inside.

There was no desk in here, just the chair and a large dark-wood wardrobe. This room was probably a dressing room and the door in the opposite wall must lead to one of the bedrooms. She tried the handle, but it didn't budge and there was no keypad.

Something about the imposing wardrobe made her turn back towards it. It was tall and polished, with intricate carvings across its panels. It seemed to suck all the light from the room, and she felt a nerve in her neck tighten. She paused, reluctant to touch it, but somehow drawn closer. *Come on, get on with it.* She pulled the door. It creaked open and she felt the room begin to spin. Sucked in a lungful of something horribly familiar.

She gripped the handle, a rushing sound in her ears, and time rolled back. She was a little child again.

Chapter Twenty-Three

Twenty-one years ago
Hannah

She's staring up at Mummy, but Mummy looks all different. Her face is red and blotchy and she's crying and shouting. Mummy never does that, never shouts or cries. She always makes Hannah feel better when she's sick or hurt. Hannah covers her ears, but her tears keep falling like drops of rain onto her new Spice Girls duvet.

Mummy keeps shouting and everything feels wobbly. It's hard to breathe.

Daddy is just staring at them. He doesn't say anything, until Mummy starts to push him away. Starts to hit him and her face is all red and Hannah has to look away. When he does speak it's so quiet Hannah can only just hear him.

'Ruby, don't be stupid.' Daddy says it really nicely, like he's going to give Mummy an ice cream, even though she's being nasty.

Then he looks at Hannah and his face is all sad. She wants to run to him, but Mummy grabs her, squeezing too tight until it hurts and she shouts for her to stop. Then the wind is blowing Hannah's hair. But it's not the wind it's Mummy's breath as she shouts and screams.

'Get away, Jack. Stay away. Don't come near us. Don't *ever* come near us again.'

And then she's crying very quietly as Daddy walks away and slams the door. Mummy's hand has gone all white where she's holding her phone and she won't let Hannah go, even when Hannah starts to struggle.

They go to the front door and Mummy locks it tight, using all the locks, even the other special one with the shiny chain. Then they watch from the window as Daddy's car drives away.

'Don't worry, my baby,' Mummy says. 'He's gone now.'

But Hannah doesn't want Daddy to go.

Then Mummy talks on the phone for ages, and Hannah has to wait for ever to get a proper cuddle and a kiss. 'It's all right, little one, he's never coming back.'

Hannah cries harder and harder and Mummy's face is all wet too. 'I'm sorry, Mummy.' Hannah feels sick inside, because she loves Daddy and now he's gone.

And it's all her fault.

Chapter Twenty-Four

Hannah slumped on the floor beside the wardrobe, her knees shaking, and that awful smell filling the room around her. In her mouth, her clothes, her eyes.

How long she had been sitting there she couldn't tell.

She wiped her face on her top and, using the wardrobe for support, dragged herself to her feet. That had been a real memory, probably her very first. The trauma of losing her dad – the dad she adored – had scorched itself into her mind. But why had it lain dormant for so many years until now?

Her parents' marriage had broken down and that traumatic moment must have been the final argument that tore it to pieces. Maybe he had an affair, and that row had been caused by its discovery. She knew first-hand just how nasty fights could become in the death-throes of a relationship.

But it had scarred her in ways she could only now begin to understand.

Her legs felt weak as she stood looking at the clothes in the wardrobe – a row of formal suits and jackets. The smell still here, but weaker now: a man's aftershave or cologne.

She rifled through a musty formal dinner jacket, a business suit in charcoal grey with a thin stripe, a pair of shoes, shiny black and coated in a light layer of dust.

But there was no stash of letters or photographs, as she'd hoped. Reaching up and running a hand over the shelf above the jackets, she came away with nothing but a dust-coated palm.

She wasn't willing to give up yet, had to keep her mind occupied, to stop herself dwelling on the past. Her father was long dead and buried, so there was no chance she could reconcile with him. No matter how unfair her mother had been in keeping them apart.

Her hands felt their way into the pockets of the dinner jacket. It was when she came to the dark grey suit that she felt a lump in an inside pocket, felt a stirring of guilt at this search through a dead man's clothes.

And yet, her hand worked its way inside and pulled out a small silver case. It was heavy, expensive. And when she flipped it open, she found business cards.

There was no writing, just an illustration, on the back of the first card. A skilfully executed sketch of The Guesthouse, drawn from the garden, looking onto the front of the building. All the cards had the same picture, so presumably the man who owned them was Lady Jane Fallon's husband.

She turned the first one over.

The rain beat against the glass window at her side, and she could only stare down at the piece of card in her hand.

The card, and the words on it. The card, and the words on it. Reading them over and over again, her brain refusing to understand:

John Roper.

Architect.

His name was on the cards – on all of them – her dad the architect. Although her mother had always called him Jack, Hannah knew that was a nickname for John. It couldn't be true.

Then she saw the inscription inside the lid of the silver case:

For Jack with love from Jane

And she watched the case fall to the floor, spilling business cards across the carpet.

It *was* true. This was her father's old home.

Chapter Twenty-Five

She staggered back down the corridor, relieved no one else was around. She had only hesitated for a moment before taking the silver case and the cards – after all, her dad would have wanted her to have them. No wonder he had never come back to England; he was a Lord, living in a place like this.

When she got to her own room she sat on the window seat and stared out. Darkness had settled over the hills and the sky, smothering the moon and the stars with a wall of driving rain.

Sandeep had said that the man he met at this house – the most recent Lord Fallon – had introduced himself as John, which meant Sandeep had actually *met* her father. Her stomach fluttered.

She needed to talk to Sandeep again, tell him who she was – who her father was – and see his reaction. Even Liam might be able to help when he returned.

All her late-night searches on Cloud BNB, poring over images of houses near the village. Not knowing that this holiday would lead her right to her father's home, to his secret life. Everyone in the village would surely remember him, the husband of Lady Fallon. After the police interviewed her tomorrow, she'd head straight there, whatever the weather.

And Rosa, she might also know something. Hannah forced herself to stay calm and went downstairs into the kitchen, where Rosa and Chloe were eating soup in silence. Rosa gestured to the Aga. 'Do try some if you're hungry.'

Hannah suddenly felt very hungry, so she ladled out a bowlful, cut herself some bread and came to sit opposite them.

After a few mouthfuls, she said, 'This is delicious. What did you put in it?'

Rosa glanced up and gave her a tiny smile. 'It's an old family recipe actually, very healthy too.' She went back to her soup.

It tasted like hedge-clippings, but Hannah finished it all and made appreciative noises. She waited until they had all pushed away their bowls, then pulled out the silver case and let it rest on the table.

'Look at this. I found it upstairs in one of the rooms, inside an old jacket – it must have belonged to the last owner.'

Chloe's eyes widened. When Hannah flipped open the case to show the sketch on the top card, Chloe leaned in closer and reached out a hand. 'Wow, cool. It's this house, isn't it?'

Hannah handed one of the cards to her. Rosa went over to the Aga and stirred the remains of the soup.

Hannah pointed at the card. 'Turn it over.'

'John Roper.' Chloe frowned. 'Who's he? I thought this house belonged to Lord Fallon.'

The feeling of excitement was irresistible and Hannah knew it showed in her voice. 'The final owner of this house was Lady Fallon, who must have been the last of the Fallon family. It looks like she married a man called John or Jack Roper, then, when they both died, the house was sold to Preserve the Past.'

'Cool.' Chloe pushed the card across the table.

Rosa had been noisily tipping the remaining soup away, rinsing the pot and putting it into the dishwasher. Now she turned to them, one hand massaging her forehead.

'I've got a splitting headache, so I'm going up for a rest. Chloe, if I don't see you, remember that you need to be in bed by nine thirty sharp. Don't make me have to come down for you.'

Hannah stood up. 'Before you go, can I just ask you something? Did you or Liam ever meet Lady Fallon or her husband? Or know anything about them?'

Rubbing her temples, Rosa shook her head. 'No. Liam's practice was in the next village.'

Chloe frowned thoughtfully. 'But didn't Dad say he knew everyone important in the area? He was always in those fancy clubs, wasn't he?'

A sharp laugh. 'You should know by now that your father is a liar and most of what he says is just to boost his ego. He's never been that important.'

Chloe swallowed, her face reddening, and Hannah grabbed her hand. 'I never told you my last name, but do you know what it is?'

Chloe shook her head and Hannah picked up the card from the table. 'Roper. It's Roper. My name is Hannah Roper. Jack Roper was my father.'

Chloe's mouth fell open and Rosa stopped at the door. 'So this house . . . it could be yours?' Chloe grinned.

'Unfortunately not, because I'm not related to the Fallons. My mum was Jack Roper's first wife and Lady Fallon was his second.'

'So you didn't know your father lived here,' Chloe said, 'because your parents broke up?'

Hannah nodded and squeezed her hand. 'But it was all right. Me and Mum got on fine. I found out where my dad had lived – that it was in this area – and I wanted to see it for myself, but I never expected to chance upon his actual house.'

Rosa's voice cut through the room. 'Come on, Chloe. You can watch TV if you want. I'll use my earplugs and mask.'

Chloe scowled. 'But you told me I could stay until nine thirty. I want to talk to Hannah.'

Rosa's hands clenched and unclenched at her sides. 'You've talked enough, I don't want you listening to any more fantasies.' She raised a hand to stop Chloe from interrupting. 'It's ridiculous. You have no idea if this girl's name really is Roper – she's a complete stranger for God's sake – and even if it is, she could have produced the cards herself. There's no proof she found them in the house.'

'Why on earth would I do that?' Hannah felt her jaw clench.

'I have no idea, to trick a gullible child, perhaps. Or because you're a fantasist, a con artist, desperate to impress that young man you've been making eyes at. I don't know, and I don't care. But my daughter won't be involved.'

Hannah was stunned into silence and, after a moment, Chloe stood up. She looked back as they left the room, then Rosa slammed the door behind them.

Chapter Twenty-Six

Hannah sat at the kitchen table and stared at the silver case, her mind going back over Rosa's outburst. What could have sparked her anger?

She stood up and sighed, rubbed tiredness from her eyes. She needed a good night's sleep, but first she would find Sandeep. Walking into the drawing room, she found only Mo, sitting beside the fire, flicking through a book. There were a few others piled by his chair. Old dusty volumes that he must have found in the library.

She sat on the sofa, taking in his tired expression, his forced smile. 'Lucy didn't mean to upset you earlier,' she said. 'She's just in a mood. It's probably work, or this place starting to get to her.'

Mo shifted in his seat. 'It's not that.' He turned the page of his book, the fire crackled, and Hannah wondered if she should go. Wished she hadn't spoken.

But then Mo closed the book and looked at her. 'I'm worried,' he said. 'About my dad. I really think I need to get him home.' His fingers drummed on the cover of the book. 'But we have to wait for the bloody police and I checked the weather forecast on the TV. It's only going to get worse.' He pushed his glasses back up his nose and stared out the window. 'There's a big storm – a huge one – rolling in off the Atlantic tomorrow. Gale-force winds, constant rain. You thought the weather was bad already? Storms around here can be brutal.'

'Didn't your dad want to stay for a bit?'

'He says he's fine, but I can tell he's not. He won't admit it, but it isn't just his physical health. It's all these memories about the house. He keeps torturing himself, going back over the same old ground. Lucy's right: we should have left ages ago.'

They fell back into silence, and the wind pressed against the French windows. Eventually Hannah pointed at the stack of books on the table. 'What you reading?'

'I found them in the library, probably left by the last owners. There's some juicy stuff about the area and its history. Quite grim, some of it.'

'Anything about this actual house?'

He passed her the book he was holding. 'Have a read of that. Check out the index.'

She flicked through and found a page about the Fallon family. There was a photo of The Guesthouse, its long driveway cutting through acres of fields, the same cold stone walls looking just as foreboding. She shivered and began to read.

When the potato famine struck in the 1840s, huge numbers of the locals died from starvation, as ninety percent of the crops they relied upon were struck by blight. The Fallon family themselves remained in England throughout this period and ignored the plight of their tenants, even evicting families who couldn't keep up with the rent.

Here we include a section of a pamphlet from the time, found in the ruins of a church on the outskirts of Fallon village in 1843:

Crying and wailing sounded across all the hills of Ireland and nowhere was more tragic than County Mayo. No village more drowned in sorrow than Fallon, where so many children died that they can be heard crying in every gust of wind that blows across the land.

Hannah stopped reading and put down the book. Her throat felt dry. Mo reached out a hand. 'What's wrong?'

'Did you read that bit from the pamphlet?'

'Yeah.' He frowned. 'Pretty upsetting stuff.' He waved a hand to take in the room and the rest of the house. 'The crying children bit certainly fits with Dad's old ghost stories about this place.'

Hannah looked into his eyes. 'Are they just stories, though?' When he blinked and took off his glasses to clean them on his shirt she went on. 'The crying child, I mean. I've heard it, Mo. Actually heard it. More than once, too.'

'Come on, Hannah.' He shook his head. 'Couldn't that have been Chloe? I mean, she's having a tough time at the—'

'I thought that at first, I really did, but it wasn't her. She's heard it too. And your dad – and Rob – they've both heard it too.'

'I don't want to sound like a dick.' He smiled and put his glasses back on. 'But maybe all these stories have set you off, you know. Maybe they're what got you thinking about ghosts, about crying children. Made you—'

'So I imagined it all. Is that what you mean?'

There was an angry silence and Mo got up to walk over to the window, running a hand through his hair. 'No, of course not. Look, I'm sorry . . . it's just all this stuff with my dad.'

He turned back to her and tried to smile. 'Tell you what. Next time you hear it, come and get me. I'm up for a bit of ghost-hunting.'

She knew she would have reacted in the same way if someone had told her that story, but still she felt humiliated. Dropping her eyes to the book again, she clenched her hands, tried to read but couldn't focus on the words. Was too aware of him still standing by the window, staring out into the dark, occasionally stroking his chin in thought. After a moment she decided she might as well tell him the rest now. She had nothing to lose – he already thought she was deluded.

'I was upstairs earlier,' she said. 'And I got into the other little room at the end of the empty wing.'

He turned to face her, smiling again. 'Nice, but don't tell Lucy or she'll have a fit. Mrs Health and Safety.' There was a touch of mockery in his voice. When Hannah didn't respond he said, 'OK, OK, spill it. What did you find?'

'Just a load of old clothes – they must have belonged to the last owner.'

He came back to sit opposite her again. 'No hidden treasure then?'

Hannah dug into her pocket and pulled out the silver case. 'No, but guess what I found in one of the suit jackets in the wardrobe?' She tossed the case over to him. 'I think even Lucy would say it was worth a bit of risk.'

He ran his finger over the embossed silver design, like a presenter on *Antiques Roadshow*, and pursed his lips. 'Solid silver.'

As he flicked it open she raised a hand. 'Before you look, I should tell you my whole name: it's Hannah Roper.'

He skimmed through the cards, raising his eyebrows when she told him who she thought Jack Roper might be. 'Wow, that's amazing. You actually belong here.' He grinned and gestured to the house.

'Not really, I'm not related to the Fallons. My mum was Jack's first wife, and she was only the daughter of a postman.'

Mo's smile grew wider and he reached out to take her hand. 'Well, I always thought you looked like a Lady.'

Hannah laughed and moved away, her face flushed, and there was a long silent moment. Then he coughed with embarrassment.

As Hannah sat wondering what had just happened he went to crouch by the grate and threw a couple of logs on the fire. Unable to look at him she stared into the flames, thinking of Ben, thinking of Ben's brother back at the funeral. Rosa had obviously noticed something between her and Mo, but she couldn't allow herself to get involved. Not yet, not for a long, long time.

The French windows rattled harder, the first signs that the storm was nearly upon them. Two nights without sleep were taking their toll and she stifled a yawn, shook herself and stood up.

'I need some coffee. What about you?'

He shook his head. 'I'm good, thanks.' He picked up his book again and turned the page, a shadow of what looked like regret in his eyes.

She was surprised to find Sandeep in the kitchen, hunched on a chair beside the Aga, drinking his usual green tea.

'Feeling any better?' she asked.

He put down his cup. 'I don't know what my son has been saying, but I'm fine. Those bloody sleeping pills, that's all. Making me feel groggy.'

Hannah poured herself a coffee and said nothing. Surely one sleeping pill at night shouldn't affect him so badly. She dragged over a chair, pulled out the case and handed it to him.

As she explained what it was and what it meant, he didn't look at her. Just opened the case and stared at the card in his hand, turning it over to see the picture, then back to the

148

wording, tracing the name with his finger. When he eventually spoke, his voice had that suspicious note in it again, just as it had when they first met.

'Is this some kind of joke?'

She blinked. 'Of course not. Why would I make up something like this?'

He passed the card back to her and breathed out heavily. 'I don't know, forget it.' He stared out of the kitchen window. 'You know, I've never been good at jokes, not really. They used to think it was a great joke sending me out here every time they got a prank call. Laughing behind my back when I tried to tell them something serious *was* going on.'

His voice got louder. 'They'd rather imagine I believed in ghosts than listen to me. I was supposed to laugh it off, treat their insults as banter, harmless banter.' He banged his hand on the table. 'And like a fool I tried to do it. To fit in. Went to the pub with them, shared a pint, bought my round, as if that would make me one of them.'

Hannah shifted in her chair, tried not to look at a tiny muscle flickering in his cheek.

'But when it came to it, I could never belong. Not like the Fallons did, not like my old sergeant did. Do you know what he said when he told me about Lady Fallon's accusations?'

His dark eyes flashed at her. 'He said he realized certain kinds of behaviour were acceptable in my part of the world, but they couldn't be tolerated here.' His speech was laboured. 'As if people from *my part of the world* believed it was fine to sexually assault a lady.' He coughed and wiped his mouth with the back of a hand.

She watched his chest rise and fall. When she spoke she kept her voice gentle. 'I'm sorry if I've upset you, Sandeep, but it's not a joke. I found those cards upstairs in a wardrobe. The reason I came here in the first place was because I knew my dad lived locally. But I had no idea until today that he might have been married to Lady Fallon.'

Sandeep closed his eyes, as if he was about to drift off, then he opened them again and stared at her. 'I suffered – for years. Thought I had settled in, become one of the lads, but it was all a joke. They thought I believed in ghosts, thought I was the ghostbuster, capable of breaking all the rules. Bringing my uniform into disrepute. Attacking a woman, for God's sake.'

'That must have been horrible.' She felt so sorry for him, so embarrassed by the behaviour of his colleagues. 'But why do you think Lady Fallon would do that? Accusing you of something so horrible when she didn't even know you?'

He sighed again, a soft, sad sigh this time. 'Yes, you're quite right, that's the question. I've thought about it a lot over the years and the only explanation is that she had something to hide.'

'And her husband? What about him? Do you think he had anything to do with it?'

When he looked up at her, his eyes softened. 'Well, I only met him that one time. Although I didn't take to him, I never heard anything bad said about him.' He shrugged. 'So who knows?' Another of those gentle smiles. 'And if he was your father you should try to think the best of him.'

Chapter Twenty-Seven

Creak, creak, creak.

Hannah stared at the ceiling, wide awake now. There it was again – footsteps – creaking above her head.

It had to be the sound of someone walking across bare wooden floorboards, someone pacing back and forth up there in those dark empty rooms in the old servants' quarters. Hannah shuddered and pulled her duvet closer.

The wind had been a low whine when she fell asleep, but now it was a high-pitched wail, gusting against the window. Her phone said 2 a.m. She listened to the footsteps for a few minutes, then swung her legs to the floor.

The sound of the wind was even louder in the corridor, and she thought she could feel a breeze, as if the wind had somehow got into the house. Above the wailing that rhythmic *creak, creak, creak* continued, right over her head.

She was tempted to go back to her room and put her head under the covers, or to knock for Mo as he'd suggested.

At that moment a creak in the hall made her jump, and a flash of blinding light illuminated her face. She held up her hands to shield her eyes.

'It's only me,' Mo whispered and the torchlight dipped to the ground. He was out in the corridor, dressed in a sweatshirt over pyjama bottoms, his bedroom light cutting across the floor behind him.

They both looked up, as the floorboards creaked above them again. He shut his door and came closer. 'Jesus. What the fuck is that?'

'Footsteps,' she whispered. 'I'm sure of it, coming from the servants' quarters.'

They headed for the stairs, Mo's torch shining a faint path in front of them. 'Did you hear crying too? I didn't.'

'Not this time.' She wanted to make sure he knew it hadn't been her imagination.

Downstairs, Mo flicked the switch that lit up the horrible green corridor, and they crept along it. Hannah went ahead of him, opening the door to the narrow back stairs. She listened for a moment to the silence.

A pale light from the little window on the landing shone down into the stairwell as they hurried up, Mo coming so fast he bumped into her at the top. As she swayed forward, he grabbed her waist. 'Sorry I—'

Creak, creak, creak.

Steady, regular, somewhere nearby. A cold breeze crept over Hannah's skin, raising goose bumps on her arms.

Mo's hands tightened on her waist and she felt him shiver. 'All right?' his whisper was almost a gasp, and she guessed the words were as much to reassure himself as to comfort her.

'Come on.' She forced herself forward, towards the source of the noise, her whole body crying out for them to turn around, for them to leave whatever it was to its own devices, go back to bed and curl up under the covers. But it was too late now.

Their shoulders brushed together as they searched the first room, Mo shining his torch into all the corners. The creaks had stopped again, replaced by the sound of their own feet on the bare boards, and the room was empty except for an old mattress and a wooden chest. Then Mo's torch shone on the floor and Hannah felt her heart flutter in her chest. A smudged footprint in the dust. They had been up in these rooms themselves, but this looked tiny, childlike.

They worked their way systematically from room to room, peering out of each window in case the sounds had come from the roof.

She couldn't remember if they had closed the doors when they were last up here, but all of them were wide open now. All except the one at the far end, the one that must be directly above her own bedroom.

They stepped towards it, their breathing loud in the emptiness, and Hannah reached out a hand towards the door. They shared a look and then Hannah pushed. It creaked at her touch and gradually swung open.

The torch shone a beam across the floor, illuminating a trail of footprints in the dust.

Mo gasped as the light followed the trail to the corner of the room, to a dark shape huddled on the floor. A slender girl, hunched against the wall, sitting staring straight at them as if they weren't even there, the light glinting in her eyes.

Hannah couldn't speak.

Mo stepped past her. '*Chloe?*'

Chapter Twenty-Eight

Hannah should have been relieved, but something in Mo's tone made her stay back, holding onto the doorframe. He tried again, his voice still uncertain. 'Chloe? How did you get up here?'

She didn't move. In her arms something shifted, a dark shape uncoiled and leapt towards them. The grey cat. It ran between their legs and out into the dark.

There was something strange about Chloe, an unsettling smile. Mo tightened his grip on Hannah's arm. Chloe's glazed eyes seemed to stare, unfocused, not registering the bright light of the torch.

'Chloe,' Hannah whispered. 'It's me, Hannah. And Mo.'

She didn't answer.

'It's cold up here. Why don't you come down with us?'

There was a moment of silence and then Chloe groaned, rubbed her hands across her face and stared blearily around her. She moved towards them, her eyes confused.

Mo went behind her towards an open window and yanked it shut. 'You really scared us, Chloe. How did you get up here?'

'I heard noises,' she said softly.

'What about the cat?' Hannah asked. 'Did you bring him with you?'

'Cat?' Chloe looked around the room again and when her eyes met Hannah's they were suddenly frightened. 'What? No. I don't . . . I don't know.' Her voice shook. 'What's going on? Where am I?'

Hannah stepped forward and wrapped her arms around her. Chloe began to shiver violently, her hair damp from the rain that must have blown in through the window.

'Never mind. It doesn't matter now,' Hannah whispered. 'Just come down with us and get warm. We were so worried.'

Still with her arm across Chloe's shoulders, she shot Mo a look and he held the door open for them. When they reached the top of the stairs, he headed down first and Hannah followed, squeezing into the narrow staircase still holding Chloe, her shoulders trembling.

Mo jerked to a stop on the stairs below.

'Shit,' he said. 'Lucy? What are you doing here?'

'I could ask you the same thing,' Lucy's voice drifted up from below.

'It's all right. It's only Lucy,' Hannah whispered to Chloe, and they carried on down.

At the bottom, Lucy stood beside Mo in the corridor in her black silk dressing gown, face as white and youthful as Chloe's. 'What's the hell is going on?' she said, her voice wobbling.

'We thought we heard noises upstairs.' Hannah didn't want to embarrass Chloe by talking about her sleepwalking.

Lucy glanced from the shivering Chloe to Hannah and tried to smile. 'Yeah, must have been the cat. It just ran past me.' She pointed down the corridor.

Hannah shepherded Chloe along it. 'We'd better get Chloe back to bed. She's cold.'

Lucy and Mo followed, and Hannah felt a surge of relief as they reached the safety and warmth of the hallway.

At the bottom of the main staircase Mo turned to Hannah.

'We'll leave you to get Chloe back to bed, shall we?' Lucy ran up and into her own room without a word and when Hannah nodded at Mo he followed, closing his bedroom door after one glance back at them.

Hannah was still clutching Chloe's arm. Through the thin cloth of her nightie it was as cold as marble.

'You're freezing.' Hannah kept her voice soft. 'Let's get you into the warm.' But Chloe wheeled round, her eyes wide. 'My dad,' she said. 'We need to find my dad. He's out there. I saw him from the window.'

Hannah took her arms. 'No, Chloe, he's in town. You remember? He'll be back in the morning.'

There was a pause before Chloe let herself be led upstairs. Hannah put her fingers to her lips as they neared the family room, but there was no sound from Rosa as Chloe keyed in the door code.

With her eyes accustomed to the dark it was easy for Hannah to see the single bed by the window, Rosa a lump, snoring lightly, in the double.

Chloe gripped her hand as she lay down but let go when Hannah wrapped the duvet tightly around her. 'You're all right now, just go to—'

'What the hell are you doing here?' Rosa sat up and switched on the light. Hannah blinked as a dishevelled Rosa came into focus, eyes wide, hair standing on end. 'Get out! Get out of my room!'

Hannah stepped forward, her palms raised. 'It's fine, she's fine. I think she had a nightmare. She must have been sleep-walking.' She gestured to the half-open door. 'I brought her back.'

Rosa went to kneel beside Chloe who, despite the light and the noise, seemed to be fast asleep. Hannah stood by the door as Rosa felt her daughter's forehead and shook her.

'What happened?' Rosa's voice trembled. 'Where were you?'

Chloe's eyes flickered open for a moment and she mumbled, 'I don't know. Hannah helped me.' Then she yawned, turned over and was asleep again.

If Hannah thought that would be the end of it, she was wrong. Rosa followed her out into the hallway, came close, leaned in and whispered into her face. 'Keep your hands *off* my daughter. Do you understand?'

Hannah stepped back, feeling oddly guilty, her face reddening. But she was tired of being bullied, tired of watching this woman bully her family.

'She was sleepwalking,' she said, jabbing her finger at Rosa. 'And you didn't notice. She was on her own in the servants' quarters, for God knows how long. If me and Mo hadn't brought her down, she could have—'

'I shouldn't be surprised.' Rosa's voice was louder now. 'I knew there was something wrong with you the moment I saw you. You came here looking for your dad, didn't you? No proper upbringing, that's what it is.' She smiled grimly. 'No father figure.'

Hannah swallowed, her face burning as if Rosa had struck her. She could only stand speechless as the woman went back into her room, slamming the door behind her.

Chapter Twenty-Nine

Hannah stood there. Her anger gone and replaced by a desperate need to hold back her tears.

Lucy's door opened and she poked her head out. 'Wow, fucking hell,' she whispered. 'Where did that come from?' She came over and rubbed Hannah's shoulders, then led her along the hall, away from Rosa's room. 'Are you all right?'

'I'm fine, just exhausted. It must have freaked her out, finding me in her room in the middle of the night.'

Lucy's door was still open, and she gestured Hannah inside.

Hannah wanted so much to be back in her own bed, but she didn't have the strength to refuse.

A bedside lamp cast a glow across the crumpled bed. Hannah's legs felt so weak she collapsed onto it while Lucy moved about picking up sheets of music, putting them into rough piles, hardly seeming to know she was doing it.

'What happened?' she asked.

'Chloe was sleepwalking.'

Lucy dropped the papers she was carrying and they scattered across the floor again. Then sat on the bed next to Hannah. 'So it must have been her all along.' Her voice quivered. 'That crying we heard.'

Of course, it made sense, and Hannah felt a wave of

relief. A young deeply troubled girl, whose parents were on the verge of divorce, who was being uprooted from the only life she knew.

That first night, when Hannah had listened outside the family room, Chloe could have been sleepwalking elsewhere in the house. And the second time, maybe the sound had been coming from the servants' quarters after all. Hannah had been half-asleep herself – she could easily have made a mistake.

Lucy stared at her, as if desperate for her to agree, so she nodded. 'It must have been.'

They sat in silence for a moment and then Lucy yawned. She lay back on the bed and they both listened to the sound of the wind and the rain on the glass. Lucy closed her eyes and Hannah stared at her, struggling to connect this vulnerable girl with the self-confident and powerful woman who had thrown off her boots in the hallway just days ago.

That crying we heard.

That's what Lucy had just said, but she had never admitted to hearing the crying. Had always claimed it must be a fox. Hannah watched Lucy sleep for a moment, her chest gently rising and falling, and then stood quietly to leave.

The next morning, Hannah woke early to the sound of the wind; even louder than yesterday, it seemed to shake the whole house like an angry toddler with a broken toy. When she went down to breakfast, she found Mo already eating scrambled eggs and baked beans in the kitchen.

He laughed. 'I thought you'd be down soon. Only managed a couple of hours myself.' He pointed at the Aga. 'Help yourself to some food.'

Although Hannah wasn't hungry, she took some and sat down to eat. They chewed in silence for a while, then Mo finished his food with a sigh. 'Right, I'd better check on Dad.'

He stood up and stretched. 'See you in a sec.' At the door he gave her a smile and went upstairs.

As Hannah tidied away the plates, the door opened and Rosa came in. There was an awkward silence and Hannah felt her shoulders tense.

'Chloe's sleeping,' Rosa said. 'She obviously needs it.' She pulled out a chair and sat, her fingers drumming on the table.

Hannah scrubbed at her plate, not bothering to reply. Eventually Rosa spoke, her hands twisting on the table in front of her. 'Look, I'm sorry about last night. I overreacted. I've been under a lot of strain – what with the house move and everything – and I guess you caught me at a bad time.'

Hannah sighed and turned to face her. 'It must have been a shock. Waking to find me in your room like that.' She tried to keep her voice level.

'Yes, well thank you for bringing Chloe back.' Rosa's smile looked forced and it was clear she had something else to say.

'It must be difficult for you being here all on your own,' she said eventually. 'I hate feeling trapped like this. And the weather's supposed to get worse, really bad from what I hear, not holiday weather at all. If I were you,' she paused. 'I'd think about leaving as soon as I could.'

'What about you? Are you planning to leave?'

She snorted. 'I'd love to, but we have nowhere to go until our new house is ready. No money, no home. I'll be glad to get to Scotland, I can tell you. And it won't take long for Chloe to get used to it. Children are very adaptable.'

'Why did you decide to leave Ireland?'

Rosa paused for a moment, her hands still. Then she stood up, a little too quickly, and went over to the kettle. She filled it and bustled around getting milk from the fridge and a mug from the cupboard. It was obviously a sensitive subject, but Hannah was beyond caring.

'I suppose Chloe has been telling you all sorts of things.' Rosa's voice was clipped. 'But don't pay too much attention to her. She fantasizes.'

Chloe's story – that her father had left his GP practice under a cloud – had sounded pretty convincing, but Hannah said nothing. And it made her think for the first time how strange it was that his situation – dismissed after suggestions of sexual misconduct – was so similar to Sandeep's.

After Rosa made her tea, without bothering to offer Hannah a cup, she stood near the Aga to drink it.

'I know you don't like me,' Hannah said, ignoring Rosa's little gesture of denial. 'But honestly I'm worried about Chloe. She seemed unstable, sleepwalking up there in the middle of the night. If she had gone outside or fallen on the stairs . . .'

Rosa swallowed, her face pale. 'I won't take a sleeping pill tonight,' she said. 'That's why I didn't wake up. I'm a very light sleeper, you see, without something to knock me out. She won't bother you again, if that's what's worrying you.'

'It isn't that at all.'

Pulling up a chair with a shaking hand, Rosa sat next to the Aga, her arms clutched tightly around her. 'I'm sorry. I really am. I should be thanking you for looking after her. It's just that I hate being here, especially now Liam's away.'

Before Hannah could think of anything to say, Lucy came through the door, fully dressed, her eyes made-up beautifully again, hair back to its stylish best. She was like a different person.

Rosa got to her feet, her voice brisk. 'Right, I'll get Chloe up or she'll sleep all day.'

Lucy yawned, went to the fridge for some juice and poured herself a bowl of granola. Slicing a banana into it she said, 'I don't know about you, but I'm about ready to leave.' She looked out the window at the dark clouds and the trees bending in the wind. 'The guards better turn up soon.'

Rosa folded her arms. 'It's all right for you, but we *can't* leave. My husband won't be back till goodness knows when. And even the new house won't be ready for another week.'

Lucy said nothing for a while and to Hannah it looked as if she was annoyed.

The windows rattled louder as a gust of rain beat the glass. 'I don't think anyone will want to tackle that footpath in this weather,' Hannah said. 'And without phone signal we'll struggle to get a taxi.'

'Mo says he's happy to give everyone a lift,' said Lucy, rinsing her bowl in the sink, 'when the weather eases, so that won't be a problem. He and Sandeep are definitely leaving soon.'

Hannah decided to ask Mo to drop her in the village. After that she could head back to London. With a pang she thought about her life at home, thought about saying goodbye to Mo. But there was no way she was staying here, not after everything that had happened.

There was a thump from upstairs and a door slammed. Footsteps thudded on the stairs, the sound of male voices shouting. Rosa opened the door wider so they could peer out into the hall.

'People can't be trusted! I told you.' Sandeep stood bellowing on the stairs, red-faced, stabbing a finger at Mo. 'You're so gullible.' He coughed. 'We're in a house in the middle of nowhere with complete strangers and you can't even take care of your stuff. Now, thanks to you, we're completely screwed. There's no way out of here. We're trapped!'

Chapter Thirty

They all stared into the hall. Sandeep and Mo were standing halfway down the stairs shouting so loudly the whole house could hear.

Sandeep almost stumbled, his hand on the rail. 'God only knows how we'll get out of here.'

Mo took his arm to help him, his voice quieter. 'Listen, keep your voice down. I've just put them somewhere, that's all. Or maybe they fell out of my pocket.'

Sandeep headed for the drawing room. 'Well you'd better find them.'

'Sit and relax for a bit,' Mo said. 'I'll bring you some tea.'

'And don't go putting any of those bloody sleeping pills in it,' Sandeep shouted, then slammed the door behind him.

Mo slouched back into the kitchen. Hannah and Lucy turned away as he went to put the kettle on, but Rosa stood with her arms folded, watching him.

'Sorry, everyone,' he said. 'He's not doing well this morning. Had a rough night, I think. He complains he's still groggy from that sleeping pill and, in the next breath, says he was awake most of the night.'

Mo dropped a teabag into a cup. 'Anyone seen a set of

car keys?' he asked, his voice a little too casual. 'I can't seem to find mine.'

Hannah shook her head, and the kitchen was silent.

'I'll have a look for them,' Lucy eventually said.

Rosa raised a hand to her mouth and let out a small sob. 'Great, just great. Your car keys *missing*. Our car's gone. No wifi or a signal, and there's a fucking gale-force storm on the way.'

'I'm sure my keys will turn up,' said Mo with a forced smile. 'I had them yesterday. They couldn't have walked away on their own.'

Hannah tried to give him an encouraging smile in return, but she knew this wasn't the first thing that had disappeared. Mo could have dropped them somewhere, or left them in a pocket, but still she felt a knot of anxiety twisting in her stomach.

And then Rosa, dramatic as usual, but this time quite accurate, voiced what they had all been thinking. 'So basically, we're all trapped here.'

No one spoke as the rain and wind thundered across the hills and the house seemed to hold its breath. Then Lucy broke the spell. 'Well, if people want to leave, we better look for those keys. Mo, why don't you go and double-check your room – and Sandeep's – and we'll try everywhere else.'

He picked up the cup of tea he'd made. 'OK, thanks, everyone. They can't have gone far.' His tone was flat. 'I'll just give this to my dad.'

Lucy turned to Hannah. 'Before the weather gets any worse, let's check outside. Mo's been collecting logs, so he could have dropped his keys there. And I thought I saw him wandering around in the rose garden yesterday.'

'What about us?' Rosa asked.

'If you want to stay inside with Chloe, you can search in here and the drawing room.' Lucy was organizing everyone as usual, Hannah noticed, but it was good to see her so confident again.

She must have guessed what Hannah was thinking, because she turned to her as they walked through the hall. 'Haven't had a cigarette for a whole day now,' she said with a grimace. 'I'm fucking dying.' When Lucy laid a hand on Hannah's arm, her skin prickled with a strange tingle, almost pleasant but not quite.

They reached the main door and Lucy stretched up to pull back the bolts. The door creaked open, letting in a huge gust of wind, and they both had to throw their weight against it. Lucy's white-blonde hair flipped and whirled around her face.

'You know, I'm getting seriously creeped out. This place is just so strange, I'm beginning to think it might actually be haunted.'

Hannah wanted to ask more, but Lucy was already through the door and heading around towards the back of the house, bent double against the wind.

Fighting her way outside, Hannah watched as Lucy managed to walk quickly out of sight.

They searched the wood pile, shifted logs and peered into every corner, but didn't find the keys. After that they separated: Lucy went to the gates and the gardens; Hannah to check around the edge of the house. The wind pressed her against the wall, whipping her hair across her eyes until she could hardly see. By the time she had finished – her hands numb with cold, her clothes soaked – she knew the keys could have been metres away and she wouldn't have seen them.

At the front door, she met Lucy and they sheltered together under the porch.

'No luck,' Lucy shouted over the noise of the storm.

Hannah shook her head and they went back inside, kicking off their shoes by the door.

'Maybe they've already found them?' Lucy said as they

looked into the empty kitchen. No sign of anyone in the drawing room either.

'Hello!' Lucy's voice echoed in the silence. She headed for the corridor that led to the padlocked area. 'You check the other rooms.' Her voice had lost some of its confidence.

Wandering around the library and double-checking the kitchen and drawing room, Hannah found no sign of the keys, or of Rosa and Chloe. They must have given up and gone to their room.

When she came back out into the hall, she saw Lucy sitting on the stairs, her head in her hands. She looked up and gave Hannah a bright smile. But just for a moment Hannah glimpsed real unhappiness on her face, even something close to despair, as if a mask had slipped.

Hannah sat beside her. 'It's all right. I bet the keys are in a pocket somewhere.' She was about to say that Ben was always mislaying his keys but stopped herself. These were the worst moments, the ones she hated most of all. When she somehow let herself forget that he was gone.

'Don't suppose you have any fags left?' she asked, for something else to say.

Lucy smiled and stood up. 'I do – but it's my last one. We could share it? I've been saving it for a rainy day, and it's definitely raining. Let's go to my room – there's no smoke alarms or anything.'

Upstairs, they both sprawled on Lucy's bed, their hair still wet from the rain. Lucy fumbled out the last cigarette and struck a match, the glow flickering in her eyes. Eyes that for a moment seemed so familiar, as if they had been friends for years.

They passed the cigarette back and forth, then Hannah took a deep drag and choked on the smoke. 'Sorry,' she coughed again, her eyes streaming. 'I think I've become a non-smoker.'

Lucy laughed. 'Good for you. It'll take me a while, but I'm determined.' She took a drag. 'Haven't had a drink since I got here either. And I used to love getting pissed. Bloody love it.' She grinned and passed the fag back to Hannah. 'Do you know there are whole months that I can't even remember? I was just plastered the whole time, completely out of my mind.'

Hannah took another, more careful, drag. 'Yeah, I was the same. This holiday is probably the first time I've been sober in months.' She chewed her lip. 'It was pretty rough to be honest. I was like a proper drunk, basically a pisshead, and I hated myself for it.' It was the first time she'd admitted this even to herself.

Lucy nodded. 'Well, after what happened to your boyfriend, it sounds like you needed it. Don't beat yourself up—'

'But it wasn't just what happened with Ben.' The words came tumbling out now. 'It was before that. I fucked it all up, ruined our relationship by drinking and flirting, because I didn't think I was good enough for him. Never have done.' Hannah swallowed, as if surprised at what she had just said.

'I guess it all starts right at the beginning,' Lucy said, squeezing her shoulder. A long stream of smoke spiralled out of her perfect lips. 'What did that poem say about mums and dads? How they fuck up their kids? Larkin, was it? One of my songs is about that.' She finished the cigarette with a few quick angry sucks and stubbed it out in the saucer.

Hannah leaned up on her elbow. '*You* had problems with your parents?'

Lucy laughed. 'Fuck yeah. We didn't get on.' When she didn't elaborate, Hannah lay back on the bed. She could understand why she didn't want to talk about it.

After a moment, Lucy heaved herself up and leaned against the padded bedhead with a sigh. 'All right, here we go, but you asked for it. Well, my mother was all right, pretty nice really. But then she . . . she died and I . . .' A pause. 'I couldn't stand living with my father, couldn't bear it, so I just left.'

'How old were you?'

'Fifteen.'

'What?'

A funny little laugh. 'That's right. And do you know you're the only person apart from my boyfriend, Damian, that I've told. Luckily I was already tall so I looked older.'

Hannah shook her head, tried to take it in, but didn't know what to say. No wonder Lucy was such a strange mix of maturity and child-like fears and emotions. Hannah couldn't begin to imagine what it was like to manage on your own at fifteen, to have no home and no family. She thought about her own mother, about how she had always been there, whatever happened, whatever stupid mistakes Hannah made.

Finally she said, 'So you've been on your own for ten years. How did you manage?'

Lucy didn't speak for a few minutes and when she began talking again, her voice was flat and controlled. 'I went to Dublin and lived rough. Couldn't get a job of course, it was like I didn't even exist. I was a non-person, had to build my life from scratch.'

'Surely your dad searched for you, told the police you'd gone—'

Lucy cut her off. 'They don't look too hard for teenagers. Just assume they wanted to disappear. Which in my case was true.' A sigh. 'Then I met up with Damian. He's a musician, you know – a violinist. Just a busker to start with, but I could sing and he taught me the keyboard. We made a bit of money, did gigs in pubs and bars, met some others and started a band.'

'That's amazing, you really made it. Wow, you should be proud,' Hannah said.

'It's no good though.' Lucy shook her head. 'I'm still a mess, still had to leave Damian. Could never really open up to him, you know?'

Hannah wanted to tell her that she did know, that she had felt the same way her whole life, but she stayed silent. Eventually, Lucy looked so unhappy that Hannah tried to lighten the tone.

'And you do wild swimming,' she said. 'That must be cool.'

Lucy stared into space for a moment and then seemed to relax. 'Yeah, I love it. Love swimming. My mother taught me and we used to go together.' She smiled. 'Not outdoors, in a pool, but I just love the feel of swimming, it's like freedom, like a kind of escape.' She looked at Hannah. 'Do you swim?'

Hannah laughed but it sounded forced. 'No, I can't. Never learned and never will. It freaks me out.'

'Your parents didn't try to teach you?'

And suddenly a stab of memory, a crystal-clear image of herself as a child in a swimming pool with her mum. Her chubby limbs moving frantically through the warm water, her legs bobbing up and down. Her mother smiling down at her, as she spluttered water and squealed with laughter.

'Hannah? Are you all right?' Lucy leaned forward.

Hannah blinked. 'Sorry, I was miles away. Yes, I'm fine. I just remembered the only time I ever went to a swimming pool.'

'What happened?'

'I don't know. It was a good memory, I wanted to go back again.'

'So how come you never did?'

'It's . . . I've just always had a phobia. Something about being underwater, about the feeling of sinking and choking. My mum accepted it and got the doctor to write me a note, so I always missed swimming lessons.'

It was only now she realized how strange this seemed. Her mother had always encouraged Hannah to be brave and to try new things. Apart from swimming.

She closed her eyes and had the sudden sense that at the back of her mind, another memory threatened to surface. She forced it away and stood up.

'I'd better go down and carry on searching,' she said.

But as she hurried from the room, she knew that other memory would not be a good one. And there was only so long she could keep it buried.

Chapter Thirty-One

In the kitchen Chloe was slumped at the table eating an orange. She turned to Hannah and her mouth wobbled. 'Mum doesn't believe I saw Dad outside, but you do, don't you?'

Hannah poured herself a glass of water, downed it and sat beside her. She took Chloe's hand, remembering how cold and strange it had felt last night. 'What exactly do you remember?'

Chloe's jaw clenched and she seemed to be on the verge of tears. 'I saw him, I really did. I knew it was him.'

'From your bedroom window?'

'I can't remember.' She shook her head, her eyes frightened. 'It's just . . . I don't know . . . Is something wrong with me? Did I imagine it all?'

Pulling her close, Hannah felt a wave of pity for her. 'It's all right, you were just sleepwalking,' she whispered. 'It's completely normal. There's nothing wrong with you, you're just upset. When your dad gets back you'll feel better.'

Chloe shook her head. 'But he's not going to come back. He's never coming back.'

Before Hannah could reply, Rosa bustled into the room and they moved apart.

Hannah chewed her lip, thinking about Liam, as Rosa made tea. He would come back – he'd have to. All the same, there had been no contact from him today. Perhaps he'd been trying to ring Rosa, but his messages weren't getting through because of the lack of wifi or signal.

Rosa took a sip of her tea and stared out the window into the rain. 'I've checked everywhere and there's no sign of those keys.' She looked pointedly at Hannah. 'I think there's a thief.'

'Well, it must be one of us, but nobody has left. If they wanted to steal the actual car, they would be gone by now.' She tried to keep her voice level. 'And me and Lucy are the only people without transport, so are you blaming this on us?'

But Rosa wasn't listening, she was staring into one of the cupboards. 'Look.' She pointed. 'Look at this, just three tins. Do you remember how many there were when we first arrived? Don't tell me we've eaten everything.'

She swung back the fridge door, and they all stared at the empty shelves. 'Oh great. Where's the food gone?' She pulled open the freezer, her movements frantic now. 'Look, a couple of pizzas and nothing else. It's all gone.'

Chloe went pale and Hannah tried to stay calm, but a ripple of fear crept along her own spine. She opened a cupboard and stared at the empty shelves. 'I don't understand. Who could have taken it?'

Rosa smiled grimly. 'If it happened a day or so ago, my money would be on that gardener.'

Hannah shook her head. 'Someone would have noticed before now. Mo's been doing a lot of cooking and he would have said something.'

Rosa paced up and down in front of the Aga, pulling her stylish white cardigan tight around her. 'Unless . . .' She turned to stare at Hannah. 'Unless it's him, of course.'

Chloe's voice was sharp. 'Mum! Stealing his own car keys?'

'He could be lying about that.' Rosa licked her lips. 'Maybe he's hidden them, I wouldn't put it past him. Just doing it to get attention. Or maybe, he doesn't want anyone to leave.'

There was a moment of silence.

'Come on!' Hannah laughed. 'Are you serious? Why would he do that? Why take the food, when he can eat whatever he wants?'

Rounding on her, Rosa began to shout. 'Of course you'd defend him.' She stabbed a finger at Hannah. 'In fact, now I think of it, I wouldn't be surprised if it was *you*.' A bitter laugh. 'You took the car keys to keep him here.'

The door opened and Hannah bit back her anger. She took a deep breath, as they all turned to see Sandeep and Mo. No one spoke. Mo and Sandeep stood on the opposite side of the table from the others.

Mo gave them a tight-lipped smile.

'Yes, Rosa,' Sandeep said. 'I heard what you said.' He stared at her. 'And I have my own theory. You see, I think there's someone here who wants – who needs – everyone to stay. I think it's someone who can't bear the thought of being left here on their own, who feels abandoned and lonely and will do anything – absolutely anything – to avoid embarrassment. That's right, it's you. You *have* to stay until that useless husband of yours gets back, if he ever does.'

Chloe put her face in her hands and began to cry.

'Please, Sandeep,' Hannah said. 'You're upsetting Chloe.'

But Sandeep and Rosa stood deadly still, their eyes locked. Eventually he spoke again, his voice gruff.

'You're the one who wants us to stay, the one desperate enough to take the car keys. So what is it, Rosa? Tell us. Why keep us at this bloody house?'

173

Chapter Thirty-Two

The room seemed to spin on its axis, and Hannah reached out to grab at the wall, holding herself steady. The sounds of the others shouting droned on around her, muffled and distant now. As if she were back in the bath upstairs, being pushed down, sliding deeper and struggling to hear or to breathe. She thought about those horrible nightmares, about all that had happened over the past few days. It was like a dream, like getting so shitfaced that you lost yourself for a few hours. She needed someone like Lori now, someone to drag her back out of the abyss and take her home to clean up the mess she had made.

Maybe that was it, maybe it was the booze after all. She'd given it up too quickly, hadn't weaned herself off it, and this was just her body telling her never to drink again.

The room stopped spinning and she opened her eyes. The colours returned to normal. She was leaning back against the wall, her legs weak. No one was paying her any attention; they were all focused on Rosa and Sandeep.

Mo was speaking, his palms raised. 'Calm down, both of you.' He turned to Sandeep. 'Look, Dad, you can't just start accusing people for something that's my fault. I've just lost the keys – they haven't been stolen – and I'm fed up with your paranoia. Sick of you complaining all the time.'

Sandeep breathed heavily for a moment. 'Paranoid? An old fool, a joke. So that's it, is it? That's what you think of me.' He sighed. 'I'm going up to my room.' When Mo didn't follow, Sandeep walked slowly up the stairs, his hand clutching the bannister.

Hannah didn't know what to think. Mo put his hand on her arm and said very gently. 'Are you all right?'

'I'm fine.' She tried to smile.

Then he turned to Rosa. 'I'm sorry about that. He's . . . he's not himself.' He looked suddenly very tired. 'I realize all this – the storm, Rob's death, my stupid keys – it's a mess, but we can't start accusing each other. We need to stick together.'

Rosa's face was pale. 'Well there has to be an explanation,' she said. 'A reason for all these things going missing. Because it's not just the car keys – it's the food, too.' She opened a cupboard and gestured to Mo. 'Have you seen this?'

He strode over and shifted a few of the tins on the shelf, as if everything else would be hidden behind them. 'Jesus, it was half-full this morning.' He opened the next cupboard and shook his head.

'And the fridge and freezer are the same,' Rosa said. Mo glanced into the fridge and then at Hannah, but she could only shrug.

The windows rattled in their frames and even the walls seemed to shift in the wind. Rosa pulled out a chair and sat down with a thump. She put her head in her hands, sobbed, and then began to cry, very quietly, her body shaking. 'I'm . . . sorry. It's just, I don't know where Liam is. And now this storm.'

Chloe went to her, patting her back and telling her it would be all right, he would be back soon. Hannah noticed that Chloe's hands were covered with scratches, presumably from the cat.

'I don't know about anyone else,' Mo said. 'But I'm hungry and we might as well eat what's left.'

He found crackers in one of the cupboards, a chunk of cheese and some grapes in the fridge and plonked them on the table with a pile of small plates. They all sat down in awkward silence, and Hannah picked at her food. Rosa still looked pale as she took an occasional sip of her apple juice.

No one spoke until Mo filled another plate with food. 'I'll take this up to my dad.' He was at the door, when he stopped. 'What was that? Shh!'

There was a scraping sound, like stone across stone. Then the shriek of an animal: a fox or a cat.

A bang, followed by a thud and the crash of breaking glass.

'Shit,' said Mo.

They stood in silence, listening to the wind. Then Lucy called from the top of the stairs. 'Did you hear that noise? It came from outside.'

Mo went into the hall, dropped his plate on a little table by the stairs and strode to the front door. But the wind was so fierce he struggled to open it.

'Don't, don't go out there, please,' Chloe said, and Hannah put her arm around her.

Lucy joined them in the hall, helped Mo pull back the door, and followed him out into the rain.

'Stay with your mum,' Hannah said to Chloe, then ran after Lucy.

The wind almost knocked her over as she stepped outside and tried to make her way along the side of the house. Her hair felt like stinging wire across her face. The grey-blue hills crouched on the horizon, dark purple in the gloom. Would the police be able to get here today? Would Liam return? She doubted it.

As she turned the corner, her eyes streaming, she spotted Lucy and Mo sheltering beside the brick outhouse. When she got to them Lucy pointed to the greenhouse.

'It's a tile,' she shouted. 'Broke a pane of glass.' The half-ruined greenhouse wasn't far from the kitchen window, which explained why the smash had sounded so loud.

Hannah shuffled towards it, her head bowed. She peered in through a broken pane of glass. A mess of broken flower pots and a dirt-encrusted trowel littered the shelf. Beside them an empty plastic compost bag swayed in the wind, waiting for a chance to lift off into the sky.

Her gaze stopped on something else, lying on the floor.

Something grey and still.

Chapter Thirty-Three

She stepped carefully to the doorframe and slid her body inside the shell of the greenhouse, avoiding the broken glass. Above the wind she heard Lucy and Mo shouting her name, telling her to turn around.

Tears prickled her eyes as she looked at the cat, lying broken and unmoving on the floor, its shining coat dulled by dust and bits of leaf blown in on the wind. She pushed the little rigid body with her toe. Mo and Lucy came to the door to stare in at her.

'What is it?' Mo said.

'It's dead.' Hannah gestured to the cat.

'Oh fuck,' Lucy muttered.

Mo pulled Hannah back outside. The three of them linked arms and gradually fought their way back to the house. Inside, the door slammed shut behind them and they stared at each other, breathing heavily.

'Don't tell Chloe,' Hannah said.

'It must have been hit by another tile,' Mo whispered.

There had been no tile or stone anywhere near it, but Hannah stayed silent.

Rosa and Chloe appeared and Lucy told them what had happened to the greenhouse.

'It was just a tile from the roof of the shed,' Hannah said. 'Nothing to worry about if we stay inside.'

She imagined herself, trying to leave the house. Running out of the front door and sprinting along the path. A tile spiralling down from above and cracking into her skull. Hannah thudding to the ground, her hand stretched out to break her fall, blood pooling around her head.

Chloe looked from Hannah to Mo and Lucy. 'The police aren't coming, are they?'

'I doubt it,' Mo said. 'But they'll be here tomorrow. And we're safe in here.' Hannah wondered if he really believed that.

Chloe's voice quivered. 'And my dad . . . he won't be back either, will he?' She stared at Hannah. 'I knew it, I just knew it. I told you he wouldn't.' There was a long pause.

'He'll be here,' Mo said eventually. 'As soon as the weather clears. You wait and—'

'I don't want to wait. I don't want to stay here. I hate it, I hate this place.' She ran up to her room, her feet thumping on the stairs. They heard the door slam, and then silence.

Lucy laughed grimly. 'Can't say I blame her,' she said.

Rosa sighed and started walking up the stairs. 'I shouldn't leave her alone.'

Hannah, Lucy, and Mo stood awkwardly in the hall for a moment. 'It's bloody freezing,' said Hannah. 'Is the heating even on?'

'Let's light the fire,' Mo said. He tried to smile, but his face was pale.

In the drawing room, Hannah went over to touch the radiator. It was cold. Stooping to twist the gauge, she realized it was on full. Behind her Mo and Lucy loaded logs onto the fire. She shivered and pulled her jumper closer, watching the rain lashing against the glass as she thought about the cat's broken body lying out there in the storm.

It wasn't just what was going on in the house; it was the things happening to Hannah's mind. Her talk with Lucy and the strange memories that kept flooding into her mind, the odd dreams that seemed so real, so vivid. And what was the other memory that seemed to linger at the edge of her consciousness?

She went to sit on the sofa and Lucy plonked down beside her.

'Are you all right?' Lucy said.

'I'm OK, just tired. And cold.' She pointed at the radiator. 'I think the heating's broken.'

Mo blew on the fire, the flames crackling. 'It's probably just the storm. Once we get this going properly, the house should warm up.' He chucked on a log. 'I'll go and look for the boiler in a minute, see if I can get the heating back on.'

'Well at least it's not as cold as it could be,' said Lucy. 'It's only autumn after all.'

Mo slumped into an armchair and they all sat for a moment, watching the flames flickering in the hearth. Mo pulled out his phone and tapped away at the screen. 'If only we could get the wifi working, find the router maybe, then we could get hold of the bloody host. He would know how to fix the heating.'

They heard a rumble of thunder in the distance.

'That'll be the real storm,' said Mo. 'It's only going to get worse.'

Heavy footsteps were coming down the stairs. They turned to listen. The thud of someone running. Then the door flew open.

Rosa stood framed by the light, her hair untidy, her face chalk-white. Her chest heaving, she reached out to the door for support.

'Mo.' She caught her breath. 'Mo, you need to come upstairs.'

'What, what is it? Are you OK?' He got to his feet.

'I said you need to come upstairs. Now.'

Hannah and Lucy followed Mo into the hall, but Rosa shook her head at them and they could only look at Mo.

'What is it?' he said again.

Rosa pointed. 'Up there in his room. It's Sandeep.'

Chapter Thirty-Four

Mo sprinted up the stairs, before anyone else could speak. They listened to his footsteps thudding against floorboards. Then the sound of Sandeep's door opening.

'Dad?' Just the one word before the door closed behind him. Rosa sighed and walked into the drawing room, shutting the door firmly and leaving Lucy and Hannah alone in the hall.

They stood waiting, glancing at each other and wondering if this was some new drama dreamed up by Rosa. A clock ticked quietly somewhere nearby and, in the distance, thunder boomed across the hills.

Lucy pulled Hannah away from the stairs. 'Come on, leave it for now. Let's talk to Rosa.'

In the drawing room, Rosa was kneeling by the fire, her face red.

'What happened?' said Hannah gently. 'Is Sandeep all right?'

Rosa bowed her head and sobbed.

'Is he OK?' asked Lucy.

'He's dead.' It was almost a shout.

Nobody said anything for a while. Hannah felt a sharp pain in her throat and she eased herself onto the sofa, trying to keep from breaking down completely. Chloe burst in the room, crying loud desperate tears, and ran to her mother. She pressed her face into Rosa's shoulder and the two of them knelt like that by the fire, sobbing.

Lucy sat carefully next to Hannah, her blue eyes wide, her face pale.

Eventually Rosa looked around at them. 'I . . . I saw him. I went to see if he wanted food, wanted to make up with him after earlier.' She wiped her eyes with a sleeve. 'But he didn't answer, so I pushed open the door and . . . it's true. He's gone.'

Hannah stood up and went back into the hall. He couldn't be dead, surely he couldn't be dead. She waited, listening, at the bottom of the stairs. If Mo was still in his father's room, he was making no sound. She walked up, her feet dragging, willing this all to be one of her nightmares, willing Rosa to have made some kind of mistake. But she knew Sandeep had been ill, knew his cough had been worsening, and heart attacks or strokes could happen with no warning.

She took a breath and tapped gently on the door. No response. Tapped again and called very quietly, 'Mo? Are you all right?'

She stood there for long minutes and was about to turn away, when the door opened. The glow from the lamp inside shrouded Mo's face in shadow, making him almost unrecognizable. His eyes glinted with dark fire.

He let the door fall completely open and Hannah put a hand to her mouth. She could make out a shape in the bed, a mound under the duvet that wasn't moving. They stepped inside.

Sandeep lay there fully dressed, the light from the lamp playing over his face – his head on the pillow, a trail of drool glittering across his cheek.

It was obvious he was dead.

A sound from Mo, a groan that seemed to come from

somewhere deep inside him. He stepped forward and knelt by the bed, sobs moving through him like waves. Hannah felt her own tears falling, trickling down her cheeks, as she crouched to hold him.

They stayed like that for a few moments, his head on her shoulder, just like Rosa and Chloe downstairs. Statues of shock and grief. She let his head rest, breathing in time with him, knowing nothing she could say or do could help him now.

Eventually she broke free and stood up, went to flick the light switch by the door. The bulb flickered and came on, shining light into every corner of the room. Sandeep's paper-thin skin looked almost translucent. On the bedside table she saw an array of plastic containers full of pills, empty blister packs that must have once contained tablets. And something else. An empty vodka bottle, its lid beside it. *Her* empty vodka bottle.

Mo stood up and pulled his phone from his pocket, his bloodshot eyes wide, his mouth twisted. 'Have you got signal? Can you check? We need a doctor.' When she didn't respond, he shouted. 'Hannah!'

She blinked, pulled out her phone, struggling to see the screen through her tears. No signal and hardly any battery. She shook her head.

'For God's sake.' Mo went to the door. 'Anyone!' he shouted down the stairs. 'Lucy, Rosa! Help!' His voice echoed around the corridors and into the empty wing of the house, where it seemed to go on reverberating. 'Anyone have signal? We need a doctor!' His chest heaved as Rosa poked her head out of the drawing room, shut the door firmly behind her and came up the stairs.

'Please, Mo, you've got to calm down,' she said when she reached the landing. 'None of us have signal, you know that. And you're frightening Chloe.'

'For fuck sake, are you joking? Have you seen him? Look at him.' He pointed at his father's dead body. 'He needs help.'

Rosa's hand went to his sleeve, but he shook it off and she stepped back to join Hannah against the far wall.

'I'm sorry, Mo, I'm sorry,' she said. 'There's nothing to be done. I was a nurse, you know. I had a good look at him – checked his pulse – before I called you.'

She paused. 'It's . . . it's far too late. He's dead, he's been dead for a while.' She glanced at Hannah, then back to Mo. 'You've had a shock. Why don't you go downstairs? Hannah can make you a cup of tea. I'd better get back to Chloe.'

Mo stood stock still as she slipped past him and headed down the stairs and into the drawing room.

Eventually Hannah said, 'Mo?' and he looked at her blankly, as if he had never seen her before.

'Mo,' she said again.

'It's my fault.' He swallowed. 'I should never have brought him here. Why did I persuade him to stay? Even after everything he said about this fucking place, even after he told me he needed to go home.'

Hannah stepped closer. 'You're not to blame.' She reached out to touch his shoulder.

He let her hand rest there for a second or two, but then he turned, face contorted with anger, knocking it away. Hannah stepped back against the wall again and Mo towered over her.

'Not to blame? Of course I'm to blame. I didn't bother to check on him properly. And the last memory he has of his son is me calling him paranoid. Can you imagine?'

This violent man was nothing like the Mo she thought she had begun to know. He grabbed one of the empty blister packs.

'And look, look at these. They're what that bastard, Liam, gave him. I bet he forced Dad to take them all.'

'Mo, you've got to calm down and think rationally. How could Liam do that? He hasn't been here.'

'Are you sure? Maybe he *has* been here all along. Or maybe he got Rosa to do it. You saw how much she hates my dad – maybe she did it herself.'

Hannah knew all about this madness, about grief and guilt tearing you apart from the inside. 'Listen to me, why would Liam or Rosa want to hurt Sandeep? It doesn't make sense.'

'He knew something about them, knew something that linked them to this house. Dad told me he had been thinking back and was sure he remembered meeting Liam all those years ago.'

'And?'

'He thought Liam was the doctor who changed his story about Rob's injury. And that was after he found out Rob worked here. At this house.' He glanced around the room. 'If it wasn't for this fucking house he'd still be alive. All I know is he would never kill himself. You talked to him, you know what he's like. Do you seriously think he would do it?'

She sighed and pointed to the vodka bottle. 'I don't know what to think. Maybe he did it by mistake, perhaps he was desperate to sleep, to stop thinking about stuff, and he just miscalculated, forgot how many pills he'd taken. I mean, it would be easy.'

His laugh sounded manic. 'You hardly knew him at all. He never drank – never – and it's just fucking obvious that someone did this to him. The idea of him having vodka hidden in his room is mad. Someone put it here.'

Hannah bit her lip. She couldn't tell him that someone – probably Sandeep – had stolen it from her. Mo crouched by the bed.

'Here, feel this.' He tapped the sheet. 'It's soaked, completely soaked, as if someone drugged him and then poured that drink down his throat. And why is the pillow on the floor? I'll tell you why: the bastard probably suffocated him.'

She forced herself to touch the soaking duvet and inhale the smell of vodka. Sandeep had seemed far from suicidal. Angry, moody, constantly complaining, but not suicidal. Even if he hated this house, he had told her that revisiting his memories was helping.

All the fight seemed to have left Mo and he stood there swaying, suddenly ten years older, shaking his head. He turned away and staggered into the corridor.

'I don't care if you believe me, but I'm done with this place. If Dad didn't want to kill himself when Mum died, there's no fucking way he would do it now. I'm not waiting for Liam. I'm not waiting for the police: I'm going to get them.'

Hannah went after him. 'You can't leave now, not in the dark in the middle of a storm.' She tried to keep her voice level. 'Wait until the morning. Let's try to get the wifi working, then we can phone the police.'

'I'm not waiting. I have to report this now. Someone killed him, you know that? Fucking killed him.'

Before she could say anything else he went into his own room and slammed the door. She heard him rummaging around and then he emerged, pulling on his coat, a little calmer now. They stood in silence for a moment, staring at each other. Then he smiled and it was as if a cloud lifted and the old Mo was suddenly with her again.

'I'm sorry. I didn't mean to shout at you like that, I just lost it for a minute.'

She reached out for him. 'I know. It's the shock. I'm so sorry.'

He took her hands and their eyes locked. 'Dad was right. There's something very wrong about this place. You should come with me.'

'I can't . . . I can't leave the others, and I'm not risking it in this weather. You shouldn't go either, you know what happened to Rob. You said it yourself: the storm's only getting worse.'

He looked away. 'You're right, it's best if you stay here. I can make better time on my own, get help faster.' Their eyes met again. 'But, Hannah, I'm right, you know I am. Two people dead in two days. Don't tell me you think that's normal. There's a killer here, I'm telling you, and you need to be careful. Don't trust anyone, especially not Rosa. She's lying about something, I'm sure of it.'

Before she could reply, he kissed her on the forehead, then ran downstairs. He paused for a moment at the door, turned to look up at her. With a smile, he pulled back the locks and heaved open the door, letting in a sheet of water and wind, like a sailor opening the hatch of a ship. And then he was gone, out into the wild night.

Chapter Thirty-Five

The others must have heard him leave because they were all – only three of them now, Hannah realized – standing by the drawing room door.

'He's insane,' Rosa said. 'Completely insane, going out in this. He'll be back soon, I'm sure he will – he won't get far.'

Chloe was taking in rapid sips of air, and Lucy put her hands on her slender shoulders, looking into Chloe's eyes. 'Your mother's right. Mo will be back soon and we'll be all right. We'll stay together in the warm down here for now, until the heating is on again.'

'But what if he doesn't come back?' Chloe's voice echoed in the cavernous hall.

Her mother put her arm around her. 'He'll be back, you'll see. Why don't we all bring the bedding down and sleep in the drawing room, next to the fire, like a sleepover. It'll be fun. But first let's sort out some dinner. Come on.'

The others filed into the kitchen, but Hannah sat on the bottom stair, so tired and miserable she could go no further. She listened to the distant thunder growing ever nearer, to the voices talking quietly in the kitchen.

Dark thoughts began to creep into her mind, even as she tried to quash them. *Not to blame? Of course I'm to blame.*

Maybe Mo wasn't the only one to blame, maybe this was partly her fault. She had done it again, first Ben, then Rob, and now Sandeep. All victims of her stupidity.

Could Sandeep have killed himself because he couldn't bear his traumatic memories of this house, memories that Hannah had forced him to relive? But it was more than that: she had made him feel guilty, pretty much told him that he hadn't tried hard enough to investigate.

And even before that – so long ago – somehow she had driven her own father away. Ruined her parents' marriage.

Now Mo was out there in the raging storm, without a chance in hell of making it. Even a local like Rob had fallen to his death, and that was on a calm evening. She should have tried harder to persuade Mo to stay. Her hand hovered over her forehead, the place he had kissed her. She thought about the way he had looked into her eyes, his gruff voice full of sadness, the way his body had felt in her arms as they crouched on the floor.

She sat there for a long time and stared into the dusk-filled hall and out through the tall windows. Listened to the wind try to tear down this old house piece by piece.

'Hannah?' Lucy said. 'There you are.' She was standing by the bannister, but Hannah hadn't heard her approach. 'Come and have something to eat.'

When Hannah didn't respond, she came to sit beside her. 'We're all upset,' she said with a sigh. 'But there's nothing we can do. We all need to stay together downstairs tonight, then leave first thing in the morning. The storm will have blown itself out by then, and the journey back to the road will be easier if we all do it together.'

Hannah swallowed. 'What about Sandeep?'

'The guards will be here in the morning, and they'll sort everything out. We might have to go to the station, but we can stay in a hotel somewhere in town.' Lucy continued speaking, filling the silence. 'There's no way we can make it to the village tonight, not in this. And we're perfectly safe here, as long as we stay together.' Her voice was strong now, as if the louder she spoke the more she would believe her own words.

They all ate together in the kitchen, sharing the pizzas that Rosa had dug out of the freezer. They ate with their hands and talked in whispers, as if they didn't want the house to know they were here. The heating was still broken, but thankfully the oil-fuelled Aga kept the room warm.

Lucy and Hannah tried to make everything seem normal, talking about what they would do tomorrow once they had left the house, but it was impossible to ignore the absence of the three men. Rosa kept quiet and checked her phone repeatedly, as if it was a sacred text that might guide her to salvation. As if it might suddenly come alive with a message from Liam. Each time she stared at the screen and sighed, her jaw clenched, not seeming to notice how this upset Chloe.

The thunder sounded closer now, the crack and flash of lightning louder and more frequent. But they carried on as if they could hear nothing, even when a particularly loud smash sounded somewhere nearby. They didn't want to acknowledge that none of them had any idea what was happening out there on the hills, or even in the dark cold bedrooms above.

Soon the heat from the Aga wasn't enough to keep a chill from spreading through the room and Hannah stood up to check the kitchen radiator. It was still cold.

'Why don't we move to the drawing room?' she said. 'Mo brought in plenty of logs, we can get the fire roaring.'

They filed out of the kitchen and into the drawing room, closing the door behind them, making sure they stayed close together. They pulled out blankets from a cupboard and moved the sofas closer to the hearth, while Hannah threw logs on the fire. She raked out the heap of ash and shifted the embers with the poker, remembering how Mo had done the same just days ago. The basket wasn't as full as she had hoped, but she couldn't face venturing outside to the log shed to fill it. When a particularly strong gust of wind rattled the window, Hannah imagined the storm rolling in off the Atlantic; nothing between Mayo and America except miles and miles of surging waves. Lucy seemed to have drifted off to sleep in her armchair, but Chloe and Rosa were talking quietly.

Chloe suddenly stood up, her blanket falling to the floor. 'What was that?' she said.

'What?' asked Hannah.

Rosa put a finger to her lips.

Something buzzed nearby, then crackled. The lights flickered above them.

Lucy sat up, her eyes wide.

Then, as if Hannah had known it was going to happen, all the lights went out.

Chapter Thirty-Six

Chloe and Rosa both screamed, and then fell silent. In the glow from the fire, Hannah could see them holding each other.

'Is everyone all right?' said Lucy.

Hannah stood up. 'I'm fine.' She remembered the matches were on the mantelpiece, groped for them and struck one, using it to peer around the room.

'What happened?' asked Chloe.

'It's probably just the storm,' said Hannah. 'We need to find a candle or something, then we can check the fuse box.'

'There's a couple of torches in the kitchen,' Lucy said, taking the box of matches from Hannah, striking one and heading out into the dark hallway. They watched the faint glow of her match disappear into the gloom. After what seemed an age, a thin beam clicked on in the kitchen and Lucy reappeared in the doorway with the torches.

She sat on the sofa and laid two torches between them on the coffee table. The pale-yellow beams shone upwards, playing across their faces. The light distorted their features until their eyes looked enormous, their noses twisted out of shape, as if they all wore crude masks.

Rosa took one of the torches and went back to the kitchen,

returning a few minutes later. 'No bloody candles,' she said. 'What a place.'

A log shifted in the grate, and eventually Hannah sighed. She stood up and stretched, trying to keep her voice calm. 'Well, I guess I should try to get the fuse box working, see if we can fix the lights.'

'Don't go,' muttered Chloe. 'Can't we all just stay here together?'

'It's worth a quick look, I'll only be a minute, and the fuse box is just through that door.' She pointed into the hall. 'I won't go far.'

She grabbed the torch, and nobody spoke as she opened the door. The hallway seemed darker than she remembered, the only sound a ticking clock and the insistent wind. Stepping carefully, the torch gripped tight, she went to the door that led into the green corridor.

Before she had time to think, she pushed it open and found the fuse box. Flicked the switches. Closed her eyes and waited for the lights to come on. Nothing. She swore and tried again, her hands slippery on the torch. Whatever happened, she wasn't going to look down the corridor towards the padlocked door.

Shit, shit. Damn thing. She flicked the switches again, but still nothing happened. The house remained in darkness. Hurrying back out into the hall and closing the door, she felt her heart rate return to normal.

Lucy was loading another log onto the fire when she got back to the drawing room.

'No luck,' she said. 'It's not the fuse box.'

'There must be some way of getting the lights back on.' Rosa pulled herself up from the sofa. 'A generator or something. And where *is* the boiler for God's sake?'

Hannah slumped in an armchair and stared into the flames. She imagined sitting here helplessly all night, listening to the house fall apart around them. Hoping not to hear footsteps on the stairs, praying not to hear a little girl crying through the walls.

The fire crackled and she thought about what Mo had said. Could Rosa really have killed Sandeep? And what about Lucy? Hannah knew nothing about either of them, not really. Could they have murdered Rob too? Paranoia crept across her mind like a bad memory, as if the house itself could control her thoughts.

They had to do something, they couldn't sit here all night. 'I know,' she said, her voice firm. 'I know what I'm going to do.' Everyone turned to face her. 'There's only one thing left, one place that we haven't looked. One bit of the house that none of us have tried. Down the end of that corridor, the padlocked door.'

'No way,' said Lucy. 'It's too dangerous.'

'How do we know that?' Hannah stood up. 'The boiler has to be in there, it's the only place left. We might even find the router.'

Lucy stared at the flames for a moment and then shrugged. 'All right, but I think you're wrong: I think we won't find anything. It's probably a dead end, some storeroom.' She ran a hand through her hair. 'You can't go on your own, though, it's not safe. I'll come with you.'

'What? You can't both go – it's stupid – what about us?' Chloe sat up, her eyes wide.

'You'll be fine. Just stay here by the fire, keep warm, and we'll be back soon.' Hannah gave her what she hoped was a reassuring smile.

'But how are you going to get the door unlocked?' Chloe asked.

'There might be a hammer in that storeroom Mo found next to the kitchen. Remember he said there were a load of old tools in there? I'm going to check it out.'

No one responded, so Hannah threw another log on the fire and checked her torch was still working.

'Take both the torches,' Rosa said with a frown. She held up her hand when Hannah went to protest. 'You'll need them more than us. We've got the fire.'

Lucy reluctantly picked up the second torch and, with a final smile at Chloe, they opened the door and went back out into the dark.

The storeroom turned out to be bigger than she'd expected, its walls lined with cleaning products and old ladders. The light from their torches flickered over a wooden chest of drawers in one corner, a row of plastic petrol containers, a stack of half-rotten wellies, then something that looked like a metal toolbox. Lucy stepped over to it, flung open the lid and rummaged around inside.

'Bingo,' she held up a hammer.

Back in the hall, their footsteps echoed as they walked towards the corridor. They stopped outside the door. The thin beams of their torches seemed to flicker hesitantly, as if the wind outside had the power to reach all the way into the house, to blow out their lights, to shroud them in perpetual darkness. Hannah could hear Lucy gulp beside her, as she stepped forward and pushed open the door.

Lucy wedged it ajar and together they walked down the corridor, the sound of their footsteps rebounding off the walls, the beams of their torches playing over the green walls. Looking back over her shoulder, Hannah could see a rectangle of charcoal grey from the hallway, contrasting with the deep black of the corridor.

Passing Lucy her torch, Hannah stepped towards the door, took out the hammer, lifted it high, and brought it down against the padlock with a smash that reverberated in her ears. A shocking sound, metal crashing on metal, like an explosion in the cramped space.

She kept going, each smash louder than the last, and it didn't take long for the chain to break and the mechanism to fall to the floor. She kicked it away, took another deep breath and shoved the hammer into her waistband.

Lucy suddenly put a hand on her arm. 'Are you sure? What if it *is* dangerous?'

'It's all right, trust me,' Hannah said, twisting the door handle with a sweaty hand and flinging open the door.

Nothing. Just a small space, another section of corridor but much shorter this time. Lucy's breathing sounded louder now, her voice hardly more than a whisper.

'It's nothing, just a cupboard. An empty cupboard.'

But Hannah took her torch and stepped towards the door at the back. She wasn't giving up now.

It was cold in here, and quiet; the sounds of the storm just a muffled murmur. When she turned the handle of the inner door, nothing happened.

'Leave it, Hannah,' Lucy said, her voice soft. 'Don't.'

Ignoring her, Hannah pulled out the hammer and stepped back. Aimed just above the lock and brought it down with all her force. The door creaked and shifted. She tried again and was rewarded with a loud snapping sound inside the lock. She threw her weight against the door and it flew open.

Something clicked and buzzed. Her heart thudded in her chest, her palms felt suddenly sticky with sweat. And then – another buzz – and they were both blinded by a burst of light.

Chapter Thirty-Seven

Lucy gasped and the hammer hit the floor with a thud. Hannah covered her face with a hand.

'What the fuck?' Lucy said, pointing up. 'It's a strip light, look.'

Above them ran a line of glowing lights, all of which must have been triggered as they opened the door. There was electricity in here.

As Hannah's eyes adjusted to the glare, she started to take in her surroundings. They were in a sleek, modern space: polished floors, tasteful art on the white walls, a Middle Eastern rug by their feet. It felt like they were in a completely different house.

'It's so warm,' said Hannah. 'There must be heating.'

Lucy had gone a deathly pale, her eyes flitting around the room, her chest heaving. 'What's going on?' she said. 'What is this place?'

Hannah said, 'It looks safe, I think. Maybe it's where the host, that Henry Laughton – maybe it's where he stays.' But Lucy still looked terrified.

They walked around the room, peering into corners, trying to understand what they were seeing. A black-leather sofa sat against one wall, a sound system, and a stack of classical music CDs beside it, mostly Wagner and Bach. Everything spotless and gleaming. The only other piece of furniture was a long steel-topped bench against one white wall. Hannah spotted a few objects lined up neatly on a small metal shelf beside it: a bottle of sanitizing hand gel and a couple of packs of medical-grade antibacterial wipes.

It was like someone had put an industrial-scale kitchen bench in the middle of their living room. 'Maybe this is where Henry does his restoration work,' Hannah said hesitantly. There were no windows in here, but the electricity seemed to be working fine, so she switched off her torch to save the battery.

Then she realized Lucy wasn't standing behind her any more; she was squatting down against the wall for support, head close to her knees.

'It's all right.' Hannah moved over to touch her shoulder. 'We're safe here. That sign was probably just to keep people out of a private area. And the lights and heating are working, so we should call Rosa and Chloe, get them to come in here.'

She pulled her phone from her pocket, but there was still no wifi. 'We might find a router somewhere.'

Lucy just shook her head, her hands clenching and unclenching. 'I don't understand. It doesn't make any sense. Who did this? What happened?'

'Preserve the Past.' Hannah spoke gently. 'Like I said – they must use this bit.' She took Lucy's arm and helped her upright. 'Come on, let's go.'

Lucy wiped her face blearily and followed Hannah to a white door in the opposite door, so sleek and flat it almost blended in.

'Let's try through here,' Hannah said.

Lucy stopped walking. 'No, let's go back. I feel sick, I can't go any further. I don't want to go in there. This is all wrong, we need to get out.'

Hannah shook her arm in frustration. 'For God's sake, get a grip. There's nothing to worry about – it's warm and the lights work. Do you really want to go back out there in the dark and the cold, when there's a fucking dead body upstairs?'

Their eyes locked and Lucy seemed so fragile and scared that Hannah felt instantly guilty for her outburst.

'Look, I'm sorry, but I want to keep going. It feels good to be actually *doing* something. If you want, you can stay here, or go back.' She pulled Lucy into a hug and then let her go.

Striding over to the white door, Hannah twisted the handle and it immediately opened. Inside was completely dark and when she groped on the wall for a light switch her fingers found only damp brickwork. In the glow from the room behind her she could see a flight of stone steps leading down into shadow.

'Wait,' said Lucy. 'Be careful.' She grabbed Hannah's jumper and pulled her backwards. 'Be careful,' she said again.

'What the fuck are you doing?' Hannah twisted away.

'It's a basement,' Lucy said. 'You could have fallen.'

They stared at each other for a moment. 'How the hell do you know that?' Hannah kept her voice firm, but she felt a shiver of fear run down her spine. She stepped back. 'How do you *know* this is a basement?'

'It's obvious.' Lucy frowned. 'There's nothing else it could be.' She switched on her torch and pointed the beam down the steep flight of stone steps into the dark. 'Of course it's a basement. And it's dangerous, look at it. God knows what's down there.'

But Hannah wasn't listening. She was staring into the cellar with the sudden unexplainable conviction that this was where the answers lay. 'Well, I'm going,' she said.

And with the torch in her hand and the comforting weight

of the hammer in her pocket, she stepped through the door and began to make her way down the stairs. A strange chemical smell came up to meet her. It burned her nostrils like medicine, making her want to retch. As she descended, doubts began to swirl in her mind.

'It's freezing,' Lucy said as she followed Hannah down.

At the bottom, the pale shaft of light from Hannah's torch illuminated a brick-walled basement, with a rough concrete floor. As the beam played along the walls, she spotted a light switch. And to her surprise, when she clicked it, a single lightbulb sputtered into life in the centre of the ceiling. The glow shone on huge cobwebs draped all around them, grey patches of web massed in corners and across walls.

'Jesus,' said Hannah.

A dripping sound echoed around the room. *Plip, plip, plip.* Her torch picked out a tap attached to the wall in a corner, with a small puddle beneath it. There was something horrible about this place.

'Let's go back,' Lucy whispered.

Hannah told herself to keep going. 'Just a quick look around, and then we'll go back.' She shone her torch to the end of the room, where the light from the bulb hardly penetrated. It looked as if there was an alcove of some kind round the corner. The stink of chemicals seemed to be getting stronger.

'Can you smell that?' she asked as they crept forward.

'What? I can't smell anything.' Lucy clung to Hannah's arm.

Around the corner, they found a long alcove crammed with stuff. One wall covered from floor to ceiling by a wine rack, the rest of the space piled with junk. Hannah's torch shone over several rough wooden chests and a heap of black bin bags. Then some big plastic crates and brightly coloured storage boxes: the only cheerful-looking things down here.

They picked their way through the junk and Hannah kicked the lid off a box. On the top lay an old blanket, which she shifted aside with her foot. Newspapers, plastic carrier bags, and torn bits of dusty cloth. In the next box she found a stack of food, cheap stuff like baked beans, tomatoes, and rice. They looked old, the cans rusted and peeling, like they had been here for years.

'Look at this,' Lucy said. She was standing back the way they had come, pointing at the opposite wall.

'What is it?' Brushing her hands against her trousers, Hannah walked closer, her torch raised. The beam picked out the line of metal shelves they had walked past on their way to the alcove. But from this angle, she could see that they had been dragged away from the wall. And behind them was a door.

When Hannah pushed it open, it felt heavy and made a shushing sound, as if a rubber seal lined the frame. As if it had been designed with sound-proofing, or to offer some kind of protection to – or from – whatever was behind it.

As they entered, strip lights flickered on, illuminating an ultra-modern, sterile-looking space lined with office furniture. Desks and tables ranged around the walls, their surfaces covered by computers, a photocopier, and a large printer and scanner.

As Hannah's eyes adjusted, time seemed to slow down. The room smelled strangely metallic, like something she knew well but couldn't name. Images came to her in a rush of colour and sound. Above one of the desks ran a series of monitors, their screens showing horribly familiar footage from the house: the gloomy hallway; the fire in the drawing room, the dark figures of Rosa and Chloe hunched together in front of it.

'Fuck.' Hannah thought about the feeling of being watched that had stalked her over the past few days.

Then she saw something else, great red pools covering a

desk and dripping down onto the floor. The smell of rotting meat hit her like a wall.

And from a long way away, she could hear Lucy's voice. 'Hannah.' It sounded like someone shouting from the bottom of a swimming pool. 'Hannah!'

She tried to respond, but nothing came out.

All she could do was gaze at the man slumped back on a chair by one of the desks, his limp hand hanging towards the floor. His dead eyes staring at the ceiling.

It was Liam.

Chapter Thirty-Eight

Dark blood pooled around his feet. So much blood. And out of nowhere she understood what the room smelled like – a butcher's shop.

The world shifted, and she was aware of nothing but a dull ringing sound in her ears. Had someone killed Liam like they killed Rob and Sandeep? Was she next on the list? Eventually the spinning room began to slow, until finally it stopped and she felt warm arms around her. Lucy holding her, muttering words she couldn't make out.

They were still standing in the middle of the room, just metres away from the horror at the desk. And when she closed her eyes, images of it flashed across her mind, so she forced herself to look at the monitors on the wall above. At the floor, the door to the cellar, the door in the side wall leading to who knew what further nightmares.

As her thudding heart slowed, she managed to break free from Lucy, stand up and take a step closer to Liam, to what had been Liam.

'We need to . . . to work out what happened,' she said.

Lucy swallowed and wiped her nose with a sleeve. 'He's dead, that's what happened. Someone killed him.'

'But why has he been monitoring the house?' Hannah

pointed to the screens. 'And why the fuck is he here in the first place? He's supposed to be staying in town.'

Lucy just shook her head and gazed blankly around at the filing cabinets, at the whole high-tech office. Eventually she got up and sat on one of the office chairs – as far from Liam as possible. She shook her head again. 'I don't understand.'

Hannah stepped closer to the body and tried to hold her breath, tried not to inhale the thick rotting smell. Liam's neck had been slit – hacked open – and blood had gushed out across the floor. A scalpel lay in a pool of blood beside his chair, as if he – or his killer – had dropped it there.

'Well, it's either murder or suicide,' she said, but Lucy didn't respond.

Peering at the blood that coated Liam's chair and clothes, Hannah realized it was almost congealed. 'That – that blood – it doesn't look fresh. As if he's been dead for hours. He can't have been away from the house for long.'

'Chloe said she saw him outside,' Lucy said. 'She must have been right.'

Hannah took a deep breath and walked away from the body to search the rest of the room, looking for anything that would answer all the questions whirling in her mind. She pulled out the hammer from her pocket and left it on a desk at the side of the room. Another metal shelf sat beside the door, sanitizing gel and hand wipes lined up on top. Underneath Hannah found a small metal cupboard and, inside, more of the same: enough to last a clean freak for months. Sandeep would have loved this, she thought grimly. She shut the cupboard door and tried to focus.

Had Liam been in this room the whole time, watching them all on the monitors, working out how to pick them off one by one? Of course he was a doctor, the obsession with cleanliness made sense. And he had a huge ego. But Rosa seemed to know nothing about it. Hannah remembered what Chloe had said about his adultery: could this place have some connection to his secret life?

She moved some wet wipes to the side to get a better look at the back of a shelf. And there, right in the corner of the cupboard, she noticed another, dark-coloured, bottle.

An expensive-looking aftershave, its label oddly familiar. She picked it up and spun it in her fingers.

'Lucy, check this out.' She opened the bottle and brought it to her nose.

Lucy stood up and her mouth began to move, forming words, but Hannah heard nothing. Because her mind was shrinking back – back to her childhood – to a place she didn't want to go.

Chapter Thirty-Nine

Twenty-two years ago
Hannah

She's all snug and cosy in bed with her teddy and her Barbie dolls. Mummy's just kissed her goodnight and tucked her in. She looks like a princess tonight, her top all sparkly and her shoes all shiny with high, spiky heels.

She's going out tonight with Sally and Rachel – they're Mummy's girlfriends, but Hannah doesn't like them because they always try to play with her hair. Daddy's staying home to look after Hannah.

She closes her eyes and holds her teddy very close, doesn't want to think about the monster that might be under her bed, might come up the stairs. The one that Mummy says doesn't exist but that she knows is real. Doesn't want to think about that now, because it's silly.

But then she hears a sound on the stairs and she squeezes her eyes tight shut. So tight they hurt and hurt and she has to open them for a second, has to let out a breath but only a tiny one. Only a really small one or the monster will hear. If she stays still like this, if she's really quiet, it might be all right.

But it isn't all right, and Hannah wants to cry. Because the door opens and the monster is in her room. She smells its smell – the one she likes when it's daytime – not now, though. Not at night when she's in bed. At night it smells of monsters.

Its voice is soft and nice, like always. 'Not asleep yet are you, princess?'

It's left the door open and she can see light through her eyelids. She opens one just a bit, just a tiny bit, pressing it closed again when she sees the monster's dark shape move across the window. It's coming closer, too close, and now it's sitting on the bed. She can feel the mattress bend. *Look how heavy the monster is. Oh no – you're not real, Mummy says you're not real – please go away.*

But it doesn't go. It leans over and touches her cheek. She feels her eyelids flutter. Why did she let them do that?

'Trying to fool me?' Daddy says. 'Pretending to be asleep? But my princess doesn't want to be asleep tonight, does she? Mummy's out so we can stay up late and have lots of fun.'

Chapter Forty

Hannah opened her eyes and saw a piece of fluff lying on the floor. Her mind readjusted, she started to remember, and then it all flooded back and she knew why she was lying curled up on the floor, just like little Hannah all those years ago. For a moment she was back there, in the warm bedroom that smelled of aftershave. The aftershave she loved and hated; the daddy she loved in the daytime, but hated at night.

'Hannah . . . Hannah!' Lucy's face loomed above her. 'Are you all right?'

Hannah managed to nod and drag herself to her feet. Lucy looked deathly pale, her face creased with worry. She pulled over one of the wheeled office chairs and helped Hannah into it.

'Here, sit down. You're all right, it's OK,' she said. 'This is messed up, I know, but we have to hold it together for Chloe and Rosa. We have to think of something to say to them.'

She was right, and not just about this, about what Hannah had remembered too. Now wasn't the time to try to understand what had happened to her when she was a little girl. What she did know was that the dreams she'd had at The Guesthouse were all about that trauma. The dark figure she thought she had seen in her room, the monster sitting on her bed; the horror of her dad's aftershave. It was all about what her father had done to her – the father who had lived in this very house.

Someday soon there would be a time to talk about it, to tell her mother and find out how much she knew. To tell Lori and make it part of her conscious life, so that it might lose the power to torture her unconscious. But not now.

'You're right,' Hannah nodded at Lucy. 'Let's go and tell them.' But as she said it she heard footsteps upstairs. And when she looked at one of the monitors, she saw the fire was still flickering in the drawing room, but the hunched figures were gone.

'Hannah. Lucy. Where are you?' Rosa shouted down to them.

The footsteps came closer. 'Hannah?' Chloe shouted. 'Lucy, what's happened? I'm scared.' They were at the top of those stone steps that led down into the cellar, heading for this room. And what was sitting at the desk.

It was Lucy who acted first, whisking out and closing the door behind her. Hannah went to follow, but her legs felt too weak, her mind too jumbled. She needed to stay where she was, to try to keep them out of this room. For now she could only stand and listen.

'No, no. The stairs are dangerous,' Lucy said. 'And there are rats down there.' Something inaudible from Rosa.

'No, seriously, Rosa,' said Lucy.

Hannah went back into the cellar and shouted up the stairs as loudly as she could: 'We're all right, but you shouldn't come down. There are slippery steps and . . . it's dangerous. There's nothing you can do in here. We'll find the generator—'

'Chloe, stop,' Rosa shouted. 'Don't—' Then a flurry of sound. 'Wait,' Rosa called. 'It's dangerous.'

Hannah hurried back through the door and stood where she hoped she might block their view of Liam. If nothing else, it might give her a chance to break the news gently.

She heard Rosa say something as they entered the cellar and then the door flew open and she burst in. Lucy was behind her struggling to keep Chloe outside, and when that didn't work, to shield her from seeing the body.

'Wait a minute,' Hannah shouted, her hands raised.

But Rosa pushed her aside and strode into the room. 'What the hell is going on? Who do you think you are? Trying to keep this secret from us, lying to . . . to . . .' Rosa's words trailed off and she stood stock still in the centre of the room, staring at Liam.

'No . . . Oh my God, no!' Rosa cried. Then she screamed and ran towards him, held him in her arms, her chest heaving.

Chloe wrestled free of Lucy and ran to her mother. At first she stood staring, her face more puzzled than horrified, and then something changed in her eyes. She let out a shriek of pain, the kind of noise that might have come from the throat of a maimed animal rather than a girl.

Hannah couldn't bear to watch, so she turned away. Lucy came with her and they stood outside in the cellar, not looking at each other. Trying to block out the awful sounds of anger and grief.

After a few minutes, the room fell silent and Hannah and Lucy came quietly back inside. Rosa was carefully examining the room. Her eyes scanned the desk, the floor beneath it, the chair, and occasionally the body in the chair. Now she turned to them, her voice cold, her face like stone.

'He cut his throat,' she said blankly. She had something in her hand and with a cringe of disgust Hannah realized it was the scalpel.

'He knew it was the best way,' Rosa said. 'Better than cutting his wrists.' She looked down at her hand, at the metal blade covered in congealing blood. 'He didn't want to fail.'

Rosa's training as a nurse must be kicking in, helping her to hold back the nightmare.

Her eyes were wild as she stared at them, daring them to challenge her. When no one did, Rosa dropped the scalpel on the desk.

Staring at her bloody hands, as if seeing them for the first time, she walked unsteadily away and sat on an office chair beside another desk, on which stood a laptop and printer.

Chloe sat in a chair, her eyes red and swollen, staring into space. Lucy left the room for a moment and came back with a blanket that she must have got from one of the boxes in the cellar room. She held it up to Rosa who nodded and let her drape it over Liam's body.

'Let's go back upstairs,' Lucy said. 'There's nothing we can do here until tomorrow.'

'Wait.' Chloe stood up. 'There *is* something we need to do.' She rubbed her eyes on her sleeve then looked at them all in turn, her voice firm. 'If he killed himself, he would have left a note.'

There was a moment of silence, then Hannah nodded. 'All right, let's look for it.' She pointed at the laptop on the desk in front of Rosa, hoping to keep Chloe away from the body. 'Why don't you get that going? I'll search the files over here.'

Chloe headed to where her mother was sitting, still just staring at the shape under the blanket. Chloe pushed her chair away from the computer and touched the mouse pad. It came to life at once.

'This is it. Come and look,' Chloe said, and the others hurried over.

A Word document appeared on the screen.

Dear Rosa and Chloe,
There are many reasons for the things I've done. One day you will understand.
I'm sorry.
Liam

No one said anything for a long moment. Rosa sobbed quietly, then Chloe broke the silence.

'No way, that's a lie. That's ridiculous. My dad didn't write that.'

Another silence. 'He must have,' Rosa whispered. 'Who else did?'

Chloe's voice was sharp. 'The person who killed him.'

Chapter Forty-One

They all stared at each other.

'Someone killed Rob,' Chloe said. 'They killed Sandeep, and now they've killed my dad. We need to find out who did it. *I* need to find out who killed my dad.' She stood, hands clenched, daring them to disagree with her.

'OK,' Hannah said eventually. 'You keep searching the laptop while we check out the other desk. See if you can access the internet. Then we can contact the police.' What she didn't say was what they were all thinking: that the killer had to be one of the people in this room.

Chloe quickly pressed a few keys and shook her head. 'The internet is down in here too, and I can't see a router. But I'll keep searching through the files.'

Hannah nodded. Approaching the body, she had to hold her breath and keep swallowing to fight off waves of nausea. She ignored the pool of blood that covered the top of the desk and searched through the drawers.

She pulled out both the drawers and carried them over to where Lucy stood beside the door. Put one on the floor next to her and started going through the other. When she realized Lucy hadn't moved, she pointed at the drawer.

'Come on. Help.' She didn't try to hide her impatience.

Lucy crouched down by the drawer and set to work.

'And keep things separate and in order. That might be important.' It felt easier to treat it like a job they had to get through as efficiently as possible.

She knelt on the floor and took papers out of her drawer, one by one, glancing over them before placing them methodically on the floor.

Most of them included Preserve the Past logo, along with a Dublin address for the charity. There was correspondence with a Dublin bank, a firm of solicitors and various building and architectural refurbishment contractors. It was clear that considerable sums of money had been paid out for work on the house.

At the bottom of the drawer she came upon an odd piece of paper torn from a notepad. It contained a list of names: all charities connected with the preservation of old houses. Every single name had been crossed out, except for Preserve the Past. In fact it had a neat little box drawn around it.

She called to the others, trying to keep her voice calm. 'Anyone heard of *Save Our Heritage*, *Saving Historical Houses* or *Preserving Ireland's Past*?'

Lucy stopped what she was doing to shake her head, and Hannah wondered if the list had been made by someone trying to invent a name for the charity.

She turned the paper over and found one name repeated over and over: *Henry Laughton*. The name of the host they had never been able to meet, the name of the man they had messaged repeatedly but whose voice she had never heard. Each name written differently, as if by someone trying out a new signature.

Could Liam really have invented Henry Laughton and Preserve the Past? She'd heard of people stealing or creating an identity, then fabricating the signature.

'Jesus,' said Lucy and they all looked round. She crouched

over her drawer, a pile of papers on the floor beside her. She had one folder open, but she hadn't taken it out of the drawer.

'What's that?' Hannah asked.

Lucy stared at her. 'The deeds to this property.'

Hannah shuffled over and looked at the document in Lucy's hands. The house belonged to Ambrose, Lord Fallon. Ownership then passed to Jane, Lady Fallon, and after another ten years to John Roper. Presumably that was when Lady Fallon died. Five years later it had gone to Preserve the Past.

Rosa and Chloe came over and sat on the desk beside them. Rosa took the document and they began to read.

'Yes,' Hannah said. 'That makes sense. Because the letter about my father's death – the one that came to my mum five years ago – the date on that letter is around the time Preserve the Past bought the house. The executor of the estate told my mum there was no money left and everything had to be sold, so it must have gone straight to Preserve the Past.'

'Hold on,' Lucy said. 'What are you talking about?'

'Didn't I tell you? About John Roper?'

Lucy stared at her. Of course, she was the only one Hannah hadn't told about her discovery. Lucy shuffled away from Hannah with a look of horror on her face.

'Your father?'

'Yes, I thought I said. I'm Hannah Roper. John – or Jack – Roper was my dad. I knew he'd settled locally, but I found evidence upstairs that he lived in this actual house. And this,' she picked up the deed, 'proves it.'

Chloe glanced up from the document. 'Hannah told us about it earlier.'

Lucy stood and looked away. She swayed, then stared at Hannah, as if seeing something unimaginable, a monster she didn't believe in, come crawling out from under her bed in the middle of the night.

'My God. Fucking hell.' Lucy began pacing up and down. 'What the fuck is going on here?' Her voice shook. 'Sandeep, Liam, and now *you*. All connected to this place.'

Hannah went towards her, but Lucy held up her palms again. 'Don't – don't fucking come near me.' Then she turned to Rosa and Chloe. 'You realize she has to be involved in this shit, don't you?'

Again Hannah tried to reach out, to calm Lucy, but she moved away, her eyes darting around the room.

'We need to get out of here. Chloe, Rosa – let's go. We need to get away from *her* right now.' She jabbed a finger at Hannah. 'I bet this is all down to her. She's the one – she's the killer – and she's going to come after us next.'

Chapter Forty-Two

Hannah tried to steady herself, tried to find the right words to defend herself, but she couldn't speak. There was a long moment of silence, and then Rosa nodded.

'Yes,' she said calmly. 'That makes sense. I guessed there was something going on with her as soon as we arrived.'

'What? You can't seriously believe this.' Hannah's hands clenched with frustration. But even Chloe was staring at her with narrow suspicious eyes.

'And she was the one who kept that poor gardener talking,' Rosa said to Lucy, as if Hannah wasn't there. 'Making sure it was good and foggy when he left, making sure he fell to his death without any witnesses.'

Hannah tried to interrupt but Rosa talked straight through her. 'And she was constantly sucking up to Sandeep and Mo, getting them to trust her, making sure she could do what she liked.'

'She was the first one to arrive, remember that? Who knows how long she'd been here, setting this whole thing up.' Lucy glared at Hannah.

'Oh fuck off, this is insane.' Hannah turned away from them and walked to the far wall. It was useless trying to defend herself. She looked back, her voice bitter. 'Whatever.

I don't care, do what you want. If you don't feel safe, go upstairs. I'll look for the generator on my own.'

They all stared at her for a moment, as the thought of splitting up settled over them like a cloud. Chloe eventually walked back to the laptop. 'I'm not going anywhere until I've checked this properly.' Her tone was firm, mature, a far cry from the voice of the little girl who had arrived only days ago.

Lucy continued pacing the room, obviously desperate to leave, but not prepared to go alone. Hannah carried on searching through the paperwork, and the others went back to work, occasionally throwing nervous glances at Hannah, as if she might jump at them with a scalpel at any moment.

After a few minutes, Lucy came back to pick up the deeds again, staring hard at Hannah. 'This executor, the man who contacted your mum, what's his name?'

Taking a deep breath, Hannah forced herself to answer. 'Declan O'Hare. I don't know much about him – he was probably a friend of my dad's or a solicitor. He wrote to my mum about five years ago, told her about the death, and then we never heard from him again. He mentioned they were selling off the house, to pay debts, but that was it.'

Lucy turned away, her arms wrapped around herself. 'I don't understand,' she muttered. 'It doesn't make any sense.'

'What doesn't? What don't you—'

'Look,' Chloe's voice cut across the room. 'Quick, look at all this.' She pointed at the laptop, and everyone stopped. They all went over to her, close enough to see the screen. 'Everything's in my dad's name,' Chloe said. 'Everything. I couldn't find anything at first. And then I checked in this one.'

She clicked on a yellow folder marked 'MISC' and a series of folders appeared, all relating to Preserve the Past. Chloe opened one and a website design popped up. The only house listed was this one – The Guesthouse – and the website hadn't been updated. It still offered just one week at a reduced price for its very first guests.

Chloe clicked on the next folder, 'Pictures', and various photos of The Guesthouse and the surrounding countryside filled the screen. Some of them had been used on the website. Within the folder was another: 'Host'. And when Chloe opened it, they saw a whole series of images of solid-looking men. One of them was the man they knew as Henry Laughton, the host, although the photo showed him standing in a mountainous, forested region that looked more like central Europe than Ireland. And the dog was no longer at *his* side, but next to a completely different man.

'Christ,' Hannah said. 'So Henry was just some random guy he found online. Then Photoshopped next to a dog.'

The final folder – 'Guests' – was just a simple list of names and email addresses. Hannah's heart stumbled when she saw Ben's name right at the top. Hers came next and then Sandeep's and Mo's.

'Ben should have come with me,' Hannah said. 'So it's the people who were supposed to be here this week, but none of you – or Liam – are on there.'

When Rosa spoke, her voice sounded strained, as if she were drunk but trying to hide it. 'If Liam did this, he wouldn't need to add his own details.' She took a breath. 'And he never showed me the website or anything. He said he . . . he said the offer popped up just when he heard about the delay to the new house.'

They all stared at her, but her eyes drifted to the body slumped over the desk. 'We've been staying here free. He told me the offer was for him to be an early reviewer. Preserve the Past had chosen him to keep an eye on things and report back any problems. Then he was supposed to comment on TripAdvisor and the rest, leave his review on Cloud BNB. He wasn't to tell the other guests, though.'

Chloe sat forward, her eyes wide. 'Can't you see? It's all fake. Why would he make it so easy for us to find this stuff?'

'But if he killed himself, maybe he wanted us to find it?' said Lucy.

They turned this over for a moment.

'There's something else,' Hannah eventually said. 'Liam's name isn't the only one missing, is it?' She pointed at Lucy, glad to be able to bite back at her. 'Yours isn't there either.'

Lucy sounded as tired as Rosa. 'I booked the day before I came, so he probably didn't bother adding my details.'

'You said yourself that we all have connections to the place . . . so what's yours?'

'I don't have one.' Her voice was sharp.

'Well that's—' Hannah's voice was cut off by a loud bang. They sat, not daring to move, and stared around the room.

'It's coming from in here.' Rosa's voice shook.

The bang thundered again, this time louder, the exact sound that Hannah remembered hearing when she stood on the stairs that very first night.

Chloe laughed bitterly. 'I did it,' she said. 'It's recorded.' She gestured to the laptop. 'It's all on here, all the weird stuff we've heard. And I bet there are speakers in the main house. Listen.'

She clicked the mouse again and that familiar mournful crying filled the air. The room suddenly felt cold, the sound so realistic and desperate that Hannah wanted to scream. In the end it was Lucy who sobbed and turned away from them.

'Turn it off, please,' she said.

The recording stopped but the chill lingered, like there really had been a little girl crying beside them. Hannah thought of that horrible aftershave, imagined Liam watching them all on the monitors, torturing them with his recordings. But why?

221

'I can't stand this – I need to get out,' Rosa said. 'I need to wash my hands.'

She looked down at her blood-smeared hands as if seeing them for the first time. Hannah gave her a packet of wet wipes from the shelf by the door, and Rosa tried to scrub her fingers and palms. But the clotted blood lingered under her nails and in the creases of her skin.

'It's no good.' She dropped the wipes with a shiver of disgust. 'I need to wash them properly. Is there a sink anywhere down here?'

When no one responded, Rosa pointed to the door at the side, the one Hannah hadn't dared to open. 'What's in there?' she said.

Without waiting for an answer, she went over and pulled at the door handle.

It swung open with a click. A gentle light flickered on, very different to the fluorescent glare above them. When Hannah walked over to stand in the doorway, she saw a small room illuminated by a lamp. A neatly made camp bed, with fresh bedding, in one corner, a wooden chest with a rail above it in the other. And a few shirts hanging from the rail.

'Great, just great.' Rosa pulled down two of the shirts and held them up. 'Look, they're Liam's. They're all bloody Liam's.' Bringing them back into the other room, she flung them on the floor. 'Now will you believe me?'

She looked between them. 'And he told me he kept losing shirts at the gym, claimed someone stole them.' A harsh laugh. 'I thought he'd left them at his girlfriend's. But this . . . this is far worse. Oh God, I never even noticed . . . my Liam . . . what the hell was he doing?'

'You're wrong!' Chloe ran to the shirts and picked them up, glaring at her mother. 'You *want* to believe this, don't you? You'd rather think he was a killer, than admit he was cheating on you.'

Rosa blinked. 'That's not . . . true, Chloe, I know about the affair. The bloody woman sent me a text to *tell* me about it. How do you think that feels?' She swallowed. 'But that's just the start of it. He's been ruining his life – and ours – for a long time.'

Rosa took a deep breath. 'A long bloody time . . . He gambled away all our money, lost his job. He was about to be struck off, couldn't keep his hands off his patients.' A nerve on her neck twitched as she paced back and forth. 'And little old me, always trying to cover for him.'

Chloe pointed to the house deeds on the table. 'If he was broke, how could he buy a place like this?'

Rosa carried on pacing. 'I don't know, maybe it wasn't the gambling that ate up our money – it was buying this fucking house. I don't know, I don't understand any of it.' She stared at all of them as if they were accusing her, rather than Liam. 'We used to be so happy. We loved each other.'

Chloe's face burned with anger. 'Well if you loved him, how can you believe he did this?' She pointed a finger at Rosa. 'You think he's a killer? That he murdered two people?' She let her arm fall to her side and turned away, her voice quiet now. 'You're all wrong. You've got it all wrong.'

'Chloe, please,' Rosa said.

But her daughter walked purposefully to the door, still clutching the shirts, and without turning back, went up the steps and into the house.

Chapter Forty-Three

'Chloe!' Rosa called after her, then ran out the door. Moments later, they heard her footsteps thunder up the stairs.

When the sounds had died away, Hannah sighed. 'Jesus, what a fucking mess. I don't know what to think.' She looked over at the little bedroom. 'Why would he do this? And why would he kill himself? None of it makes sense.'

Lucy shook her head, her face pale. 'I don't know and I don't care; I just want to leave. We should go back upstairs, let the police sort this out.'

As they walked out of the cellar, Hannah suddenly stopped. Instead of carrying on to the steps, she stood listening, wondering why she hadn't heard it before. A humming noise seemed to be whirring somewhere nearby.

Lucy paused at the bottom of the steps. 'What is it?'

'That sound, can you hear it? Listen.'

It was a machine-like sound, something working steadily. 'That could be the generator. We should still try to find it if we can.'

Hannah switched on her torch and walked towards the sound. It seemed to be coming from the L-shaped alcove at the back of the cellar.

Lucy paused for a moment, and then came after her. Hannah thought about what they could do with electricity in the rest of the house, maybe they could get hold of the guards. Maybe Rosa and Chloe could begin to make some sense of their family tragedy.

As she stepped into the alcove and flicked the beam of her torch over the piles of junk, she wondered how long had passed since Mo left the house. How long he had spent out there in the storm. Whether he was still lying out there somewhere, being picked apart by foxes and birds.

A cold hand gripped her from behind, so suddenly she let out a yell. Lucy's fingers bit into her arm, twisting her round to face her.

'Listen,' Lucy said, her face close in the gloom. Hannah's torch dropped to the ground.

'You're hiding something,' Lucy hissed. 'I know it. You were so keen to come down here, to lead everyone else down here too. You *knew* it was here, didn't you?'

'What? What are you talking about?' Hannah shrugged herself free.

'Liam, of course.' Her head moved closer until one bright blue eye filled Hannah's vision. 'Liam and all that convenient evidence against him.'

Hannah could smell Lucy's sour breath. 'Why would I plant evidence against Liam? I didn't even know him.'

Lucy's mouth twisted in a smile. 'You told me you didn't know this house, but that was just another fucking lie. You're his daughter. That man, Jack Roper – *his* fucking daughter.' She almost spat. 'What a coincidence.'

Hannah stepped backwards and bumped into the wall. The beam from her fallen torch bounced off the wall and cast Lucy's face in shadow. Hannah tried to speak, but her throat felt dry.

'It *is* a coincidence,' she said at last. 'It isn't me, Lucy, I'm

225

telling you. I'd never fucking heard of this house before I saw it online, and I didn't even know my father.'

Lucy started pacing back and forth. 'After you got the letter and found out he was dead, you didn't come over here? Didn't go to the funeral?'

'No. My mother didn't tell me about the letter until it was too late. I never met Declan, or had contact with him. I'm telling you: I'd never met any of the guests. This has nothing to do with me.'

Her words seemed to have some effect at least, because Lucy stayed quiet for a moment, her shoulders hunched. 'What can you remember about your father?' She spoke quietly now.

Hannah blinked, tried to control her thoughts. Tried not to think about it. 'Hardly anything,' she said weakly.

Lucy turned to stare at her and the only sound was the *drip, drip, drip* of the tap in the corner of the room.

'His aftershave,' Hannah said suddenly, before she could stop herself. 'I remember that. And I can't get it out my head. It's fucking everywhere, on his old clothes, on the carpets and armchairs. That was the bottle I found in that room, too.' She pointed behind the shelves. 'So maybe it was Liam's after all.'

'No,' Lucy said. 'Liam didn't wear it, we would have noticed. But I've smelt it too. It's all over the house, in my room, in my bed.' She shivered and looked up at the dark ceiling above them, at the grimy pipes running along the ceiling. 'Your father.' She stared at Hannah. 'Did you love him?' Hannah remembered her asking this once before.

'I . . . I think so. At least . . . I've always told myself I did.'

'And he loved you?' Lucy's voice was barely a whisper, but so intense it sent a shiver through Hannah.

She felt confused and could only say, 'I don't know. I thought so, but I was very young.'

A long pause and Hannah waited, not daring to move or speak. She told herself she had nothing to fear from Lucy, the killer had been Liam and now he was dead. Lucy was just in shock after everything that had happened. But Hannah couldn't stop herself from inching away towards the bottom of the stairs. Towards the others. She no longer cared about the humming, wasn't even sure it was a real sound.

'I'm going back up,' she said gently. 'I can't stand being down here any more. We can talk properly in the light by the fire.'

Lucy gave her a tiny smile that did nothing to calm the thump of her heart. 'OK,' she said.

Picking up the torch, Hannah hurried ahead without waiting for Lucy, up the steps, through the immaculate white-walled room, along the green corridor and out into the hall. She felt a wave of relief to be back in the main house. Away from the cellar, away from that constant dripping and the stink of chemicals. Away from what was left of Liam, away from Lucy.

The hall was still shrouded in darkness, the sound of thunder much louder now, booming right on top of the house. She walked into the empty drawing room, went to stoke up the fire that was now just a few smouldering embers. This was the only warm room in the house, so where had Rosa and Chloe gone?

She looked out into the hallway calling again. 'Rosa!' Her voice echoed back at her. 'Chloe!' The only sounds were the wind and the rain. She clenched her hands to stop them shaking. And had to sit on the sofa to still her trembling legs.

Lucy had been acting so strangely. She had seemed so distant ever since they entered that other section of the house, so desperate to keep them out of those rooms. Hannah thought back and realized it had always been Lucy who had objected, who had steered them away from the padlocked area with subtle hints or suggestions. Then, when Hannah had refused to listen to her, Lucy had made sure she was there beside her every step of the way, as if she had something to hide. Hannah shivered and another crack of lightning lit up the sky.

She imagined Lucy all alone, wandering around in those cold empty rooms in the cellar, listening to the drip of the tap. Or she could have slipped quietly past the drawing room and gone upstairs to find Rosa and Chloe. Gone to talk them round, whisper lies about Hannah until they thought she was the killer. They could be sitting up there now, muttering about Hannah the lunatic, *the girl who thinks she's a Lady*. Whispering just like the girls did at school, just like all those people on social media. Hannah shook her head, she needed to get a grip.

She heard a sound and stood up, her heart racing.

A bang, and then another. A creak and then a huge crash that seemed to shake the walls of the house.

For a moment she thought it must be Lucy, back by the monitors, turning on the recordings again.

But the sound was coming from just outside the drawing room, in the hallway: someone was banging on the front door.

It must be Mo, or the police, they'd finally arrived. She was going to be all right, they were all going to be OK.

'Mo! Mo, in here!' she shouted as she ran out into the hall.

But then she stopped, dead still. No – there was no one here – the bangs were made by the door itself, crashing open and closed in the wind.

Someone had run outside and left it ajar.

Chapter Forty-Four

Chloe, it could have been Chloe. Maybe Rosa had followed her out there, maybe Lucy had gone after her too. All three of them could be outside right now, hiding in a ditch somewhere. But who – or what – were they hiding from?

She stepped outside and pulled the door shut behind her. Stood in the doorway and stared out into the night, strained to see along the gravel driveway to the slopes beyond. Twigs and bits of leaf and grass, even small stones, whipped past the building in the wind. No one could get far in this.

She pulled her collar close and made her way along the side of the house to look through the French windows into the drawing room. With the curtains open and the fire blazing, the room was lit up like a beacon; people could see it from miles around. It made her shiver to imagine them all sitting in there by the fire, oblivious as someone peered in from outside. A flash of forked lightning lit up the hillside and she saw rows of twisted trees, bent double by the wind.

'Chloe!' she shouted. 'Rosa!'

There was no answer. And as she walked around the house, shivering in the cold, she thought again about Mo out here on his own. He would never have made it to the village.

The wind tore her words away as she called for Chloe. It

stung her cheeks and filled her eyes with tears. She clung to the wall as thunder boomed and lightning flashed, getting closer.

After she passed the back door, she saw something she hadn't noticed before: a flight of steps with a door at the bottom. It must be another way into the cellar. She went down, grateful to be out of the wind, and rattled the handle. But it was locked and there was no sign that anyone had been here. She stood for a moment, savouring the calm and quiet. Then climbed up and carried on towards the outhouse.

As the old building loomed into view, another peal of thunder rolled across the hills and the air crackled. A flash of lightning split the sky, illuminating the outhouse, and beside it a shadow standing in the rain. The figure seemed to be trying to get through the door.

Then the night descended into darkness again. She ran towards the building, shouting. 'Rosa, Chloe! It's me, Hannah.'

But as she got closer, she realized that the figure had looked tall, too tall to be Rosa or Chloe. It could have been Lucy, or maybe Mo, or a policeman. She ran faster, hoping to see Mo, hoping to see his smile. But when she reached the building, the figure was nowhere to be seen. She shone her torch around her, held her hand up to shield her eyes from the rain.

She was sure someone had tried to open the outhouse door. Her hands numb from the cold, she tried the handle, but it was locked. The beam of her torch played along the grass around her, flickering against the trunks of trees, but she could see no one. The weight of the torch in her hand felt comforting as she walked back to the house, heavy enough to do some damage if it came to it.

She couldn't stop replaying the moment in her mind. The flash of lightning, the tall shadow struggling with the door of the outhouse. Shrouded in dark clothes. Something about it seemed familiar, but her jumbled mind wouldn't focus.

Back in the hallway she slammed the door and shot the bolts.

'Lucy! Hello, Rosa?' Her voice echoed in the empty hallway.

She went to the stairs and called up again but was met with only silence. Something told her not to go upstairs, not to walk up there on her own. But she took a deep breath, held out the torch and began to walk towards the first floor.

'Rosa! It's me, Hannah. I'm coming up.' Her torch beam flicked across the family room, its door firmly shut. 'Lucy . . . Chloe . . . Where are you?'

She felt alone, horribly alone, as the sound of her voice died in the silent corridors. Her legs heavy, as if her body knew what she would find at the top of the stairs, as if it was trying to stop her, trying to protect her. Her palms sticky against the torch, her heart thumping in her ears. She wouldn't go in there yet, she couldn't, she would check the other rooms first.

She shone her torch along the corridor towards Sandeep's room. Mo's door was half-open, just as he'd left it, and inside was empty. She checked his bathroom, stared at his clothes lying on the floor, wondered whether he would ever wear them again.

Closing the door behind her, she walked to Sandeep's room and made herself glance inside. The bright torchlight picked out his body and seemed to make his face glow. His half-open eyes glinted with what looked to Hannah like suspicion, or maybe even reproach. Had she done this to him? Was this her fault?

A creak on the stairs made her spin round, torch raised.

'Hello? Who's there?' she shouted. The torch shook in her hand as she pointed the beam along the corridor towards the stairs again. Step by step, she walked silently back and raked the beam of light from her torch up and down the staircase. Nothing, just dancing shadows. But then, at the top, she noticed the door to the family room. It was open.

Someone had been inside that room in the last few minutes, while she was checking the corridor.

She pushed open the door to look inside.

It seemed empty, but in front of the half-open bathroom door lay a crumpled shirt. One of Liam's from the cellar, she thought. And on the double bed was another. The duvet lay twisted and crumpled on the floor, broken glass strewn across the room, bloody handprints smeared across the wall.

Hannah felt everything begin to spin, her knees turning liquid. She stepped towards the bathroom with her torch held high.

Its beam reached through a crack in the door and played across the linoleum floor, reflecting off a pool of blood. Someone else was dead.

She pushed the door, but it didn't move.

Someone – or something – was behind it.

Chapter Forty-Five

The room roared with sound as she kicked at the bathroom door, flinging herself hard against it, convinced the killer was waiting for her on the other side. But the door hit something too soft to be human. There was no one there.

And when she stepped in and pointed her torch down behind the door, all she found was a pile of towels.

She stood for a moment, making her whole body still, listening for any sounds in the house around her, eyes fixed on that pool of blood. The torch felt slippery in her hands, so she wiped the handle on her jeans and tightened her grip.

There was something lying on one of the towels. A scalpel, just like the one they had found beside Liam's body, bleeding scarlet onto the white fabric.

She moved the beam of light from the towels along the floor to the pool of blood. And followed the trail of red up the side of the bath, to the shower curtain that had been pulled completely across. She knew what had to lie behind it. *Please God, please God.*

With a gasp of breath, she slid back the curtain.

Rosa.

Her body limp and pale, empty of life. More like a

crumpled heap of clothes than a woman. One leg bent at the knee, the other stretched on the edge of the bath, as if she was trying to climb out. Dead eyes staring.

Her neck was slit, just as her husband's had been, her clothes soaked with blood. The tiles around the bath splashed with vivid red.

Hannah staggered against the wall, pulled herself away from the body, through the bedroom and on to the landing again. She was numb, unable to feel anything more. As if this was one of her awful nightmares and she was about to wake up.

She stumbled downstairs and into the drawing room, her mind refusing to come to terms with what she had seen, refusing to think about what might have happened to Chloe. She crouched beside the hearth and threw a few logs on the fire, huddled close to the flames, shivered with cold.

Sitting on the sofa, she tried to piece together the events of the evening, tried to make herself feel human again. Leaning her head back and closing her eyes, she forced herself to think logically, to narrow down the list of possible suspects.

Chloe had been so angry with her mother, had been behaving so strangely and sleepwalking at night. Could she have murdered Rosa in a fit of rage? Or even done it in her sleep? No, it wasn't possible, Hannah just wouldn't believe it. Chloe was a child, what possible reason could she have for killing Sandeep or Rob?

She shook her head, couldn't let this house twist her thoughts and turn her against people she had grown to trust. But she had to face facts and Liam couldn't have done it all. She had wanted to believe his death was suicide, that he had been the killer, but she knew that wasn't true.

Someone else had done it, someone who had been in the house the whole time.

And there was only one person left. The person Hannah

had never really been able to understand. The one who had shown them all two entirely different sides to her personality.

Lucy.

It had to be her, there was no one else. It could have been her out there in the storm by the outhouse, wrestling with the door. She could have been the person creaking down the stairs as she fled the scene of Rosa's murder. Hannah stood up and walked back to the hearth and threw another log on the fire, crouched closer to the flames to warm her numb fingers. Lightning flashed across the sky, and Hannah stared through the windows. Should she go back out there to search for Chloe?

No. There was no way she would find her now, especially if Chloe didn't want to be found. She would just have to hope she was somewhere safe, that she wasn't lying dead out there too. Lying dead somewhere close to Mo. Killed by the storm, the night, by the sucking bog. Or by whatever monster was stalking them.

There was only one part of the house where she might find Chloe, one place she might be hiding. Pushing her hair behind her ears, she stood up and grabbed her torch, searched around for a weapon. Where was the hammer that had been in her pocket? She looked at the clumsy poker on the floor by the fire, but decided it would be too heavy.

She went into the kitchen, still half-hoping she would find someone there. But it was empty, the table littered with remnants of pizza. Cups with their dregs of cold coffee, one with a trace of lipstick on the rim, and Chloe's half-drunk orange juice. *Mary Celeste*, Hannah thought. No one had survived that either.

But she *was* going to survive this, and she would make sure Chloe did too. Clutching her torch, she went through the hall and into the green-walled corridor. Going first up the back stairs to the bare servants' rooms. Keeping her torch low as she crept up, trying to move silently. If someone was hiding here, the sound of her footsteps would give them enough time to get away.

Her hand shook as she moved from room to room, playing the torch around each dusty space, finding nothing. Deep down she had known there would be no one here, that she would have to go back through the padlocked door.

In the green corridor, she took a deep breath and hurried through the open door, moving the broken padlock aside with her foot, careful not to rattle it. She blinked as she entered the first brightly lit room. Still clean, modern, and apparently undisturbed.

Pausing at the top of the stone steps, she took a breath and listened for a moment to the thumping of her heart. Then went down into the L-shaped cellar, alert for any signs of movement, wishing she had brought the metal poker after all. The door to the computer room was closed, but she knew she had to go in there again. Chloe might have wanted to be near her father.

She stopped.

Someone *had* been in here. The L-shaped alcove had been disturbed, all the black bin bags pushed aside. And as the light from her torch settled on a large carpet-covered box, she saw what had been hidden by the rubbish. Another door. If anyone was down here, that was where she would find them.

That humming sound was still here, growing louder in the alcove. As she pulled the carpet off the box beside the door, she realized why. Underneath sat an old chest freezer, still working. She lifted the lid, releasing a cloud of cold air. On top, a layer of frozen food: cheap bags of fish, sausages, burgers, frozen vegetables. All budget brands, all years old.

She lowered the lid and moved towards the door. But as she stepped over the crumpled piece of carpet, she saw something that must have fallen on the floor.

A black oblong shape. A book.

She stooped to pick it up and flicked it open. It was hand-written, the cover torn, several of the pages ripped out and scattered on the floor by the door. She collected them up.

The writing was very neat – old-fashioned looking – so it could have belonged to one of the past children who'd lived in the house. Maybe the last Lady Fallon when she was a girl, or even a child from a previous generation. Each entry was written in pencil and headed with the day of the week. The writing appeared to mature as the entries went on so presumably the journal spanned some time.

She was about to close the book and get back to her search, when she spotted a couple of references that made her pause.

She began to read.

Chapter Forty-Six

Tuesday

Mummy says she won't punish me if I promise not to do it again. I spoke to a stranger and you must never do that. It isn't safe, because there are bad people out there. They walk in the gardens, or stand behind the trees. They walk across the hills. And sometimes they come into the house. I have to hide then, have to make sure no one can see me, have to make sure I don't make a sound.

We were doing lessons upstairs when Mummy went down to the kitchen. I stood at the window and breathed against the glass, wrote my name there and then wiped it out, like I always do when it's raining outside. But then I saw a man in the garden. I watched him digging there for a while and I thought he was so wrinkly and grey he must be the oldest thing in the world. But then he looked up and saw me. He fell backwards into the mud, his face all funny, and I wanted to talk to him, wanted to play a game with him, so I tried to call out. He stared at me and said something, but I couldn't hear him. I put my hand against the glass and tried to tell him my name, but he just went all white. I waved for him to come closer, but he just ran away into the trees.

Then Mummy came back up and she knew what I'd done.

She was so angry. She was crying too and said she ought to beat me for being so bad. If I ever did anything like that again, she would have to punish me, even though she loved me.

'Is he one of the bad people?' I asked.

'No,' she said. 'He's just Rob the gardener.'

Then she sent me to my room and told me to stay there and to remember that she would beat me if I did anything like that again.

But she won't beat me. Mummy never beats me. Only he does that.

Thursday

Sometimes I'm allowed into the garden with Mummy. I love that, but I've never seen Rob the gardener out there, never had the chance to talk to him. He doesn't come every day, but he must get lonely up here all on his own. Like me, I guess. I need to find out when he comes, so I can talk to him properly. I want to ask what he knows about the bad people. Why he can be outside, but I can't?

Tuesday

I spoke to Rob! Mummy wasn't well today, so I was looking after her. Then she fell asleep and I saw him from her bedroom window. He was digging in the garden and I ran down to the door, slipped out and went into the garden.

He looked scared when he saw me, like Mummy does sometimes when I do something bad. He dropped his spade and I thought he was going to run away again.

'Please don't go!' I said. 'I'm Maddie and I just want to talk to you.'

He didn't want to, though, I could see that. He kept moving away from me, as if I was a bad person. Then he said that he thought I was a ghost and I laughed. That made him laugh too, but I could see that he still thought I was scary. Then Mummy came to the door in her dressing gown and she was really angry. I've never seen her so angry. I had to go back inside and this time I thought she would beat me. But she just kept crying and saying it was all her fault, saying that she had ruined everything. She said if I ever spoke to anyone like that again something really really bad would happen.

But I don't care, because Rob is my friend now. And I've never had a real friend.

Chapter Forty-Seven

So this was Maddie. The name in the diaries Hannah had found in the office next to her room. Those diaries had ranged from twenty to ten ago, so this Maddie was presumably around at that time. It still wasn't clear when these entries had been made, but she remembered Sandeep and Rob both talking about the crying child fifteen years ago.

So Maddie was the pale little girl from the stories, the one Mo and Sandeep had talked about, but she was real.

It changed nothing, though. The only definite thing Hannah knew was that the alcove had been cleared to let someone through this door, and they'd done it recently.

Perhaps it was Chloe. She could have realized that the storm was too dangerous and taken her chances in the cellar. Hannah stuffed the book in her pocket and opened the door. Inside she found herself in a dark tunnel. Her torch picked out a long corridor with rough walls covered in stained white tiles. Pipes lined the ceiling, rusty streaks of liquid formed dark brown puddles on the floor. She spotted a light switch and turned it on. A row of strip lights flickered for a moment, illuminating a wide-open space at the end of the tunnel, then died.

Her breathing sounded loud, her footsteps echoed along

the corridor. And that chemical smell was almost over-powering. A memory seemed to be tugging at her mind, trying to show itself, but she shook her head and clamped it down. She needed to focus.

On the left was a door, a space in the wall that led into what looked like a shower room. The torch flickered over a rotten wooden bench and a pool of brown liquid. More grimy white tiles, some of them smashed, others streaked with rust-coloured stains.

At the back of the room, she could see a dark alcove – a walk-in shower. She approached cautiously, listening to the steady *drip, drip* of a tap somewhere nearby, and shone her torch into the back of the shower. On a metal shelf lay the slimy remains of a bar of green soap. An old threadbare towel hung on a hook attached to the wall. The floor was slippery, streaks of green slime making it difficult to keep her balance.

And then she heard a sound behind her. A tiny splash as if something had fallen into a puddle of water. She twisted round and pointed her torch at the door. Nothing. She crept out into the corridor, listening hard, and shone the light left and then right. The only sounds were the *drip, drip, drip* of a leaking pipe, and the thump of her heart.

Chapter Forty-Eight

'Chloe,' she whispered. Her voice echoed in the tunnel. All she wanted was to go back, but she had to check the space at the end of the corridor – the yawning black hole at the heart of the house. She owed it to all the others she had let down: Ben, Rob, Sandeep, even Mo and Rosa.

There were no more rooms, but the corridor carried on to the big space at the end. The smell of chemicals grew stronger as she inched her way further along the tunnel. Her mouth felt dry, her stomach churned. It could have been her imagination, but she thought the torch might be growing dimmer.

If only her phone was here, not back in her bedroom, completely dead. Without it she could only guess it must be sometime in the early hours of the morning. A wave of exhaustion made her stumble, her limbs heavy, as if she were trudging through mud.

And that thought brought Mo back to mind. She prayed he was in a cosy hotel room somewhere, waiting out the storm until he could come back with the police. A hard lump rose into her throat, but she swallowed it down.

Because she had to face the possibility that she was the only one left, last on the list.

If only she could make sense of it, understand what had happened and who was to blame.

At the end of the corridor, a few steps led even further down, into another much shorter tunnel, its walls covered in the same stained white tiles. More rusty pipes along the ceiling, dripping brown liquid into dark pools on the floor.

Then she stepped out of the tunnel into a wide-open space. It seemed enormous, like stepping into an empty cathedral in the dead of night. She lifted her torch, its light even dimmer now. It reflected off tiled walls, a high ceiling, and a huge expanse of water. Of course. The horrible chemical smell that churned her stomach was chlorine – this was a swimming pool – and even as she realized it her torch sputtered. It flickered, flashed on for a second, and then died.

She stood there in complete darkness, wanting to turn and run. Along the corridor, groping the slimy walls to find her way, back up those stairs, back through the cellar room and into the main house. Then out into the storm.

But Chloe might be down here.

She tried to control her breathing, shook the torch. Fumbled with the plastic case and took out the batteries, shifted them around and replaced them, clicked the case back into place. Took a deep breath and turned the torch on. It worked, the light dim, but strong enough for her to shine a beam into the yawning black space again. She stepped closer to the edge of the water. Under her feet slippery white tiles stretched away to the left and right. When she lifted her torch its light flashed against the water. Deep, green, scummy water full of dark floating bits of leaf, twigs, and mould. How had they got inside?

She blinked and the torch slipped from her hand. It fell through the air and crashed into the floor. And the memories hit her like a wave.

Chapter Forty-Nine

Twenty-one years ago
Hannah

She's at the pool with Mummy and she is so happy. Then Daddy is there too. He takes her into the deep water, even though she doesn't want to go and her mummy says he shouldn't. But he whispers to her, telling her she should shout back that she likes it.

'We can have fun,' he says, and he sounds just like the monster. The monster she hates, the one who comes to her bedroom at night, or when she's in the bath.

But it's different this time because Mummy is near and Hannah struggles, kicking and fighting to get away. She pokes him in the eye and he lets go. But now she's going down, down, into the blue water. She can hear shouting and screaming, but it sounds all muffled and strange. Her eyes open and all she can see are white tiles at the bottom. If only she could breathe. Mummy told her water was fun, but you had to be careful. It's dangerous at the deep end. And she knows that word. Drowning, she's drowning.

But strong arms come around her and pull her up, choking and spluttering. It's him, though, still him, and she fights and coughs and cries. Then – at last – she's lifted out and into a warm towel and Mummy is holding her. Telling her she's safe and calling Daddy bad names. 'You idiot, Jack, what were you doing?'

And Daddy touches her hair and whispers in his sweet soft voice, 'I'm sorry, princess.'

But that's what the monster says at night when he frightens her, when he hurts her. And she screams and kicks him and Mummy takes her to the changing rooms.

And when she's dry and warm, Mummy asks why she was so scared. 'It was just Daddy being silly. He won't do it again.'

Then she tells Mummy about the monster. She asks Mummy if she can tell him not to do the other things as well. The things he does to her in bed at night and in the bath.

Chapter Fifty

So that was it. That was what had destroyed Ruby's marriage and eliminated Jack Roper from their lives. No wonder she had wanted him not just gone but forgotten.

The shock of the memory washed over Hannah and she reached out for the damp wall behind her. Leaning her shoulder against it, she forced herself to breathe deeply, to ignore the taste of chlorine, to ignore the fear of falling forward into the pool.

Eventually she moved on with unstable legs, keeping close to the walls, feeling her way along the slippery tiles, the torch still clutched to her chest. Praying and breathing in tiny sips of air. Blood pounding in her ears.

She swung the torch across the pool, its beam catching reflections of the water on the walls and ceiling. And she saw again how green and mottled the water was, more like a stagnant pond than a swimming pool. Its surface rippling slightly, disturbed by her movement, or maybe by something living in its depths.

Creeping onwards, one hand still on the wall, she looked across the water. And stumbled over something. She fell to her knees and gripped the torch as she went down.

She had fallen over a wooden bench. It had shifted out

of position, so she pushed it back into its alcove by the wall. She was going to be all right, it was all going to be OK. Her knee ached from where she had fallen, her mouth felt dry. This whole place was rotting away, its walls and floors eroding under layers of water and slime.

When she reached the far end of the pool, she spotted yet another door. It must lead outside, to that flight of steps where she had sheltered from the wind. Chloe might have got out that way, but when Hannah tried the handle, it was locked and there was no sign of a key.

She carried on down the other side of the water, groping her way along the wall, the light of her torch growing weaker by the second.

A tiny noise like a foot stepping in a puddle. She swung the torch back to the entrance, illuminating the empty black hole of the tunnel. Pointing the light across the pool, along the way she had walked, she could only see the wooden bench in its alcove. No one there either, at least no one in sight.

She carried on, her breath clouding around her in the cold. There was another alcove just ahead, the twin of the one on the other side. Another little sound, maybe just the echo of her own breathing. Or maybe a tiny sob barely louder than a whisper.

It might be Chloe, terrified, hiding somewhere in the dark. Hiding from Hannah, perhaps, believing what Lucy and Rosa had said. It didn't matter any more, everyone else was dead. Chloe needed help and she would soon remember that Hannah was her friend.

'It's me, Chloe,' she whispered. 'It's Hannah. Don't worry.' Her voice echoed around the pool. As she spoke, she moved forward as silently as she could.

What if it wasn't Chloe? What if it was something else entirely? What if someone else had been in the house with them this whole time?

Cold sweat ran down her neck, a prickle of fear along her spine. She held her breath and crept closer to the alcove. As well as another wooden bench, there was a door at the back, with bolts at the top and bottom. They were on the outside, so the room must have been used for storage.

Her hand shook as she reached out to touch the door handle. 'I'm coming in now.' Her voice wavered. 'Coming to help you.'

The room was empty.

As she shone her torch across the bare concrete floor, a large spider scuttled away. A dingy towel or blanket lay crumpled by her foot. Kicking it sent dust motes spinning up the shaft of torchlight. She watched them for a moment as they glittered and danced. But she felt sick inside. This place reminded her of a prison cell.

The torch flickered and she breathed a silent prayer that the battery wouldn't give up on her now. It picked out a couple of pictures attached to the brick walls.

She held the beam closer and realized they were photos of people. One of a man, the other, a woman and child.

Then she noticed a grey canvas lump next to the blanket on the floor. She braced herself and reached out to pick it up, her fingers recoiling at the touch.

It was a rucksack, threadbare with age, and inside she found a plastic bottle with an inch of green-tinged water at the bottom. Then she pulled out a few pieces of paper with childish drawings on them: a house, trees, a woman holding hands with a little girl. Hannah guessed a tramp had somehow broken into the house and been living down here. These pitiful things someone's mementoes from a previous life.

Right at the bottom of the bag lay three books and something made of wool that had her fingers twitching again. She dropped it on the floor, thinking it was clothing of some kind. But it was a toy, a stuffed woollen elephant, another sad keepsake.

The largest of the faded books was a children's picture book she remembered her teacher reading to them in school when she was very young. The next a small English dictionary.

As she turned away and moved back towards the door, she heard something else.

She flashed the torch towards the tunnel, but nothing moved. Then to the door at the back that she thought led outside.

Another sound, this time much closer.

Suppressed breathing, coming from behind her.

Someone or something was in the room with her.

Chapter Fifty-One

Her groping hand touched a wall switch. A bare bulb hanging from the ceiling flickered on, its weak light dazzling her for a second. She shielded her eyes. When she looked again, she saw a sleeping bag propped in the far corner of the room.

Someone was huddled inside it. They'd pulled it so high that only the fingers of one hand were visible. But Hannah could see a lock of hair.

A lock of white-blonde hair with a hint of blue at the roots.

Lucy.

Strong, bossy Lucy with her stylish clothes and beautiful make-up, cowering under an ancient sleeping bag.

'Lucy?' she said tentatively, thinking about how sure she had been that Lucy was the killer. But as the silence stretched on, the figure in the corner looked so fragile that Hannah's fear began to fade. 'What are you doing? Are you all right?'

The sleeping bag rustled again, and Hannah took a step closer.

'Go away,' Lucy muttered.

'It's all right, it's me, Hannah.' She inched nearer. 'What are you doing in here? We need to look for Chloe.'

Lucy pulled down the sleeping bag and stared up at her.

Her eyes were red and swollen, make-up smudged, streaks of dirt on her cheeks and forehead.

She clung to the sleeping bag like a child with a security blanket. Her eyes were clouded and she flinched away when Hannah tried to touch her arm.

'I won't hurt you,' Hannah said gently.

Lucy just stared at her, with something like horrified wonder in her voice. 'Hannah, yes, it's you. I should have known.'

Hannah shuddered as she thought about what might have done this to Lucy. Had she found Chloe's body? Or even seen her murdered?

She crouched on the filthy floor. 'That's right, I'm Hannah and you know me. I'm your friend.'

But Lucy seemed to look right through her, as if seeing someone else. Her words were muffled, so quiet that Hannah could barely hear her. The only word she caught was 'sister'.

'What? What about her?'

A giggle, a tiny broken laugh. 'He told me about her. How he loved her, but didn't love me.'

Hannah swallowed and tried to think of something to say. But Lucy had let the sleeping bag fall, shuffled forward and reached for the rucksack on the floor. She pulled a crumpled piece of card from a small pocket at the front. When she held it out, Hannah realized it was a photo.

Creased and torn as it was, she could see that it was the picture of a little blonde girl. Three or four years old at most, holding a Barbie doll, smiling into the camera. She could have been a very young Lucy. And anyone else might have assumed it *was* Lucy.

But not Hannah, because she recognized that dress and that doll.

Because the little girl in the photo wasn't Lucy.

It was Hannah.

It took a few minutes to process what she was seeing and to try to make sense of it. When she looked back, Lucy was fiddling with the rucksack, focused on pulling at a loose thread.

'This is me. It's a picture of me,' Hannah said. 'Did you find it in the rucksack?'

Lucy shook her head, wouldn't meet her eye. 'He gave it to me.'

'Who, Lucy?' Hannah felt sick, her throat numb. 'Who gave it to you?'

Another mutter, reaching out for the photo. 'My father gave it to me.'

Then those bright eyes met hers and they were clear and sane and almost like the eyes of the Lucy she thought she knew. 'Your father gave it to me,' she said.

'You mean . . . Jack Roper gave it to you?'

'Yes.' Lucy took the photo. 'Jack Roper, your father.' Pressing and rubbing the photo between her fingers, as if that might smooth away any imperfections. 'Your father, my father.' Lucy was studying the photo as if it held the answer to a complex puzzle. 'Because he loved you, but he didn't love me.'

Chapter Fifty-Two

The world disappeared. All Hannah could see was Lucy.

It was as if she was lit by a piercing spotlight, so bright Hannah had to close her eyes. Behind her lids flashes of colours and a whirl of black dots, teeming and twisting, made her reach out to stop herself falling.

The rough floor under her hand was real and solid. It brought her back to herself and she was able to look again. And see the tiny dark room around her and Lucy, pale and dirty, huddled in the filthy sleeping bag. Everything was the same. And yet totally changed.

'You . . .' Hannah's voice cracked. 'You're Jack Roper's daughter too?'

Another nod.

Hannah rubbed her forehead, as if that might clear her thoughts. She went back over what Lucy had told her over the past few days, how she had left home after her mother died because she didn't get on with her father. She hadn't said that her father was dead, so Hannah had assumed he was still alive.

Then she thought about what Sandeep had told her. 'But Lady Fallon had no children,' she said.

Lucy picked at the woollen elephant, removed bits of fluff

from its eyes and trunk. When she pulled at a loose strand of wool, some of the stitching started to unravel. She patted it back into place and put the toy carefully in the rucksack.

She let the sleeping bag fall down to her waist and when she spoke it was more like the adult Lucy. 'That's what he told everyone. He didn't want me, you see, didn't let Mum register me. Didn't let anyone see me.'

Oh dear God. Another question that she knew the answer to already. 'What's your real name?'

'Mummy called me Maddie.'

Hannah pulled the journal from her back pocket. 'So this . . . this is yours.'

Lucy looked at it with something close to hatred. 'I don't want that.'

She must have ripped it up herself and Hannah could understand why.

'But, I don't get it. Why are you so sure Jack Roper loved me?'

'He told me,' she smiled. 'You were the good daughter, I was the bad.'

'How long have you known who I was?'

It was almost casual. 'Only since you told me Jack Roper was your father. Before that, when I realized everyone here was linked to the place, I . . . I wondered. I felt a connection to you, from the start, I guess.'

Hannah remembered feeling something like that too. 'But you didn't guess, even when I said my dad lived near here?'

'I had no way to guess. I never knew your first name, you see.' Her voice hardened. 'He – Jack – always called you just his daughter or his *princess*.'

Hannah's mind whirled. So many things still didn't add up. 'But . . . you're the same age as me, and Jack didn't leave my mum until I was four. It doesn't make sense.'

'I lied.' A tiny smile. 'When I ran away, I told everyone I

was five years older. I was only fifteen, but I said I was twenty.' The smile turned into a headshake as if she'd surprised herself. 'You're the only person I've told the truth apart from Damian. I was fifteen and that was five years ago, not ten, like you thought.'

That meant she was just twenty now, hardly more than a teenager, which explained why she looked so young, sometimes not much older than Chloe.

'But why did you come back here if you were so unhappy? Did you want to claim the house as yours?'

Lucy leaned against the damp wall, calmer now, almost resigned. She pulled something out of her pocket. 'Rob. I kept in touch with him. He sent me a note to say I had to come back.'

Now Hannah saw why Lucy had been so upset when Rob had died, why Chloe had heard her calling his name from the window. Little Maddie called him her friend in the journal, the only person from the outside world that she had ever known.

Hannah was kneeling and the damp from the floor began to seep through her trousers, but she barely noticed. She was thinking of that scribbled note.

She's been fed so DO NOT give her any more. Just some water. J.

She had assumed the words referred to a pet, but what if they were about the child that nobody even knew existed? The child who was warned never to go outside and never to tell anyone her name.

She looked around at the horrible cell and saw again the photos taped to the wall. Now she could see that the pale little child, dressed in a simple dress, could be Lucy as a seven year old. The woman looked equally wan and thin, fitting Sandeep's description of Lady Fallon. It must be Lucy and her mother.

She didn't want to look at the other photo, the one of the man in dark clothes, but she couldn't stop herself. His face blurred in a sunbeam that slanted across the room, as he stood in what could have been the hall of this house. Behind him a tiny figure – Maddie – the pale little girl people talked about. Huge eyes, a white face, she looked like something from another world.

Lucy was the shell Maddie must have built around herself to protect the neglected child inside. Saving herself when even her mother couldn't help her. Hannah remembered Ruby screaming at Jack after Hannah told her what he'd done, and she offered a silent thanks. But no one had been able to protect Maddie.

'Did you have to sleep down here?' she asked gently.

Lucy nodded. 'When I did something wrong, or when people came to the house. He always said they were bad people.' The hint of a smile. 'But I liked it better down here, away from him. Mum would come down when he went out and we'd go swimming.' She gestured towards the pool. 'Then I was happy. He didn't like the water. And sometimes when he was out, I'd sneak into the garden and see Rob.'

Rob had given no hint of knowing Maddie, when Hannah had first spoken to him, instead muttering about the pale little girl as if she were a ghost. He must have been trying to protect Lucy, trying to scare the guests away so they didn't find out about her.

Lucy said, 'Sometimes when *he* . . . when *he* was out, Mum let me go into the garden. Never when Rob was there, though. But if she wasn't watching me or when she was ill – my mum was always ill – I used to try and sneak outside to talk to him.'

Chapter Fifty-Three

Thirteen years ago
Maddie

In here there are no windows, but Maddie knows it's Tuesday because Mummy brought her baked beans on toast. That's what she always has on Tuesdays. Mummy whispered that it's OK to take her time: Daddy won't be home for a while. When he is home, Maddie must eat her dinner in half an hour. Then he looks at the plate, to make sure she hasn't wasted any food.

She always eats everything anyway, but it's nice to make it last today. Mummy sits on the sleeping bag with her while she eats and talks to her about the sea, about how big it is and how you can swim for miles and miles without ever reaching land. Maddie has seen the sea and beaches, but only in books. Mummy has brought a book from the library upstairs for her to look at today. Maddie used to go upstairs for lessons, but she was bad: she went to the window and saw the gardener.

Another day she sneaked out and talked to him. She did it a few more times after that too. But she's not allowed up there any more: she has to stay down here. It makes Mummy cry sometimes, but she says that one day they'll run away and go to the sea.

It's so nice cuddling up to Mummy, but suddenly the upstairs phone rings. It's probably *him*. And Maddie's plate is empty, so Mummy grabs it and leaves her alone. She hates it when Mummy goes, but at least she left the book.

When she gets into her sleeping bag to read it, she realizes that the door is open – Mummy has forgotten to bolt it.

Out of her room, hardly breathing, she creeps through the cellar and upstairs. The big door into the hall doesn't have a lock, so she comes out and without stopping she opens the front door and runs into the garden.

The sun is shining and it feels so warm on her skin. She looks down at her legs, all dirty from the floor in her room, and wishes she had a clean place to sleep.

But Rob is always dirty too, so it doesn't matter.

And she sees him and runs over. He smiles down at her. 'Hello, little un. Where'd you spring from?' They laugh because he always says that. It's a joke. Then he looks sad. He pulls at his beard and shakes his head. 'I'm sorry, darlin', I ate me lunch already.'

She's still hungry. She's always hungry. 'It's all right,' she says. 'I've had my dinner.'

He pokes around in his pocket and brings out something wrapped in silver foil. 'Don't suppose you want this then?'

As she stuffs the chocolate in her mouth, it starts to melt and she wants to cry. She loves it so much. Standing on tiptoe she looks into Rob's kind eyes. And, instead of crying, she jumps up and down forgetting herself and shouting, 'Thank you, Rob. Thank you!'

She isn't allowed to shout, but she feels so warm and fuzzy and Rob is laughing too as she runs around the garden.

Then they hear it, the sound of an engine. And Rob's face

looks suddenly very old. It's the Land Rover, the only vehicle that ever comes here. It's him.

She knows she should run back inside, but she can't move. She feels all strange and tingly, like she hasn't stood up for a whole day. And Rob puts his hand on her shoulder. The Land Rover comes fast now, kicking up a shower of stones, and pulls to a stop at the front door. He gets out.

'What the fuck?' He points his finger at them. 'Is going on here?' His face is bright red, like it always is when he's angry. Only even redder today, as if it might split open and let his anger pour out and burn them all. 'Did you hear what I said?'

She moves closer to Rob. Big and strong Rob might just be able to help her, even when Mummy can't.

But everything explodes in pain and darkness and the ground comes up to hit her face. All she can see is the dirt and his boots. Her face hurts and she knows she has to get up, has to run away. Then a boot moves and she curls up, knowing what's going to happen next. But at the last second the boot stops.

'No!' Rob shouts. 'Don't touch her. That's enough. Let her be.'

Blinking through tears and the grit in her eyes, she sees Rob holding Daddy's arm, saving her. And she gets up and runs to the outhouse. If she can hide right at the back, he might never find her. Then Rob will chase him away and she and Mummy will live happily ever after.

Heavy footsteps as she gets inside and shuts the door. Please let it be Rob.

'Get out of here now you little bitch.'

She knew it would be him, because no one can beat him. The door rattles and then flies open. His big fingers grab her arm so tight it feels as if they might break her in two.

He opens the back door and throws her into the kitchen,

leaving her bleeding there on the hard tiles. 'I'll deal with you later.'

She's so scared, but she needs to save Rob. She pulls a chair up to the window. Rob's out there, saying something, coming towards the back door. But then a flash of metal hits him and he flies back, landing on the floor by the log store. Her father stands over him, a spade in his hand. Rob tries to pull himself up, holding onto the shed. And then the sun glints off the spade again as it comes down fast. It hits his hand over and over until Rob's screaming is all Maddie can hear and Rob's lying on the floor.

Chapter Fifty-Four

Hannah swallowed and wiped a tear from the corner of her eye. 'And Sandeep found him like that. But who called the police?'

'My mum. She phoned them, then ran out and told Jack what she'd done. He hit her and said he was going to kill her. Then he leaned down and said something to Rob. My mum came in and wrapped me in a blanket and we all got in the Land Rover. I had to lie down in the back under the blanket as we drove away. And after what seemed like hours, we stopped and I looked outside. It was getting dark, but I could hear the sound of waves and seagulls nearby. We were in this deserted car park near the sea.

'That was the first time I saw the sea.' She smiled. 'I wanted so much to go closer, to walk on the beach, to swim.' A bitter laugh. 'But I couldn't even get out of the fucking Land Rover.

'We slept there all night. I cuddled up with Mum under the blanket and in the morning we went home. I thought he'd beat the shit out of me, but it didn't happen.' She paused for a moment. 'I think he was actually scared, for the first time in his life. But when Rob's hand was fixed, he just came back to his cottage as if nothing had happened. He had nowhere else to go and Jack let him stay as gardener. As a reward, I suppose, for keeping quiet. What happened to his hand was my fault, but he never blamed me. He always helped me, and now he's dead and that's my fault too.'

'I'm sorry.' Hannah reached for her again, but Lucy shuffled away. A shadow seemed to fall over her face and she looked at Hannah with a flash of something like hatred.

'Our father loved you,' she said, her voice harsh. 'Said you were like him, his perfect girl, but I wasn't. I was nothing.' She touched the photograph. 'He made me put this picture of you up on the wall. Do you know how many years of my life I've spent fucking staring at it? Trying to figure out why you were better than me?' Her chest heaved. 'But I kept taking it down, when he wasn't here, couldn't bear it. You were just so fucking perfect. You still are. And you told me you loved him.'

Hannah stayed silent. She wondered how much hate Lucy must have bottled up inside her and thought about what that sort of hate could make someone do.

Lucy rubbed away a tear with a dirty hand. 'He said he would have done the same to you too, if he hadn't loved you so much, been so proud of you. He told my mother she was a coward, but your mum was brave and strong. He never needed to beat her, *she* always did what she was told. It was Mum's fault he got angry, because she was so pathetic.'

'Why didn't she do something?'

Her eyes glinted with anger. 'She tried. Of course she fucking tried. But we were so isolated, she had no one to turn to. There used to be a proper driveway to the house, but he had Rob dig some of it up and let the rest go wild. His Land Rover was the only thing that could get close.'

Lucy stared out towards the pool. 'She called the police the day Rob nearly lost his hand, hoping they might get suspicious, and she rang them at other times too, but nothing happened. When Sandeep came into the house, *he* was always hiding in the other room, listening.'

'But why did she make those accusations against Sandeep, when he was trying to help?'

Lucy laughed. 'Why do you think? It was him. He made the complaint – the lord of the fucking manor – and of course everyone believed him. And when they came to interview Mum, there he was with a hand on her shoulder.'

She shook her head. 'You know what the worst thing is?' Her eyes bored into Hannah's, daring her to respond. 'He told me this – all of it – with my mum sitting there next to me. Making sure we both knew there was no hope. There was no way out. We belonged to him.'

She fell silent and they listened to the drip of a pipe somewhere in the darkness. Eventually Lucy sighed. 'But Mum did keep trying.'

'So what happened?'

Lucy stared at her, her expression blank. 'He kept his promise. He killed her.'

Chapter Fifty-Five

Ten years ago
Maddie

She hurts everywhere, but it's going to be all right. They're in the Land Rover, Mummy took it when he was asleep, and she's driving really fast. They're going to the hospital and the doctors will make it better. As long as Maddie doesn't say anything and only Mummy talks.

She's frightened as they pull up at the hospital, its car park full of cars, millions of cars. Inside there are so many people, more people than she's ever seen before. She didn't know they could all fit inside one building at the same time. Although she's in a little cubicle with Mummy, she can hear them all outside, their voices talking and shouting like a thousand arguments between Mummy and Daddy all happening at once.

The doctor is kind, but he looks sad and worried. He asks their names, but Mummy tells him the wrong ones. The doctor does some stitches and other things to make her feel better. He says he will get her a bed, because she has to stay here for a while.

But when he goes out, Mummy gets up to leave.

'Daddy will find us if we're not back by morning,' she says.

'Can't we stay here?' Maddie points at the mattress. 'He said I can sleep in a bed.' And Mummy starts to cry and puts Maddie's coat around her and they walk out.

A nurse asks if they're all right and Mummy says, 'Yes,' then whispers to Maddie to hurry. But they're not all right, not really. And when they get outside, she tells her to run and they run, with Mummy lifting her off her feet when she can't go fast enough.

As Mummy drives, she keeps looking over her shoulder. Maddie asks her again, very quietly, if she can stay in the lovely hospital. But Mummy says he will find them if they stay there and things will be worse.

When Mummy brings her food a few days later her face is all bruised, like Maddie's face sometimes is. That's never happened before to Mummy. He never hurts *her* face.

She's crying. 'Even though I gave a false name,' she says. 'Someone at the hospital must have recognized me and told the doctor. The doctor contacted social services and they called round this morning.'

A wild little hope. 'Are they going to help us?'

Mummy shakes her head, tears dripping onto Maddie's hands. 'I'm sorry, darling. He was there and made me say it wasn't me, it couldn't have been, because we don't have any children.'

Maddie touches Mummy's eye where it's all purple and red. Her finger comes away wet with tears. 'Can't we run away?'

Mummy shakes her head. 'I want to, I want to get you away from here, but it's impossible. I don't have any money and he'll never let the Land Rover keys out of his sight again.'

Maddie puts her arms around her, resting her head against

Mummy's poor face. 'I have to go now,' Mummy whispers, and she looks suddenly very serious. 'But I want to show you something first.' She gets up, goes to the door, and shows Maddie how to open the bolts to her room from the inside. 'Just in case,' she says. 'In case something happens.' And Maddie feels sick, like she's eaten all her food in one go, but she watches what to do. 'You can practise when I'm gone, but don't let him find out.'

Tonight Maddie is so hungry she can't sleep. Then she remembers what Mummy taught her about the bolts. It's the middle of the night so it will be safe. The doors out into the house are never locked, Mummy makes sure of that, in case there's a fire or something. So Maddie creeps out, across the cold, cold hallway and into the kitchen.

In one of the cupboards she finds an open packet of biscuits and stuffs one into her mouth. Then another, crumbs falling onto her T-shirt. Her hand shakes as it hovers over the packet. She can't, not another one, he might notice. There's an open loaf of sliced bread in the bread bin, so she takes a piece and bites into it.

A tiny laugh from the doorway, a sound she knows so well. Maddie feels like she's been slapped already, her face goes all funny and her hand shakes even more. She tries to swallow the mouthful, but can't get it down. Keeps chewing. He just stands there in his silky dressing gown, watching her, with a little smile on his face. She hates that smile.

There's nothing to do or say, it never does any good, she just has to hope it's over quickly.

He grabs her arm in one hand and her face in the other, squeezing her cheeks until she spits out the bread onto the floor.

'Leave her alone.' It's Mummy's voice. 'She's just hungry because she's growing. Let her go back downstairs.'

He doesn't answer, just pushes Maddie onto her knees. 'Pick it up,' he points at the piece of soggy bread. 'Eat it if you want it that badly.' When she does what he wants he slaps the back of her head. 'All of it, you filthy little—'

But Mummy pushes him out of the way. 'Maddie, go back downstairs now.' She can't move. 'Please, Maddie, just go,' Mummy says.

Then Maddie goes as quickly as she can, so she doesn't have to hear what happens next. She climbs into her sleeping bag and closes her ears, but the bangs and crashes seem to go on forever, even longer than usual. Until, finally, it's all quiet. Quieter than it's ever been before.

Chapter Fifty-Six

Lucy stopped, her face like stone. 'Later that day he came down and said she had fallen from an upstairs window. He was actually smiling when he told me, as if he couldn't wait to see what I would do, told me she was dead and they'd already taken her away, so I would never see her again. "Be careful," he said. "Or the same thing will happen to you."'

Something in her eyes made Hannah look away. 'So how did you escape?'

'Things got worse after that and I was hardly ever allowed out of this room. But I was only ten years old, so I didn't even think of trying to get out for years. I was used to it, you see, scared of the outside world. Whenever Jack was away I would see Rob in the garden. Sometimes he would bring me some decent food, or I would manage to steal some from the larder or the fridge. I would swim and try to remember my mother. But as I grew older, I got braver, and I knew I had to get out.'

Her hands fiddled with the hem of her top. 'Rob wanted to help me, but I wouldn't let him, not after what Jack did to his hand. And his little cottage was the only home he'd ever known. Jack used to say he would kill Rob, if I ever got away, and I believed him. He said he'd created evidence that proved it was Rob who killed my mother. Told Rob the same, that he would take the evidence to the police if Rob ever talked about what happened here.'

'Fucking hell.' It was all Hannah could say.

'I was terrified of the outside world,' Lucy went on. 'Kept thinking about all the bad people out there.' She laughed grimly. 'They seemed so real. But as I got older, I began to realize that everything I had been told was a lie. I knew Rob and the doctor and nurses at the hospital weren't bad, and the policeman had tried to help. There were good people in books as well.'

'What happened when you finally got away? Didn't he come after you? He could have killed you.'

A tiny sniff, a sharp movement of the eyes. 'I knew I had to make sure he couldn't do that.'

That must have been why she had changed her name. 'So did you come back when you found out he had died?' Hannah asked.

Lucy looked down and shook her head.

Hannah's hands felt suddenly sticky. 'Did you even know he was dead?'

'Oh yes, I knew.'

'So why return after all this time? I mean, even if the rest of us were fooled by the website, you must have recognized the place for what it was.'

Lucy reached into her pocket again and pulled out a crumpled piece of paper. She handed it to Hannah without a word. Hannah turned it over and looked at the barely legible note:

Deer Maddie. There doing up the house. You need to come bak and see bout your dad. Rob

Hannah rose to her knees and slowly moved back, desperately trying to convince herself she was imagining this – it couldn't be. 'What? What does he mean? *See* about your dad?'

Lucy sighed impatiently. 'Rob thought Preserve the Past was genuine. And he knew I needed to take care of things back here, before they did any more renovations.'

Take care of things.

Lucy smiled, but there was no warmth in it. Her fingers played with the hem of her top, back and forth, back and forth. The only sound was the drip of a pipe somewhere nearby. A cold hand reached into Hannah's heart and squeezed.

'Lucy,' she said, as she began to edge away towards the door. 'What did you do?'

A grim little smile. 'I killed him. I killed Jack Roper. I killed our father.'

Chapter Fifty-Seven

The room exploded into colour and movement, as Hannah found herself on her feet scrabbling at the door. She was already halfway through it before Lucy jumped up.

'Hannah, wait!' Lucy called.

Hannah stopped, ready to run if Lucy moved. 'You killed him!' She stood, shaking, her hand on the door. Desperate to get away, but desperate to make sense of it all.

She stared at Lucy. 'You killed my dad and then you killed all of the guests. I knew it – I knew it was you.'

Sandeep and Rosa would have been easy, and she remembered Lucy coming in windblown on the morning of the walk. That must have been when she attacked Rob, to stop him betraying her, to clean everything up this time. She had lured him to that grove of trees and knocked him into the ditch.

'You're not listening,' Lucy said. 'I didn't do it.' She took one step forward, but stopped and raised her hands when Hannah got ready to run through the door. Hannah was holding her breath, but Lucy's was loud in the silence. 'I only killed *him*,' she said. 'I had to. It was the only way out.'

Hannah kept a tight grip on the door, her hand slippery. 'Then why did you come back?'

'To get rid of evidence,' Lucy said.

'Couldn't Rob have done it for you? I mean, he was still here.'

'I left it to Rob the first time and . . .' She shook her head. 'I had to do it properly, get rid of it forever.'

A lump of lead had settled in Hannah's stomach. 'I don't understand.'

Lucy spoke in a low monotone and a smile crawled across her face. 'Rob gave me a hammer.' She seemed more in control now, more like the Lucy Hannah had met when she first arrived – what seemed like years ago now – but Hannah wasn't sure if that was a good thing or not. 'And I got out and hid in the kitchen behind the door. When Jack came in, I beat him over the head.' Another tiny smile.

Hannah inched backwards, millimetre by millimetre, hardly daring to breathe.

Lucy didn't seem to notice. 'But he looked so awful and I was so scared, I just sat there crying. After what seemed like hours, Rob found me and told me he would take care of the body. He said everything was going to be all right, that no one would ever know, that he deserved to die and that I wasn't to blame.' A deep shaky sigh. 'Then I ran to the road and hitched a lift to Dublin.'

She walked over to the wall and ran a finger over the picture of the little girl. 'And I wasn't Maddie any more – I was Lucy. When I got there, I had to live on the streets, begging for money. Damian found me and looked after me. We made music together and for the first time I was happy. My friends knew my age, knew I ran away from home and had no documentation. They looked after me.' She smiled. 'Eventually I told Damian some of it – about the way Jack Roper had treated me – and I couldn't believe it, but Damian said he still loved me.'

'So Rob buried Jack for you?'

'I thought he would, but when I sent him a letter from Dublin, asking if everything was all right, he wrote back and said he was too scared to take the body outside. The ground was so hard it could only be a shallow grave and there were too many walkers about.'

Her eyes flitted back towards the cellar and Hannah tried to swallow. *Oh God.*

'He thought it would be safer inside the house where he could keep watch over it.'

Hannah inched further away. 'The freezer?' She choked out the words, and Lucy nodded. 'So that was why,' Hannah said. 'That's why you stopped me checking that humming sound, why you tried so hard to keep us out of the cellar.'

But Lucy carried on as if she hadn't heard. 'Everyone thought Jack had gone abroad and the house still belonged to him.'

But something didn't make sense. 'And Preserve the Past?' Hannah spotted her torch on the floor by her foot.

A suspicious sideways glance. 'I knew nothing about that, until Rob contacted me. It must have been someone who found out Jack was dead and pretended to be his agent, to cash in maybe. It could have been Liam.' The blue eyes flashed at her. 'Or . . . it could have been you. After all, you were one of the only people who knew he was dead.'

Hannah stepped back. 'I don't believe you. I think you did it.' When Lucy didn't respond, she thought of something else. 'Or Declan O'Hare. It could have been him. He wrote to my mum to say Jack had died.'

Lucy's smile was almost a smirk. 'It wasn't him,' she said very softly.

'*You* . . . you wrote that letter?'

'I had to make sure his other family – the one he was always praising – didn't come looking for him. I knew about your mother's job. With Facebook and all the rest it wasn't difficult to find your address.'

'But you suggested I come to the house.'

'I couldn't resist.' Lucy smiled again and Hannah felt her body tense. 'I wanted to see this perfect daughter,' Lucy said. 'The daughter he always told me about. Just once.' A hard accusing look again. 'But you didn't come.'

'And what would you have done if I had? Would you have killed me too?'

Lucy laughed. 'I don't know.' A chill went through Hannah. 'Maybe I would have explained everything to you and we would have talked together.' Lucy took a step closer, speaking almost pleadingly. 'Talked like this. Like sisters.'

The light switch, on the wall only a foot away from Hannah. If she could just . . . But Lucy was muttering again, holding up the picture of little Hannah.

'I used to talk to you, every fucking night, tell you all my secrets. Ask you to come and help me.' Her mouth twisted. 'You should have come. Why didn't you come?'

A sick wave of fear washed over Hannah and with a jerk and a snap she reached out and hit the light, enveloping them in complete darkness. As she turned to run, she heard Lucy scream but didn't pause to find out why. Slamming the door behind her she shot the bolts home and stepped away from it. Listened, her blood roaring in her ears, but not a sound came from inside the room. Nothing.

For a moment she almost convinced herself that the room was empty, that the whole thing had been some warped nightmare. But then she heard a tiny sob coming from behind the door. Stepping back, her movements slow and quiet, she began to creep away. Hannah needed to find Chloe and get her out of here fast.

Moving as silently as she could along the pool, shining the torch in front of her, Hannah headed to the only section she hadn't checked. If Chloe wasn't there, she might be back in the cellar, or somewhere upstairs in the house.

The smell of chlorine made her stomach churn, but she forced herself to keep it together. The torchlight grew dimmer and dimmer, but she kept searching.

After what seemed like hours, she reached the tunnel entrance again. She'd done a full circuit and Chloe wasn't here. To be sure she gave one more flash of the torch around the whole pool. Her heart stopped as the beam faltered. It flickered on and then off again, buzzed, and then died. She stood in the pitch-black and fumbled out the batteries, felt their reassuring weight in her sticky hand. Switched them round and clicked them back into place, hit the switch and waited. But nothing happened. She shook the torch and tried again, her hands slippery with sweat, her heart thudding. All she could see was darkness and the only sound was her own harsh breathing.

Work, fucking work. She kept glancing towards Lucy's cell, but the light never came on. She thought about her sitting in there in the dark, in complete silence, about what it must be like to be Lucy. The child who didn't make it.

Another shake of the torch. 'Yes!' she whispered, as the light came on and she felt a rush of relief.

But then she heard a sound behind her, like a sharp intake of breath, and something hit her hard in the back.

She dropped the torch and stumbled to her knees. Thought about how close she was to the water, how green it had looked, how many dark shapes floated in it.

Something slamming into the back of her head, harder

this time, and she fell forward. Her mind registered for a split second the sensation of spiralling through darkness, and then she hit the water. Ice-cold water. And she was sinking – slowly and peacefully – down to the bottom.

Chapter Fifty-Eight

Her eyes opened wide and her head throbbed with pain. The torch must still be on, lying where she had dropped it, because there was enough light for her to see the water above her, clouded with bits of algae and leaves. And above that the dark ceiling. Her lungs were still, shocked into stillness. A thought – a thought that seemed like a revelation – came to her. If she didn't breathe, she would be fine down here, lying peacefully at the bottom of the pool.

But the need for oxygen gradually became unbearable and she began to choke and struggle. Kicking herself off the floor she reached up towards the light. And broke the surface, mouth wide, spitting water. Gulping air. A moment of blessed relief. *Thank you, thank you.*

But she sank again.

She couldn't swim.

Ben's words came to her: *It's easy, Hannah, nothing to be afraid of. Just relax and kick your legs.* She tried to stay calm, to move her limbs, and she came up to the surface again. Sucked in another breath. Maybe Ben was here with her now – at the end – maybe that's why she felt so peaceful, like she could float down and lie there on the bottom forever.

But as she went down again she remembered how she

came to be here. The smash into her back, someone throwing her in.

Her calm acceptance disappeared and in its place she felt cold terror. She thrashed the water, trying to keep above the surface. And heard something else above the splashes. Something that sounded like a laugh, a low cruel laugh.

Then a muffled splash from the other side of the pool and a wave of water hit her. She was no longer alone in the water. Someone else was in here with her, moving fast along the bottom. And she had a sudden flash of memory, of Lucy crouching in the cell telling her story. *Mummy showed me how to open the bolts from the inside.*

It was Lucy.

Hannah could feel her close by, a dark shape gliding towards her, and it was just like all those years ago with her father. She kicked out, her foot connecting with something soft. Then her hand struck what she hoped was a face and she gouged and scratched at it blindly.

As Lucy kicked off for the surface, Hannah clung to a piece of clothing and felt herself rise with her. Before Lucy could recover, Hannah lashed out again, hit her in the stomach and sent her back down under the water.

Grabbing the side of the pool she pulled herself along to the metal ladder. Reached out for it and hauled her body up, hand over hand, until she lay panting on the edge. The torch had gone out, shrouding the room in darkness, the only sound the frantic splashing of Lucy clawing her way to the side.

Water sloshed across the floor as Hannah staggered to her feet and ran. Slipped on the slimy tiles, smashed into the ground again and felt her arm shriek in pain.

Running again, along the edge of the pool and into the tunnel, the echo of her footsteps thundering after her in the dark. The stomach-churning smell of chlorine and mould followed her too, all the way along the tunnel. In the pitch-black she missed a bend and collided with the wall, her head throbbing, her wet clothes weighing her down.

Back through the cellar, up the stone steps and past the sterile room, her footsteps pounding against the floor. A few times she thought she caught the sound of panting behind her, of Lucy in pursuit, of another set of feet thumping into floorboards. Never far away, closing the distance fast. She smashed through the padlocked door and into the green corridor and then she stopped. Gasped for breath, leaned against the wall. What was that smell?

It was smoke. The smell of burning plastic and stone, bits of the house crumbling to ash. She carried on, her pace slower now, and when she entered the hallway she saw smoke billowing out of the corridors upstairs. Hot air hit her like a wall, despite her sodden clothes, and she felt her lungs begin to contract. With her top pulled over her mouth as a shield, she looked into the drawing room, just as the ceiling splintered and began to collapse in flames. The curtains had gone up, spreading heat and fire across the room and onto the floor above. Her eyes streamed and she coughed in great heaves. Chloe wasn't here, but on the floor lay an empty can of petrol – one of the cans she had seen in the storeroom.

Lucy had said she needed to get rid of the evidence, but why do it in the house rather than the cellar?

Unless she wanted to kill everyone left inside.

'Chloe!' She coughed again. 'Chloe!' She bent double and went to the kitchen, but was met by another even fiercer wave of heat. Her eyes stung and her vision began to cloud. She needed oxygen. 'Chloe! You have to get out!' Down the green corridor, something shifted. A shadow moved, someone walking towards her, and she turned to run. Then:

Hannah's trainers skidded on the marble floor of the hall

and she almost fell. Grabbed at the wooden rail that ran along the wall to steady herself. Had to keep on her feet, had to get out.

Running on again, she strained to see through drifts of smoke. Sweat trickled down her neck in the heat. Smashed paintings and blackened fragments of chandelier littered the floor. And the huge front door loomed at the end of the hall, smoke coiling around it in the gloom. She fumbled back the bolts, wrenched it open and took in a lungful of fresh air. Paused to listen for any sounds in the hallway behind her, any signs of life inside the house. Flames crackled and the building groaned as it began to crumble and fall apart in the heat.

Stepping outside, she pulled the door closed behind her. Leaned against it and took another gasp of clearer air. The storm had calmed, but rain was still beating down onto the empty hillside that sloped away before her into the night.

She went to the heavy garden bench beside the door, gripped the cold metal of an armrest and dragged it forward. Her muscles burned, the iron legs of the bench screeched against paving stones. Hands shaking, she turned to the electronic security pad beside the door and tried to key in the code to lock it. *Hurry up. Hurry up.* The sound of her heartbeat was loud in her ears.

Then she heard something else, a noise that cut through the howling wind. Footsteps inside the house. Hard shoes beating against marble floor, coming towards the door.

She turned and started to run.

Chapter Fifty-Nine

Five minutes later, Hannah was lying face down in the mud with her leg trapped in a trench of icy water. Dawn would be breaking soon and the worst of the storm was over. She had almost made it, but not quite. Because further up the hill, just below the burning house – coming ever closer – was someone walking towards her. Coming to kill her, she knew that now. She wanted only to lie in the mud and cry, but she had to keep trying.

She twisted her leg and pulled, but the mud only clutched tighter. Sobbing gently to herself she tried again, exhausted now, barely able to move. And then she stopped and stared back up the hill, to watch the walking figure, to meet her fate with at least a measure of calm. Lucy must be closer now, poor damaged Lucy – a girl with whom Hannah could have shared a lifetime, a sister she could have grown to love – reduced to a killer with only one victim left on her list: Hannah.

Looking up at the house she saw the flames were no higher than earlier. Perhaps the rain had dampened them down, perhaps Lucy's plan was going to fail and some of the house would survive. That freezer and its contents might still be there when the police arrived. And she had to hope that, whatever she had done, Lucy would survive too.

But . . .

That walking shadow was too tall to be Lucy, too broad and heavily built.

It was a man and with a huge surge of relief she realized it must be Mo. Not dead but here with the police to carry her home.

But the man wasn't wearing Mo's clothes; he was dressed all in black, wrapped in threadbare winter clothes. As he reached the nearest cluster of trees, he stopped and Hannah finally saw his face. It was Rob.

He had survived somehow, crawled back to his cottage and then come to help them. Maybe Lucy hadn't hit him hard enough because deep down she loved him, and here he was. The police would be here soon and they might be able to find Chloe.

He reached the top of the trench and peered down at her, his grey hair moving in the wind. 'Stay put!' he called. 'I'll come down.'

He shuffled across the muddy slope, his back hunched, and dropped down beside Hannah. He sat there panting, one hand on his chest, the other resting on his knee.

'Thank God, you're alive. What happened?' Hannah asked. 'I thought you were dead.'

'I survived.' His voice quiet.

'Well you need to help. My leg, it's trapped. Here, take my hand.' Hannah held it up to him.

But Rob didn't take it.

'Pull me out!' She was shouting at him now. 'We need to get help.'

'But I want to talk to you, Hannah.' It was less his words than the way he spoke that made her pause. No longer the

283

monosyllabic communication she was used to with Rob. And he had never before used her name.

Her stomach jolted. Her vision fixed on one point, and the whole world shrank until that was all she could see:

Rob's hand. The hand that rested on his knee; the hand that was stretched out as strong and undamaged as the other one.

This wasn't Rob.

'Who are you?'

The man didn't respond. He got up and stretched with a yawn, as if suddenly very bored. He stood tall, the hunch no longer visible. Then he smiled down at her, a twisted smile that was at once strange but familiar, like meeting a distant relative for the first time and seeing some version of yourself reflected in them. It was her father – Jack Roper.

'So you've finally realized. Well hello, Hannah.' He smiled down at her. 'Hello, princess.'

She struggled to crawl away from him, to free her leg.

He came closer. 'You can't leave yet, princess. The fun's just getting started.'

Chapter Sixty

A searing pain in her skull, a throbbing just above her temple. When she moved her head a fraction the throb became unbearable. She tried to shout, but the only sound was a muffled *mghhhhhh*. She tasted rough cloth against her lips, her mouth was gagged, her hands bound to a bench behind her back.

She was in Lucy's cell. The light from the bare bulb above her head illuminated Rob – or the man she'd thought was Rob – standing in the doorway, his hands in his pockets. He had knocked her unconscious, then carried her back to the cellar. Back to this nightmare.

He looked down at her. 'Wakey, wakey,' he said.

After a moment he knelt and pulled down her gag. She gasped for air, spitting out foul-tasting saliva, and he smiled.

'What do you want?' Hannah eventually said. 'Why are you doing this?' His bright eyes stared down at her, full of intelligence.

'It's a long story,' he said. His hand reached to touch a lock of her hair.

She flinched away. 'Get off me! Get the fuck off me!' But when he stood up again and went to the door, Hannah called out. 'Wait! Where's Maddie?'

'Maddie?' He looked back at her. 'What a disappointment she was after you. So weak, so pathetic, just like her mother. Look around you, I mean this was her fucking bedroom. It's disgusting. In fact I was never sure she actually *was* my child. She was like the runt of a litter, you know. Not worth keeping but hardly worth killing either.'

Hannah could smell smoke, but it was only faint. How long had she been unconscious? She needed to keep him talking.

'You're so wrong about her. Maddie managed to get away from here – when she was only fifteen – and you couldn't even find her. She made a career for herself, out of nothing. Or didn't you know?'

'Of course I did.' He laughed. 'I've been watching her for years. But, my darling, you wouldn't have made the mistakes she did. You wouldn't have trusted poor old Rob here for a start.' He patted his chest and laughed again, an awful sound that echoed off the walls. 'Can you believe she used to write to Rob from Dublin?'

'What did you do to him?'

He walked back into the room and leaned against the wall in front of her. 'They were both fucking useless. She couldn't kill me, could barely even knock me out. When I woke up she was gone and Rob was trying to decide what to do with my body.' His eyes glittered under the light of the bulb. 'He must have had a nasty surprise. I used the same hammer she'd used on me, but a lot more effectively. I made sure he was dead.'

Hannah looked away and thought about poor Rob, a man who had done so much for Maddie.

'Maddie thought Rob would tidy everything up for her – bury me – and that would be the end of it. But I needed her to come back home eventually, so I came up with a plan. I wrote to her and told her I'd cut up the body and stored it in the freezer.' He grinned at Hannah. 'Of course I didn't say which body.

'There was no way I was going to bury it. That body was my way of getting her back, having her all to myself again – I knew she couldn't let it get discovered. It was a kind of insurance policy, you know, because as far as she was concerned it was proof she murdered her dad. But I missed her, that's the truth, I missed Maddie and I was angry with her for running away.'

The soft way that he spoke – so warm and comforting – brought Hannah back to those long-ago days in her bedroom. She shivered.

'That's why I brought *her* back,' he said. 'But aren't you dying to know why you're here too?'

She swallowed but didn't respond. 'Of course you are,' he grinned. 'Well, apart from wanting to see my little princess again, I thought you just had to be part of this little gathering. You see, you all have something very special in common.'

'What? What do we have in common?'

'You pissed me off.' He laughed again. 'That fucking policeman, hanging around all the time, trying to make people suspicious of me.'

'His name was Sandeep and he was just doing his job.'

He cocked his head at her. 'Took to the old bastard, did you? Well I sorted him out. Got him off my back and out of the job without much trouble, but there always seemed to be some other do-gooder popping up.'

Hannah flinched as he touched her face, running his finger down her cheek and cupping her chin. 'You all tried to ruin things for me. Although you, Hannah my darling, you have the unique distinction of being the only one who managed to do so.'

There was not a trace of *Rob* left now and the voice was the one she remembered only too well.

'And you've met your sister. I have to say it was great fun watching the two of you just now. You really thought she killed all the others?'

He straightened and pointed at the photo of Maddie on the wall. 'You thought *she* tried to drown you in the pool?' A chuckle. 'She tried to *save* you. It's a good thing she's a strong swimmer, or you might have finished each other off. And that would have been a great shame.'

Hannah began to shake with a chill that reached all the way into her bones. She tried to move, to work her hands free from the bench, but the rope had been tied too tight by too practised a hand. He talked continually, his words spilling out of him as if the days as Rob had built up a torrent of language.

He touched the picture that showed The Guesthouse in the background. 'I've always hated this house. I thought about setting fire to it for years. Then I had a better idea, the perfect way to do it: a group of Cloud BNB guests ignoring all the warnings and throwing petrol on the fire when the generator failed.'

Hannah watched him walk back and forth across the cell. How could she have been so stupid? There was no possible reason for Lucy to do any of this, to kill those who had tried to help her. But she needed to keep him talking, give herself enough time to plan her escape.

'But why Liam? How did he piss you off? I thought he helped cover up what you did to Rob?'

'Haven't you worked that one out? I have to admit he helped with the Rob incident. Just needed a quiet word with the right person to get him to back down on that one. Sadly for poor old Liam, he was also the doctor who saw Maddie at the hospital and that was a bit too much for his tender, sentimental heart. He had the nerve to alert the child protection people. Just a nuisance, but it annoyed me. So I decided to ruin his precious career, get him struck off the medical register.'

'But how? How did you do it?'

'The gradual drip, drip of anonymous complaints and allegations. More words in the right ears. In the end they had no choice but to fire him. Then I watched his life collapse more disastrously than I could ever have hoped.'

He laughed. 'You know, watching was the best bit. Watching you the whole time in this house. It was my own personal experiment. I made sure you weren't getting enough sleep, made sure you couldn't escape.' His voice grew louder. 'And then I left a trail for you to follow that turned you all against each other.'

'But why go to all that trouble? Why not just light a fire on the first night and get rid of us?'

He stopped pacing and smiled down at her. 'Now where would be the fun in that? No, I didn't just want to kill you, I wanted to own you. And, I wanted you to know I was doing it.'

Hannah tried to swallow but her throat was too dry. 'What about the others? The ones who didn't even know you?'

'The families? Call that guilt by association. Or a bonus for me. And they didn't have to come. I sent the offer to the policeman, not his son. Hardly my fault if the lad couldn't resist a cheap holiday.'

'You're insane. You're fucking insane.' She struggled against the rope for a moment, and then fell still.

He just chuckled and turned back to the photos. 'I'm not insane, I just like to live freely.' He carried on, the sound of his voice echoing in the silence. 'I decided not to plan anything too rigidly, so even I didn't know how it would all pan out. That's the best thing about experiments, you never know what might happen. What you can use. When that annoying little cat started hanging around the place a few weeks back

I thought of bashing its head in there and then. But I left it in case it came in handy later. And it did.

'Rob's little accident on the hill is another example. I watched you all from the trees and it suddenly came to me – like an epiphany – a way to stage his death. And it worked out better than I could ever have imagined.'

'So you made Liam tell us Rob had died. Then forced him back into the house and killed him there.'

'It wasn't difficult,' he chuckled. 'But it was a long road with Liam, you see, I had to ruin his career just to get him here.' He laughed. 'And even that wasn't enough.'

As he stood there by the wall, something about his shape and size sent a memory flickering into Hannah's mind. A tall shadow standing in the storm by the outhouse, wrestling with the door.

'I saw you!' Hannah said. 'When I went out in the storm.'

Jack laughed. 'You almost caught me, but you always were clever. A chip off the old block.'

'But what were you—'

A sound cut Hannah off. The sound of something collapsing in the house above them. He went to the door and looked out. 'Not long now, princess, not long now. The flames will be here soon, so it's about time we lit the final fire.' He rubbed his hands together. Relishing the moment.

Hannah closed her eyes and remembered those words from another time. A little girl with her daddy on the way to the circus. *Not long now, princess, not long now.* And she had screamed with delight when he had lifted her up and tossed her into the air. 'Higher, Daddy, higher,' she had said, and he had laughed. But there was no laughter in his voice now.

'Time to go,' he said. 'Time to find your sister.'

He untied her from the bench, but kept her hands bound together. Dragged her out towards the swimming pool, a torch in one hand, and led her towards the tunnel. She limped behind him, her head thumping with pain. No fight left in her.

She could only guess what he was planning. Perhaps he needed her and Lucy in the same room, to make it look like they started the fire. There was no point in trying to get away. He was much stronger and she was exhausted and injured. *Later*, she told herself. She would fight back later.

As they entered the tunnel, the smell of smoke grew stronger, blending with the stink of chlorine and algae. His torch played across the slimy walls as he dragged her along, closer and closer to the fire. All those doors between here and the drawing room would protect this area, but only for a while.

And Chloe. Where was Chloe? And what had he done with Mo?

She made a sudden lurch forward, but he grabbed her waist and lifted her off her feet, threw her against the wall. The air punched out of her and she collapsed on the floor. Gasped in a breath. Tried again to kick out at him, but he just laughed and tightened his grip.

'That's my girl, always a fighter.'

As he lifted her to her feet, she snapped back her head and felt it connect with his face. A yell of anger and he spun her round. The back of his hand cracked against her cheek and her face whipped to the side. Then he frogmarched her forward. She screamed out in pain and frustration, hating him more than she thought possible.

Along the tunnel they went, her dragging back, him jerking her forward. She heard a rhythmic thumping sound as they passed the shower room and he laughed. Leaned close to the door and shouted, 'Not long now, Maddie.'

They went up the final passage and into the cellar. A dim

light flickered from the ceiling, a hanging bulb casting shadows in the gloom. He threw her onto the stone floor and disappeared back down the tunnel to get Lucy from the shower room.

As she lay there staring up at the steps, she saw smoke creep in under the door above them. It pooled across the ceiling, growing by the second. She had to escape. Her feet thudded on the steps as she charged to the top and slammed into the door. Pushed at the handle, but nothing happened. Of course it was locked.

Back at the bottom of the steps, she collapsed against the wall, fighting the tears, and watched him drag Lucy through the door and throw her to the floor. She crawled across to Hannah and their eyes met.

'I'm so sorry,' Hannah whispered, and Lucy squeezed her arm.

'Well, isn't this lovely?' Jack spoke in the soft, kind voice she hated so much. 'The whole family back together.'

They watched him walk away from them and open the freezer, throw bags of frozen food to the floor and reach inside. Lucy started to shake.

'I have something for you, Maddie.' He pulled out a small package, held it up to the light, and then tossed it to Lucy. 'Don't say I never give you anything.'

Lucy caught it, sobbed, then let it drop to the floor.

It was a hand, a frozen human hand curled almost into a fist, a hand with two fingers missing:

Rob's hand.

Chapter Sixty-One

Hannah tried not to breathe, tried not to look at the brown lump on the floor. Lucy was trembling and Hannah pressed her shoulder against her, trying to give her strength, to give herself strength.

Jack strode towards them, his face in shadow, and took something from inside his coat. It glinted under the light, a flash of thin metal. A scalpel. She thought about the scalpels she had found beside Rosa and Liam, imagined her own body being butchered in a corner somewhere.

Jack stepped closer, flipped the blade up and down in his hand, pointed it at them. 'Look at you. You're both pathetic.'

He stared at the lump of frozen meat on the floor and his lips curved. 'What is it they say about revenge being best served cold?' As the grin spread over his face, Hannah surprised herself by noticing that he was still handsome.

'I've enjoyed writing to you, Maddie.' He pointed the blade at her. 'Keeping in touch. But it couldn't go on forever: you were doing too well for yourself, you might have got right away and never come back. I *had* to have you back.' His eyes drifted to Hannah. 'Both of you.'

Still watching them, he reached behind one of the plastic

boxes and pulled out a can of petrol. Hannah felt her chest begin to heave.

He looked up at the smoke gathering along the ceiling and checked his watch. 'We need to light the final fire, to speed things along a little. It's been so lovely spending time with my girls I almost forgot the time.'

He moved towards them, unscrewing the lid of the can, sloshing petrol across the floor.

'They'll know you set the fire, they'll know it was you,' yelled Hannah.

He laughed, carried on pouring, soaking the piles of junk in the alcove. 'They won't, because I'm Henry Laughton and I'm miles away from here, with a solid alibi.' He tipped petrol into the freezer. 'It's not my fault a mad woman murdered a group of innocent strangers and then killed herself in the fire.'

Lucy had stopped shaking. She stood up and Hannah noticed her hands weren't tied. Perhaps Jack thought she wouldn't put up a fight.

'You're wrong,' she said. 'No one will believe it was me.' Her voice was calmer now.

As he swung round to face her, some of the petrol spilled onto the floor. 'Well, look at little Maddie all grown up.' He shook his head. 'Oh, they'll believe me all right.'

He glanced over at the computer room, and Hannah felt a flicker of hope. If he went in there, they had a chance. But his eyes narrowed, as if he'd read her thoughts, and he moved forward to grab her. Yanked her to her feet.

One muscled arm across her chest, one hand at her throat – the blade touching her skin – he shuffled them into the computer room, keeping an eye on Lucy.

'Stay there,' he said. 'We won't be long.'

His touch felt delicate, but it would take just one move-ment, one slash, to kill her. Inside the stink of rotting meat was overwhelming. Flies buzzed around the blanket that hid Liam's decomposing body.

Around the room they shuffled in what felt like a ghastly dance, him splashing petrol and her trying to wiggle the rope around her hands loose. She flinched when he showered liquid over the hump that had been Liam and her stomach churned as the smell of petrol mixed with rotten meat. The blade nicked her throat and she froze. Forced her body close to his, forced her mind away from the memories the closeness threatened to bring back.

In the cellar, Lucy hadn't moved. He let Hannah go and she took in a shaky breath, went to Lucy's side. Her hands were still bound, but she could feel the knot loosening.

As he put the petrol can down, Lucy spoke, her voice strong. 'I thought you loved Hannah. You don't want to hurt her.'

For a moment he looked at her with an expression that might have been pity. 'Did I tell you that? Granted, she's superior to you in every way.' Another grin. 'But she's to blame for the whole thing, you know. If she'd behaved like a proper daughter, none of this would have happened. And you never know, you might be lucky, they might even blame all this on her instead.'

He kicked the half-empty can across the floor and wiped his hands on his filthy coat. Looked around slowly – satisfied – getting ready to set the fire.

'Everyone knows poor Hannah's been off her rocker since Ben's accident.' That horrible grin. 'That was a lucky break. But then, you make your own luck, don't you?'

'You! You killed Ben?' Hannah screamed. If only she could get to him; to hurt him the way he hurt people.

His tone didn't change. 'Like I said on Facebook, I think he wanted to die. When the opportunity presented itself to make his dream come true, I took it. Even turned off the lights on his bike afterwards.'

Hannah couldn't speak, but Lucy stepped forward. 'That crying we heard,' she said. 'It was me, wasn't it?'

'Ah, clever girl, you recognized yourself. I hoped you would. That was another brainwave. You see, I recorded it all those years ago – a video of you crying in the cell and your mother bringing you food. I kept it, in case I ever needed to prove she was responsible for keeping you imprisoned. Just another piece of evidence to make her toe the line. But it turned out to be perfect for my little experiment.'

'You bastard!' Lucy shouted. 'You pathetic bastard.' And that did get to him. He moved towards her, his hand flexing on the scalpel.

Hannah struggled again with her hands, the knot getting looser and looser. Just a few more seconds. 'My mother used to tell me all about you, about how needy you were.' It was a lie, but it got his attention.

As he turned to her, the blade raised, she shot a quick glance at Lucy. Urging her to do something. A moment's hesitation, a lifetime of fear flickering across her face, and then Lucy moved. Leapt forward and hit the light switch, throwing the room into darkness.

Hannah dived to the ground, but she wasn't fast enough. Jack rushed forward and she heard the slash of a blade. A jagged pain exploded in her leg and she screamed. Rolled away, clutched at her thigh, felt warm blood against her palm. She bit her tongue and held her breath. Listened to Jack swear and grope around on the floor for her.

'Where are you? Come here you little bitch.'

She shifted away quietly and half-crawled, half-limped to the side of the room. He stopped and stood still, listening. Silence. Then Lucy made a rustling sound at the side of the room.

He charged towards it, and Hannah threw out a foot, sending him sprawling to the ground. His head cracked against concrete, and Lucy was on him. She screamed and hit him repeatedly. Hannah heard his head bashing against the floor, the sound like a drum in the dark. Silence once more.

She heard Lucy get up and walk across the room. Then the slosh of liquid as she picked up the can of petrol. As her eyes adjusted to the gloom Hannah watched Lucy stand over Jack. Heard the gurgle of liquid being poured across his body. Then she raised her foot for one final kick and a stamp.

After that the only sounds were Hannah's gasps and the drip of petrol. Then a crash from upstairs and the door burst open, letting in a rush of heat and light. Clouds of smoke billowed in.

'Hannah, come on,' Lucy said. 'We've got to go.'

They clung to each other for a second then headed into the tunnel. Hannah could barely walk, had to cling onto Lucy. Blood dripped from her soaking jeans, her vision blurred. But Lucy paused at the door to look back at the body lying in a pool of petrol on the floor. Flames reached the door at the top of the stairs and with a whoosh they hit the petrol vapours and leapt down into the cellar. In seconds the whole room was ablaze.

Lucy paused to watch Jack's body go up, and then they hobbled away, a wall of heat chasing them. They groped along the tunnel, choking for air. Daggers of pain cut through Hannah every time she put down her foot. Past the shower room they staggered, along the little tunnel and then the side of the pool. It seemed like miles.

Thank God. The door at the end was unlocked. They burst through it and up the steps into the garden. Into the brightening dawn. Hannah blinked back tears and her head whirled.

At the garden gates, they stopped and stared at the house. The top half was smouldering now, but she could see the fire taking hold in the cellar. Great waves of heat rolled off the building. It looked as if most of the house would survive, the rain would make sure of that. Perhaps Jack had figured that he didn't need to destroy it completely, so long as the murders could be blamed on one of them.

'It's all right,' Lucy shouted, and for the first time she looked really happy. 'He's dead. The bastard's dead.' And through the haze of pain, Hannah smiled too.

They staggered along the slope, but Hannah kept stopping. Her shoe sticky and wet with blood, her strength fading.

Lucy slowly lowered her to the ground. 'I should run for help.'

Hannah's vision blurred. 'Maddie,' she said. 'Don't go yet.'

Lucy gave her a tiny, very sweet, smile. 'It's Lucy, your sister Lucy.' She pointed at the house. 'I left Maddie back there. She's gone.'

Then the world started to fade and Hannah's eyes closed. Something warm wrapped around her. 'I'll be back soon,' Lucy whispered.

And as the world turned black, Hannah felt something touch the top of her head. She thought it was a kiss.

Chapter Sixty-Two

No pain, just warmth and the need to go back into the darkness.

A hand touched hers. 'Hello, love, it's Mum.'

Hannah forced her heavy eyelids open and the world blurred. She couldn't speak.

'It's all right, I'm here,' Ruby smiled down at her. 'You hurt your leg, remember. You hit your head and you got too cold.'

Memories flickered across her mind: bumping along in an ambulance, a hospital full of staring faces and probing hands. And pain, lots of pain.

She tried to sit up but fell back against the pillow. Her sore eyes took in the little room, a space she vaguely remembered. Tears began to fall as she stared at Ruby. Her mother leaned over and dabbed at her cheeks with a tissue.

'Thank you,' Hannah whispered. 'I'm sorry.'

'It's all right, you're going to be all right now.'

The memories hit her like a blow. The Guesthouse, the fire. *Jack Roper*. She took deep breaths and tried to struggle up again.

'Hannah.' Her mother touched her shoulder. 'It's OK, calm down.'

'Jack.' She wasn't sure if she'd said the name or just thought it.

Her mother's hand tightened on hers. 'He's gone, love. He's dead.'

Hannah shook her head and wiped away a tear. 'He was a monster.'

'I'm so sorry. Sorry I wasn't honest with you. I should have told you the truth, but I didn't want you to remember it.'

'You saved me.' Hannah looked at her mother.

Ruby brushed a hand against Hannah's cheek. 'I should have done more. He used to write to me, telephone me, beg us to come back. To let him see you. That was one of the reasons we kept moving, why you had to go to all those different schools. Why you had trouble making friends.'

'It wasn't your fault.' Hannah tried to smile at her.

'For a while it all stopped. He sent me a letter saying he had remarried and wouldn't be bothering us any more. But another letter came about five years ago.' She looked away. 'It said he would make us pay for ruining his life. But then I heard he had died, and I was so relieved. Should have told you everything then.'

They sat together in the little room holding hands. Three names swirled through Hannah's mind: Lucy, Chloe, Mo. But she was too afraid to ask if they were alive. Just for now she would let herself rest.

When a doctor came to check on her, Ruby stepped outside. He asked how she was feeling and she managed to nod.

'You're going to be fine,' he said. 'We stitched up your leg, but you lost a lot of blood. You had concussion when you came in, but otherwise you'll be back to normal soon. The police want to talk to you, but I'll hold them off until you're ready.'

After he had gone, she slept again, but dreamed of the swimming pool and the rooms under The Guesthouse, dreamed of a little girl still lost down there crying in the dark.

When she woke her mum was with her again. 'It's all right, you're safe,' she said, helping Hannah swallow some water. 'Lori will be in to see you later on.'

This time Hannah had to ask. 'Lucy?' The word came out as a whisper.

Ruby's hand gripped hers, and she suddenly wanted to forget it all. Go back into that wonderful dreamless sleep again. But, no. 'Please, Mum.'

Her mother said, 'Lucy is here. In the hospital.'

She couldn't breathe. 'But she wasn't hurt. She wasn't hurt, was she?'

It was almost too soft for her to hear. 'She's in a psychiatric ward.' Hannah went to speak, to say Lucy was fine, but Ruby held up her hand to stop her. 'The doctors say she's doing very well, but it will take some time.'

Hannah could tell that wasn't all. 'Mum?'

'Well, she's under police guard too. They still don't know what happened, how those people were killed. You've been out of it and there's no one else who can tell them.'

No one else. Oh God. The names burst out then. 'But Chloe and Mo?'

'After she left you, Lucy ran to get help, but didn't have to go far. The emergency services were already coming up the hill.' Hannah heard the door open. 'And look who was bringing them,' Ruby said.

Mo stood there smiling and smiling. 'Did you think you'd got rid of me?' He took a seat beside her bed and she reached for his hand. She looked from him to Ruby. 'Chloe?'

Very gently her mother said, 'Chloe hid in the outhouse.'

Cold fingers probing her heart, as she remembered that figure standing by the door of the little shed. So that's why he was trying to get in there.

'I called her, but she didn't answer. I tried to find her.' No one spoke and Hannah closed her eyes.

Then Mo gave her hand a little shake. And when she looked again, he was beaming at her. 'And here she is at last,' he said.

Chloe ran into the room and thumped against the bed. 'Careful,' Ruby said. 'Gently now.'

Hannah held her for a moment, feeling the tears well up. Chloe looked different, her eyes darker and her face thinner. There was a tightness around her lips that Hannah knew would be there forever.

'I'm so, so sorry about your parents,' Hannah said.

Chloe smiled, a brave smile. 'I'll be all right. I'm staying with my best friend's family. Going to live with them in Ireland until I finish school.' Her eyes glistened but she didn't cry.

'I called and called for you,' Hannah said weakly. 'Did you hear me?'

Chloe nodded. 'I didn't trust you. Mum . . .' Her chest rose. 'My mum said it might be you.'

Hannah squeezed her hand. 'It could have been anyone.' As Chloe went to speak she squeezed again. 'No need to talk about it now.'

Hannah looked from her to Mo and back again. 'What about Lucy? Did you tell the police it wasn't her?'

Mo said, 'Apparently my evidence doesn't count. I left there too soon. I'll never forgive myself for leaving you in danger because I was in such a state about Dad.' He bit his lip, then went on, 'I was sure she had nothing to do with it, but they need to talk to you.'

'I tried too,' Chloe burst out. 'But they wouldn't listen.'

Hannah could smile properly now. 'Well they'll have to listen to me. I was there.' She turned to her mother. 'And, after all, I have to protect my little sister.'

Ruby nodded and smiled back at her. 'And Lucy has already told them what Jack said about Ben. That he had lights on his bike and that Jack killed him.' She looked long and hard into Hannah's eyes. 'His family knows he didn't want to die, and I've spoken to them. They're very glad about that, and his mother says you can come to see them when you're better.'

It wouldn't be easy and it didn't make her any less guilty, but Hannah knew it would help.

Ruby kissed her forehead and went to the door. 'I'm going to have a break. You have some time with your friends.'

'Please,' Hannah said. 'Tell the doctor I want to see the police.'

When Ruby was gone, they sat there in silence for a long time, holding hands.

Epilogue

Two years later

As green mile after green mile sped by Hannah stared at the thick red neck of the taxi driver in front of her, wondering if he was the same one as last time. Two years ago, but seeming like twenty.

She felt sick. Had felt sick even before the plane took off from Heathrow. And when she saw the first signpost for Fallon village she almost screamed at the driver to turn around and go back. Instead she closed her eyes and tried not to think. But that was impossible.

When she'd woken up in hospital after the horrors at The Guesthouse she'd imagined that was the end of it. But as her body got better, so much else got worse. Sure, she'd made some kind of peace with Ben's family, and her friend Lori was there, as well as her mum, but the people she most needed were those who'd been through it all with her. The only ones who could truly understand. And as the weeks went by they had gradually faded from her life.

At the inquests only Hannah and Mo had been present. Chloe was allowed to give written evidence and Lucy was still in the psychiatric ward, not even able to talk.

At least the police had soon discovered how Jack Roper had set up the fake charity, Preserve the Past, and how he'd kept track of Hannah, Sandeep, and Liam over the years. And what they'd found matched Hannah and Mo's evidence and the statement Lucy had managed to give before she broke down. So Lucy was cleared of blame for any of the deaths, including those of Jack Roper and Rob the gardener.

Mo had visited Hannah every day in hospital, but after the inquests he said it was too painful to keep seeing her. He needed time alone to focus on forgiving himself for his dad's death.

Chloe had stayed in Ireland and Hannah had tried to keep in touch with her through WhatsApp and Skype, but for months Chloe hardly responded. Only recently had she begun to open up, admitting how hard she had found things. Now she seemed much better and said she was longing to see Hannah.

But Lucy. Poor Lucy. She'd spent over six months in a psychiatric unit. Hannah had gone over to Ireland twice to see her, meeting Lucy's boyfriend, Damian, who was always there and who said her visits helped. 'She knows you've been here and she knows you're her sister.' Hannah wasn't sure. Lucy never reacted to her presence, staring out of a window, but seeming to see nothing. Her doctor said what happened at The Guesthouse had forced her to confront the years of abuse and her mind was struggling to cope.

Hannah only learned Lucy had been released when she'd had a message from Damian, to say she was slowly recovering and that she'd be in touch when she felt up to meeting people.

Then nothing – until now.

Hannah came back to herself when she spotted a signpost for Fallon ten miles away. Mo, sitting beside her in the taxi, squeezed her hand. 'I still don't think this is a good idea.' His voice was croaky. 'What's the point?'

She could only shrug, too tense even to speak. But she squeezed back. They'd met up for the first time in ages a couple of months ago and, very cautiously, seemed to be moving into something that might turn into a real relationship.

Sunlight so bright it hurt Hannah's eyes flashed through the taxi window, turning the fields around them a luminous green; the strip of sea in the distance a vibrant blue. As if to mock them it was a beautiful day – summer edging into a glorious autumn.

She sat up when she saw what must be the layby she remembered and Mo reached for the door handle.

But instead of stopping at the layby the taxi drove on, took a sharp left turn and headed down a newly metalled lane that wound through the fields. Mo turned to look at her. He hadn't been expecting this either.

And as they crested the brow of the hill it was there.

Not The Guesthouse of course. The ruins of that were completely gone. But the iron gates with the gardens behind them and in the hollow, where the old house had stood for centuries, a new building.

It was very modern, with lots of glass, yet looking surprisingly at home in the landscape. As the taxi passed through the gates, slowed and stopped, the white front door opened and Lucy stood there, smiling.

Hannah couldn't move. Couldn't believe what she was seeing. When Lucy had asked them to come here today she'd explained that her psychiatrist had suggested she return to the site of The Guesthouse to exorcise her demons. Hannah had imagined she wanted them there to support her during a quick visit. This was different. Lucy must have started coming months ago. But why would she choose to rebuild on this spot?

The taxi driver turned to them with a smile. 'Here you are. Nice job they've made of it, haven't they?'

Hannah's legs were shaking as she stepped down and she was grateful for Lucy's arms coming round her. Holding tight, as if she guessed Hannah needed support, Lucy whispered, 'Hello, sis. It's been too long.'

When Lucy stepped away to embrace Mo, Hannah was able to look properly at her. Her hair was longer and slightly more golden than before, but she was as beautiful as she'd ever been. Nothing like the drained husk Hannah had seen staring at the wall in the hospital.

And then the whirlwind that was Chloe burst through the door, kissing Hannah hard on the cheek before rushing past to do the same to Mo. 'Come in. Come in and see this place. It's wonderful. Lucy has her own recording studio.'

Chloe, at sixteen, was a tall and pretty young woman, but her giggles were still those of a little girl. She dragged Mo inside as Lucy put her arm around Hannah's waist, holding her back. 'Damian told me you visited when I was in the hospital. But I was lost. Lost in the memories.'

Hannah swung round in front of her. 'You look wonderful. Are you really all right?'

When she nodded the hank of hair fell across Lucy's eyes just as it used to. She pushed it back. 'I think so. As all right as I'll ever be. Don't suppose any of us will get over it completely.'

Hannah turned to properly take in the house. She was back working for an architectural firm in London now, but it didn't take any expertise to see how good the design was. 'This place is amazing, but why, Lucy? Why rebuild here?'

A flash of blue from the huge eyes. 'It's where I belong. Where my mother belonged. Officially I inherited it from him, but this place was her family's home. Nothing to do with him.'

That was right of course. As she was also Jack Roper's

307

daughter, Hannah had legally been entitled to a share in his estate and the lawyers had told her Lucy wanted her to take half, but she had refused. Lucy was right. Jack Roper stole it from her mother. The woman he'd tormented and murdered. It was nothing to do with him.

Now Lucy said, 'I wondered how he got the money to renovate the place when he turned it into The Guesthouse.' A quiver of disgust as she said the name. 'Apparently the family, my mum in other words, owned loads of land all over Ireland. He sold it off and it was the time of the Irish property boom, with developers desperate for building land, so he made a packet. There was easily enough left for me to build this place and buy a flat in Dublin.'

Inside could hardly have been more different from The Guesthouse. The long living room was filled with light and sweet-smelling breezes. The whole of one wall consisted of glass doors folded back completely, meaning that the scents were wafted in from a terrace dotted with pots of herbs and flowering plants. It was only when Hannah glanced past the terrace that she saw with a pang the view she remembered. The grass rippling like a green sea to the blue-grey hills in the distance. The gardens too looked almost the same.

As if guessing her thoughts Lucy said, 'The garden is the only part I wanted to keep as it was. The way Rob loved it.'

Then she clapped her hands. 'OK, time to show you what I really brought you here for.' And she headed through the glass doors and round the side of the building.

Glancing at each other, Mo and Hannah followed her and Hannah saw she had been wrong about the garden. There was one change. A group of slender, silver-barked trees, their delicate leaves still green and fluttering in the breeze, replaced the bare rose garden. Lucy stood in front of the trees, hands clasped as if in prayer, her face anxious.

She looked first at Chloe and then at Mo. 'If you don't like it . . . If you don't want this I can have them taken away, but I thought . . .'

There was a sob from Chloe and she ran to one of the trees and flung her arms around it, then did the same to its neighbour. Mo made a sound deep in his throat as he moved to lay his forehead against the trunk of a third tree. When Hannah looked back at Chloe she was standing between the two trees she had hugged, encircling each with an arm. A family group.

Because beneath each tree was a silver plaque and each plaque was engraved with a different name. *Rosa, Liam, Sandeep*.

Lucy walked over to two other trees, stroking them with gentle fingers. The plaques below them read: *Jane, Rob*. Her mother and her childhood friend.

She looked back at Hannah as if for reassurance. And when Hannah nodded she turned to the others, smiling. 'I can add extra wording if you want.'

Mo shook his head, his eyes glittering. Chloe said, 'Thank you, Lucy. I love it.' And Mo, 'Sandeep would have been very happy with this.' He held out a hand to Hannah and when she came to him he dropped a kiss onto her hair.

They stood amongst the trees for a long time. Hannah felt the flecks of sunlight filtering through the slender leaves caress her face with warmth as she watched motes of dust spinning through the air.

Lucy's voice was very gentle. 'These are the people I want to be remembered here.'

After another few minutes, Chloe moved away and, with a sudden peal of laughter, Lucy clutched at her waist. Chloe let out a delighted giggle and Lucy said, 'Right, inside now. Damian's been hiding out in the kitchen and he should have food and drink ready for us. So let's get to it.' She ushered

Mo and Chloe inside, but took Hannah's hand and led her back to the front of the house.

Beside the front door she pointed to another plaque on the wall that Hannah hadn't noticed before.

It was the new name of the house: *Two Sisters*.

'Thank God, we don't need a plaque under a tree,' Lucy said. 'But I wanted us here too.'

And still holding hands they went inside.

Acknowledgements

Thank you first and most of all to my co-conspirator Finn Cotton. To Rhian McKay and all the lovely people at Harper Collins.

To my Irish ancestors and friends for the inspiration. Please forgive me for any liberties I've taken with your history and your wonderful island.

To everyone who loves reading and supports books and authors by buying or borrowing from libraries. And very special thanks to all those bloggers and reviewers who take the time to share the book love. You are wonderful.